# THE BEGINNING OF ME

Fred Wambolt

Sometimes, I feel the past and the future pressing so hard on either side that there's no room for the present at all.
　　　　　—Evelyn Waugh, *Brideshead Revisited*

# SECTION 1 — SEPTEMBER

# Chapter 1

I think my English teacher slit his wrists while reading my essay. The paper is practically dripping red ink, and I can't really make sense of most of his comments. The C+ at the top is huge and circled. I've worked my ass off for the first three weeks of senior year, and a C+ is not going to cut it. Trevor Banks, 12th grade English teacher, is young and cool, but he's a really tough grader. Still, I expected at least a B.

I mope my way through the other grumbling seniors and slink into my seat near the back. Andres and Brayden are sitting right behind me, and Andres is running off at the mouth as usual. Today he's going on about how he hates gay people and how gays should just keep their shit to themselves. I'm determined to ignore him, not take the bait. I zip up my hoodie and pull up the hood. I'm taking things out of my backpack – book, pen, notebook – when he says, "Man, we have gays in every class."

"For real," Brayden replies.

Andres snorts, "Yeah, look at this one."

I stand up and turn around and say, 'Yo, you got something you wanna say to me?'" Andres and Brayden both stand. Andres says, "Nah *Gay*-briel, sit your ass down, bruh."

"Chill with that shit, man," I tell him.

Trevor calls out from the front of the room, "Everything okay back there?" I remind myself of all the things my counselor, Karina, has been telling me for the past three years, how I can't let people push my buttons. How I need to walk *away* from trouble instead of walking *into* it.

I say, "Yeah, everything's cool, Trevor." I glare at Andres and sit back down. Trevor will make us put our phones away in a minute, so I take a quick last peek at my

Instagram photography page. Over 300 likes for a photo of my cat staring at my little brother sleeping that I posted this morning.

But then, Andres leans forward and whispers, "Punk ass faggot."

Next thing I know, Andres is on the ground with blood streaming out of his nose, Brayden is trying to get to me but is being held back by a couple of guys, and some other guys are dragging me to the door. I'm struggling against them and Trevor is standing in front of me saying, "Gabe. Gabe. Let them get you out of the room. Zach is on his way up."

The last thing I hear as I'm dragged into the hallway is Andres yelling, "Imma get that maricon."

An hour later and I'm still in Karina's office, waiting for my mother to arrive. It's never a good sign when they make you meet with a parent, and the assistant principal, and the counselor. They're going to dish out some punishment and layer it with "social-emotional support." So much for rocking senior year.

Zach comes in with my mom. To say she's not happy would be an understatement. I take deep breaths and try to avoid looking at her. I stare at my bitten fingernails. My knuckles are swollen and red and starting to ache. My mother and Karina are chatting about the weather in Spanish. I wish someone would get this started so we can get it over with.

Finally, Zach kicks it off. "Thanks for coming in, Isabel. We want to get this sorted out as quickly as possible so we can get Gabriel on the right track for his senior year." Zach's not bad. Young white guy, sorta surfer dude-ish. Has a dope sneaker collection. Today he's wearing vintage Adidas, white with red stripes.

I'm still looking down at my hands, so he says, "Gabriel? Can you look up please, so we can talk?"

I mumble, "It's Gabe." I lift my head but don't make eye contact.

"Right, sorry about that, Gabe. I slipped up again."

Karina jumps in. "Gabe." Thank God she didn't call me *Gabriel* with the Spanish accent like she does sometimes. She's pretty good at sensing when I'm extra tight. "Do you know why we're all here?" *Seriously? I had a fight. You think I don't know why I'm here?* I take a deep breath and nod.

"¡Habla cuando alguien te haga una pregunta!" My mother spits this out. I still can't speak.

"Gabriel, ¿qué pasó? Me estoy cansando de todo esto. I can't be leaving work to come to school for you getting in fights. I thought we were done with this, done with the fights and the drama."

"I'm sick of all of this too, Mami. I thought we were done with it too. But people can't just leave me alone."

Karina has a bowl of yellow stress balls on her desk. I reach over and grab one. It has a smiley face on it. I want to throw it against the wall and wipe the smile off its face, but instead I start squeezing the shit out of it. When Karina first gave me a stress ball in ninth grade, I thought it was corny, but boy have I used a shitload of them in this office. Not gonna lie, they definitely do help. My right hand is hurting from the punch, so I switch the ball to my left.

Karina says, "Let's start with what happened in Trevor's class with you and Andres."

"He pissed me off, so I punched him."

"What did he do?" asks Zach.

"He was talking his usual shit. I remembered what you both always tell me about using my words to solve conflicts, so I told him to chill. When he kept on, I made him shut up with my fist. I used my words first but that didn't work."

Mami asks, "¿Qué dijo mijo?"

"I'm not a snitch. Ask him what he said. See if he admits it. But it's over, it's done, I'm finished with Andres. Can I just go back to class now? It's almost last period and I don't want to miss my Physics quiz." I start to stand.

Zach, with his sorry-to-be-the-bad-guy expression, says, "Unfortunately, we can't let you go back to class. You punched another student, so I'm sending you home with your mom. You know it's district policy that—"

"What?" I interrupt, standing up. Now I'm mad heated. "He started this shit. What's gonna happen to him?"

I sit back down. I imagine smoke is coming out of my ears like in the cartoons. I look at the wall behind Karina and see this month's inspirational poster: TODAY IS A GOOD DAY TO HAVE A GOOD DAY! *Hold it together, Gabe.*

Zach says, "We're meeting with Andres and his family too. Now let's just get you home to cool off and then when you get back, we'll have a restorative circle with you and Andres to work it out."

"I'm not meeting with that asshole." I quickly correct myself since I'm already in deep shit. "Sorry, that *jerk.*"

"We'll work it out when you get back. You have to fix this so you can concentrate on finishing strong and getting into college."

Mami rolls her eyes, shakes her head, turns all shades of red. She's been down this road before with me, but not for a while. It's a damn bumpy road, with a shitload of potholes. She looks like she's ready to just slam on the brakes, get out of the car, and walk in the opposite direction.

"How long is the suspension?" she asks Zach.

"Two days, not counting today."

I snort and shake my head. Mami glares at me.

"You can come back on Friday. I'll let all your teachers know so they can email your work."

"Vamos," Mami says softly.

When I don't get up, she repeats it a little more forcefully. "Gabriel, vamos."

As hard as I try, I can't hold back the tears. "Mami, I'm sorry you had to leave work. I'm sorry I messed up on the first day. But I didn't start it. I came ready to start senior year. Everybody's acting like I wanted to get suspended on the first day."

I stand, grab my coat and backpack dramatically, and head to the door.

Mami says, "Gabriel, espérate."

I stop and turn, thinking that maybe I should tell them what Andres said to piss me off so much. But I'm not a snitch, so no.

Zach and Karina hang back as Mami comes over and wipes my cheeks.

"Let's go, mijo."

Karina says, "I'll walk you out."

In the outer office, Andres is waiting. He's with a man in dirty jeans and a bright yellow shirt. Construction worker. Probably his dad. The man looks as happy as Mami. Andres and I look at each other for a second. I look away.

It's passing time just before last period, so the halls are packed. I avoid making eye contact with anyone. Kids move aside and make way for Karina and Mami to pass, and I follow. Karina holds the door and I walk out into the warm September sun. Beautiful day, all shot to hell.

I throw my backpack in the back and hop into the shotgun seat. As Mami starts the car, she and Karina are still chatting in Spanish. They say their final words, their goodbyes. Karina pokes her head in and says, "Hey Gabe. It'll get better."

Well, it can't get much worse. Can it?

# Chapter 2

My little brother is the best. I guess most big brothers don't say that. I bet a lot of them think it, but it's not cool to admit it. We're supposed to talk about what a pain in the ass little brothers are, and of course mine can be a royal pain and he's super hyper, but he's really an amazing little bro. His name is Nicolas. Nicolás with the Spanish pronunciation my mother uses. He used to go by Nicolas, but when I started going by Gabe, he decided to start going by Nic.

In the car going home with Mami, I get a text.

*Nic: what happened? Mami left me a message that she had 2 go 2 ur school and might be late getting home*
*Me: got in a fight punched a dude*
*Nic: gtfoh. Mami pissed?*
*Me: hella mad*
*Nic: what was fight about?*
*Me: tell u later. Mami yellin @me to get off the phone*

The rest of the way home, we ride in silence. I keep my phone in my pocket so she doesn't go off on me anymore. I'm hungry and want McDonalds but I don't want to ask her for any favors right now.

When we walk in the door, she tells me that she has to think about what the punishment is going to be, but for now she can't even talk to me because she's so mad. I grab a slice of cold pizza and head to my bedroom—*our* bedroom. Nic and I share a room. I know I said I really like him but being seventeen and sharing a room with a nosy, hyper twelve-year-old is not the greatest. And I'm neat and he's messy so we fight about that all the time.

Nic is on his unmade bed reading *Aristotle and Dante Discover the Secrets of the Universe* when I walk in. Ever since I came out to him, he reads a lot of books with gay characters. It's pretty sweet. Señor Gatito is on my bed, curled up on my pillow. Nic looks up, puts the book down and rushes over and looks real close at my face. Like way too close. I push him away. "Doesn't look like you got in a fight," he says.

"I threw the only punch. Everyone jumped in and broke it up."

"Who was it with? Was it John again? Malcolm? I bet it was Malcolm."

"Jeez Nic, calm the f down. It was that jerk Andres."

"The one you had a fight with in ninth grade? Tell me everything," says Nic. He sits back down and he's bouncing up and down on the bed. It's like he's living vicariously through me. He never gets into fights, which is a good thing because it means that maybe he's not looking at me as his role model like my dad told me he would.

Señor Gatito wakes up when I sit down on my bed. He meows as I pick him up and put him in my lap. He's purring like a madman.

I describe the scene for Nic, and he interrupts me the whole way.

I wrap it up, telling him how Mami looked so pissed when she walked in the room with Zach. Nic is hyped from hearing the story. Just keeps repeating, "Oh my God, oh my God, I can't believe it, I can't believe it."

"Jesus, it's not the first time I got in a fight at school for God's sake. Chill."

"Yeah, but this is the first time you got in a fight over being gay."

"Well, I haven't been out at school for a long time. Guess it was bound to happen."

Truth is, I didn't really think it was going to happen. They say we're a "diverse urban public school" whatever that means. I guess it means that we have a lot of black and Latino kids. A lot of kids who speak Spanish. There's a small number of other white kids like me. We all seem to mix pretty well. I don't see a lot of bullying. Kids curse a lot but not really at each other. And before today, I never heard anyone call someone a faggot. Kids don't even throw the word fag around. Sometimes I hear the Spanish speaking boys say maricon, but they don't really mean it in that way.

My coming out wasn't all that dramatic. I didn't get on the school loudspeaker and say, "Good morning, this is Gabe Meyers. Just wanted to let you all know that I'm gay. Have a good day." Last February, I decided that I would tell a few friends. I told Lulu, Francisco, and Mariya and of course, none of them were surprised. I told them I wasn't swearing them to secrecy, so slowly word got out. A few people asked me if it was true, no big deal. I know some people were talking shit behind my back, but this is really the first time it got dramatic.

"What happens now?" Nic asks.

"I got suspended for two days."

"What about Andres?"

"Dunno."

"That's messed up. He started it."

"He may get in trouble if they get him to tell them what he said. Or if another kid who heard it tells them."

"You didn't tell them what he said?"

"I'm not snitching."

"You gotta tell 'em. He can't get away with saying that."

"He didn't get away with it. He got a bloody nose and got knocked on his ass." I wink at Nic and laugh. Nic laughs.

We sit in silence for a few minutes. I scratch Señor Gatito's neck as I notice that Nic's eyes are welled up. "I'm sorry that happened."

I say, "It's okay." Even though it's not.

# Chapter 3

I started high school three weeks after my father was convicted of vehicular homicide and sentenced to five years in prison. The night before the sentencing, my dad took me out to the backyard. It was a clear, crisp night, cool for early September. He put logs in the fire pit and balanced them like a little tent. He said, "Gabriel, grab some of that newspaper there, wouldya. Crumple it up, not too tight, and start packing it under the logs there. Good. Put a little more on the back side there."

He inspects my work. "Looks good. Here," he says, handing me the long lighter. "Slide the little safety button on the top and then pull the lever thing with your finger. It's like pulling a trigger."

After a few tries I get it to light. He tells me to light pieces of newspaper on all sides, and the paper starts to go up in big flames. "Okay, now you have to blow on it to get the flames to touch the logs." Before long we have a pretty good fire starting.

We sit for a while staring at the flames. I look up. A half-moon shines a bit off to the east, and the black sky is littered with bright stars. I locate the constellation Cygnus, the swan, with the Northern Cross. I imagine the Greek friends Cygnus and Phaeton racing across the sky, coming too close to the sun, their chariots burning and them falling to earth.

Dad finally breaks the silence. "Gabriel, I think...I'm pretty sure that I'm going to jail for a while."

I just keep staring at the Northern Cross.

"Your mom's going to need you."

I nod.

"Nicolas is really going to need you." His voice cracks a little. "You need to set a good example. He's always looked up to you. Now he'll look to you for everything. You'll be his role model."

More silence. More stars. More half-moons. More not the right words. More no words at all.

He breaks the silence again. "Here, use this stick to move the logs around a little." I take it and stand up. "You have to move things around to keep the fire going, give it more oxygen. Good, the one on the right, push it to the center. There you go."

I sit back down. We sit in silence, and I get lost in the flames.

"Good fire." He doesn't know what else to say to me.

I can't find the words to tell him. How angry I am. So mad. At him. At Mami. At their fights. At him getting drunk. At Mami saying, "I hate you, get out and never come back." At him calling her a bitch. At him sneering, "Getting you pregnant was the biggest mistake of my life. You fuckin' trapped me." At him for storming out. For getting in his car, getting behind the wheel wasted. For driving the wrong way on the highway, hitting a car head on. At him killing a woman. And her 3-year-old daughter. At him surviving and making us live through the aftermath.

# Chapter 4

My punishment for getting suspended is that I have to clean the garage. And the basement. But I like cleaning and organizing, so it's not the worst punishment in the world. Also, for the next week, I can only have my phone from 7am to 7pm. Mami will take it at night and give it back to me in the morning. She also tells me that I have to agree to meet with Andres and work it out. I haven't told her yet that he's the same kid I had the fight with in ninth grade. We never really worked that out then, but we've managed to just keep our distance and ignore each other for a few years.

I still have almost an hour before I have to put my phone in Mami jail for the night, so I text Lulu. Earlier, she texted me to find out what happened, but I was in the car, so I told her I'd text later and time got away.

*Me: sorry. things got crazy. can u talk?*
*Lulu: yep. call me in 5*

I head out to the backyard. The sun is just disappearing behind the Macedonio's house next door. I love this time of late September when it's warm during the day and cool at night. I hop into the hammock and FaceTime Lulu. She picks up right away.

"Boy, I know things got crazy, but you can NOT leave me hanging like this ever again. I've been going crazy over here waiting to hear FROM YOU what happened. Someone posted a video of you being dragged out of class and Brayden or Andres screaming something in the background. Someone said they heard that he called you gay and someone else said they heard that it was Andres. And that it wasn't gay, it was fag. If he really said that he better get suspended. There needs to be justice. I mean, what did they do to you? What did your mother say? She must be losing it with you fighting again. Did you get in trouble? I guess she didn't take your phone, that's a good sign, but—"

"Jesus Lulu, will you let me talk?"

"Sorry, I'm just really worked up, especially if it's true that he called you that."

"Yeah, it's true. Well, actually it wasn't fag, it was punk ass faggot…"

"NO!"

"Yep. And maricon."

"Are you okay?"

"Yeah. I mean, I gotta admit that it really pissed me off. Obviously, since I punched him in the face."

"You know how I feel about violence but I get why you lost it. I'm so sorry this happened."

Lulu and I have been friends since we were really little—like playdate little. We lived on the same block until her family moved to the other side of the city. We were friends for a little while longer but then sort of drifted apart because we went to different schools. Then on my first day of high school, I'm sitting in the cafeteria by myself when I look up and see this beautiful redheaded girl walking toward my table. She's wearing a Smiths T-shirt, with the picture from the cover of their album Meat is Murder.

"Is this seat taken?" she says.

I stare at the beautiful face for a few seconds. She sees the recognition hit me and smiles. "Lulu? Oh my God. I haven't seen you in a minute. What's it been? Five years?"

"Sounds about right," she says as sits across from me.

"You look great, by the way."

"You too. I heard that you were going to school here. I heard about your dad. I'm so sorry."

"Thanks."

"How are you doing through it all?"

"I'm okay."

"How's your mom? And Nicolas?"

"They're good. Nicolas is in fourth grade. He's still a pain in the ass," I laugh. I notice that she doesn't have a tray. "Not eating?" I ask.

"God no. I never eat school food. That stuff will kill you."

We sit quietly for a minute. I pick at the brown mush on my plate. Lulu says, "You seem really sad. You sure you're okay?"

"I don't really wanna talk about it," I murmur.

"Okay." More silence. Then, "I have to run to the office. My mom is dropping something off for me. What's your number?"

I give it to her.

"Can I call you later?"

I nod.

"So good to see you Gabriel," she smiles as she kisses me on the cheek, grabs her bag, and rushes out of the caf. And the rest, as they say, is history. She's been my BFF since.

I go through the whole thing with Lulu on Face Time. The meeting with Karina, Zach and Mami. How I got suspended for two days and I have to do a restorative circle with Andres even though I don't want to. Lulu, of course, thinks that restorative circles are the best thing that ever happened to high school. She's one of the Restorative Student Facilitators. She's always trying to get me to solve my problems by talking them out. I'm not big on talking it out with people who piss me off.

"I'm going to help you prepare for your circle. I know you're super mad right now, but you have to work it out so you don't get into any more fights this year."

"You sound just like Karina and Zach," I groan. "I have to give my phone to my mother. Thanks for being there for me always, Lu."

I'm about to hang up when Lulu cries, "Oh, wait wait. I almost forgot. Do you remember Billy Sachs?"

Of course I remember Billy Sachs. And his blue eyes. And his curly hair.

I pretend to have a vague recollection of Billy. "Yeah, I think so. Wasn't he in our English class for the first half of freshman year? Then his family moved somewhere? Florida?"

"Yep, that's him."

"Why?"

"He moved back. He's going to Wallace."

Billy Sachs, back?

"Really?" I ask, trying to sound nonchalant.

"I ran into him at Whole Foods. Umm…....wait til you see him Gabe." Her eyebrows lift high on her forehead.

"What? Why?"

"Well, let's just say that Billy Sachs has matured into...umm, a handsome young man. Check out his Insta: theonlybillysachs."

I hang up and immediately open Instagram. I'm about to search when my mother comes to the back door. "Gabriel, it's 7:00. El teléfono, por favor." Damn. Billy Sachs will have to wait until the morning.

# Chapter 5

Mami leaves for work at 7:00 every morning. She usually wakes me and Nic up at 6:30. I was hoping she'd let me sleep in today since I'm suspended, but nope. She got a message from Zach that all of my teachers are emailing work to me, so in addition to cleaning the basement and the garage, I have to do schoolwork. And she's going to check with Zach to make sure that I do it. At least I don't have to fight with Nic for bathroom time this morning.

I grab the box of Honey Nut Cheerios and the carton of milk. I think about asking Mami if I can have my phone but it's only 6:48 and I don't want to push it. She could get pissed and say she's not giving it back at all. I sit, shoveling cereal into my mouth and reading the back of the box. I haven't read the back of a cereal box since I was a kid. It's actually pretty interesting. They removed their mascot, Buzz the Bee. There's just a white space the shape of a bee now. There's all this cool info about how bees are disappearing and why, and why they are important and what we can do to bring them back. They're doing a #BringBacktheBees campaign and there's a packet of seeds in the box.

Mami comes into the kitchen. "Nicolás, vamos," she yells. "I'll drop you at the bus." She gives me a kiss and says, "Bye, mi amor. Don't go back to bed. I'll be checking." She starts to leave and says, "Oh, tómalo," and hands me my phone. I put it face down on the table and go back to my cereal, pretending that I haven't been in withdrawal for twelve hours.

Nic comes rushing in, looping his backpack straps over his shoulders. One of his shoes is untied.

"Hey stupid, don't you know how to tie your shoes?"

"Gabriel!" my mother chastises me.

"I'm just joking, Ma."

"Stay out of trouble today," I wink at him.

"Yeah right," and they are out the door.

I pick up my phone. I have a ton of texts, everybody wanting to know if it's true what they've been hearing but I can't really deal with any of that right now. But I can check Instagram. I open it and see that a bunch of people have posted videos of the fight. There's the one Lulu told me about, with me getting dragged out of the room. There's one of Andres on the floor, wiping blood from his nose saying, "Imma kill that maricon." There's even one of me landing the punch. I'm not proud of losing my temper, but not gonna lie, it was a pretty good right hook.

I start to read comments. Some of them focus on me being gay, with not the nicest language. Others talk about how badass I was and how Andres deserved what he got. I can't go down this rabbit hole and get worked up again. Instead, I search: theonlybillysachs.

Lulu was right. Billy has really grown up very nicely. He was super cute in ninth grade with his blue eyes, long lashes, olive skin, curly hair, and gap between his teeth. Now he's taller, dark, and handsome. Seriously handsome. Most of his pics are him with family and friends. Some of him playing tennis. A trip to New York in the summer—him and his older sister in Times Square. Him with his mom on the Brooklyn Bridge. No videos of him partying. Not a bunch of selfies posted like a lot of guys do. No shirtless pics. I keep scrolling. No evidence of a girlfriend either.

*Okay Gabe, easy there.*

I close Instagram and grab my laptop to check my email. There are assignments from three classes—Physics, Economics, and English. The work is attached in each email, but the only one with a message is from Trevor:

*Hey Gabe,*

*I hear you're not going to be with us for a couple of days. Attached is the assignment for the next 4 chapters of Catcher in the Rye. We'll be having a discussion on Friday, so just do*

I work most of the morning. I'm already in the shit with Mami, so when she checks in with Zach, I want her to get a glowing report. She's a real hardass about grades. She's never had to push Nic since he's always liked school and always does good. I used to be good until high school. I got off to a bad start, barely passing my classes in ninth grade. I even had to do summer school for the first time in my life.

I was really angry in the beginning of high school. It's hard enough adjusting from middle school to high school; add your father going to prison on top of it and you get one really pissed off, testosterone-fueled, sexuality-questioning fourteen-year-old. I didn't go to school for the first three weeks of the year, so when I finally started, I was already behind. I knew a few people from middle school, but I didn't really hang with them. Then I reconnected with Lulu on my first day. She was a big help, but I still struggled. I wanted to do good in school, but the emotional stuff kept getting in the way. I would snap at teachers, walk out of class, cut class and hang out in the bathroom. Mami didn't know what to do with me. She was struggling too, and I was making everything worse.

That's when they made me start meeting with Karina. I resisted at first, saying "I don't need to talk to anyone. I'm fine. I'll be okay if everyone just leaves me alone." When I got in my first fight, they really ramped up on the pressure for me to see a counselor. I gave in. Not gonna lie, it's a damn good thing that I did. Who knows where I'd be right now if it wasn't for Karina? She's the one who taught me to take my temperature when I get heated. I kinda judge it on a scale of 1 to 10 and that helps me to stop for a minute and figure out what I need to do to cool down.

So, about that first fight. I'd only been in school for a couple of weeks. I knew that some kids were talking about my dad. No one said anything directly to me, but they looked at me weird, so I was paranoid that everyone was gossiping. We were in gym class, the only class I ever wanted to go to. We were playing basketball, and I was playing hard and aggressive. I got a steal and made a breakaway down court. Just as I went in for the layup, I was fouled hard from behind and knocked on my ass. I bounced right up and got in the face of the guy who fouled me. I was jawing at him about the dirty foul, probably threw in a few curses. He told me to back off and pushed me away. I pushed him back. We postured a little more, puffed up chests and all like the NBA players we all watch. Then it was over. Until he walked by me and said, loud enough for me to hear but soft enough so everyone else didn't hear: "You the dude with the baby killer father?"

My temp shot up to a 10. I lost it and started wailing on him. He landed a few good ones too before the gym teacher jumped in and broke it up with the help of some of the kids.

I got suspended because I threw the first punch. And that's when I had to start seeing Karina.

I never told anyone what he said to me, just said I was pissed off about the foul. And Andres and I avoided each other since then, until yesterday.

# Chapter 6

The rest of the day, I alternate between schoolwork, naps, organizing my closet, and social media—especially obsessing over a particularly hot IG pic on Billy's page. Mami calls to make sure I am awake and doing schoolwork and chores. Lulu texts to make sure I'm not wallowing in self-pity. Nic texts me a meme of Jesus. It says: JESUS SAYS MAKE GOOD CHOICES. I text him back: *don't get caught w/ ur phone. Mami's pissed as it is.* I shoot back a meme that says: BAD CHOICES MAKE GOOD MEMORIES ;). I demolish a bag of Takis for lunch with a jumbo Arizona. I lie in bed feeling pretty shitty about the whole situation, really beating myself up, and with a Taki-Arizona belly ache. Señor Gatito keeps me company. "Thanks for always having my back, Señor Gatito," I tell him. He just blinks his orange eyes at me and goes back to cleaning himself.

I feel really guilty about the way I treated my mother. She works so hard just to keep us in a house with food and clothes. She hates taking money from Uncle Andy but she has to so we can make ends meet. I help out with the little bit I make at Dunkin' Donuts, but she won't let me take too many shifts because she wants me to concentrate on school and getting into college. And now I go and get in another fight and get suspended and embarrass her in front of Karina and Zach.

How can a single word hold the power to provoke such anger? Faggot is not a word that has a history in my life. It's not a word that I've had hurled at me, not a word that I have hurled at others. I know that the word has a long, dark history, but it's a history so far in the past, so far removed from my 17-year-old world. I've grown up in a world of Ellen, Ru Paul,

Queer Eye, Lil Nas X. In my world, my reality, the word faggot shouldn't hold so much power.

But history can weigh heavy on a word, and I felt that weight in Trevor's class. And I probably shouldn't be, but I am mad at myself. I'm mad at myself because I don't give a shit what that asshole Andres thinks of me. And I don't want to let a word—an ugly, hateful word, but just a word—set me off like that. Karina tells me that words only hold power if you give them power. I don't know if that's true. I don't know why it made me snap so fast. I didn't even think. The word was a finger that just flipped a switch.

And Nic. I'm supposed to be setting a good example for him. I have the weight of being his role model, a weight that was piled on me because my father messed up. And I know that he looks up to me, I know that he needs me there for him, and I'm trying my best, but I keep messing up. And it's hard. And I don't know if I can do it. But I know that I have to find a way to do it. And it's not fair and I know that life is not fair. And in my brain, I know that my father was really angry and drunk, but my heart believes: I'm a mistake. I. Am. A. Mistake.

I dozed off for a while and when I woke up, I decided I should clean the basement before Mami got home. I hardly ever come down here. My dad, Nic, and I used to play ping pong down here, but for a while now it's been a big mess, with boxes piled up everywhere, including on top of the dusty ping pong table. Mami wants me to put all of the boxes along one wall and then sweep the floor and get rid of all the cobwebs.

As I'm moving boxes, I check what's inside. There are a few boxes of adult clothes, things that Mami and daddy had not worn in years. I look through to see if there is any of my dad's old stuff that I would want. Some of it is definitely never coming back into style, but I find a few cool t-shirts. One is the faded album cover of Nirvana's *Nevermind* album, with a picture of a little baby swimming underwater and reaching for a dollar bill. There's another that's from a concert, The Smashing Pumpkins Infinite Madness 1996 Tour. I figure out that my dad would have been 16 or 17 then. How the hell did he get to go to a rock concert at that age when I don't get to do shit? Jeez. I put the two shirts off to the side and continue sorting.

Finally I come to the last two boxes. In the first one there are a lot of old papers, things that might be important, things that I should set aside for Mami to go through. There's also an envelope marked: RINCÓN 2002. I open the envelope to find a stack of photos. My parents in Puerto Rico, the year I was born. Dad in his board shorts, his long, sun-streaked hair pulled back in a ponytail, posed next to his surfboard, smile gleaming in the sun. Mami in a blue bikini emerging from the water, looking like a swimsuit model. The two of them together at a beach bar, surf crashing in the background. The last photo—my dad standing behind Mami, his arms wrapped around her, hands on her belly; not the flat, swimsuit model belly from the other pics, but a small, rounded belly. A belly with the beginning of me inside. They both look so happy. The look on dad's face on this beach in Puerto Rico in 2002 does not say: *this is the biggest mistake I ever made.*

# Chapter 7

Friday morning. Suspension is over. Back to school. I'm lying on the floor in the basement. Last night, I grabbed my sleeping bag and told Mami and Nic I was going to crash downstairs. Nic got all worried and then a little hurt when I told him I needed space. I've got headphones on, and they're attached to dad's old Discman. The final box in the basement had a bunch of his old CDs. I've been listening to the Smashing Pumpkins, the one from the tour t-shirt. I'm imagining 16-year-old dad with his friends. They're probably stoned. They're so excited to be there. Maybe it's his first concert. I want to ask him. I've been listening to this track called Thirty-Three. Billy Corgan is singing about tomorrow, pulling his collar up, alone and cold, facing it.

I take a quick shower and decide not to eat breakfast. I say goodbye to Nic and Mami and try to rush out the door. Mami stops me and reminds me that she has my phone. I was so lost in the music that I didn't even think of my phone. She also reminds me that I have to work it out with Andres. She'll be checking with Karina later to make sure. I kiss her and head out.

Lulu is waiting for me outside of school. I take a bite of her apple. Before we head in, she gives me her Restorative Justice Facilitator pep talk. How I need to be open and honest. How I need to listen to Andres and respect his perspective. How I have to assume good intentions (not sure how I can assume his intentions were good when he called me a punk ass faggot, but whatever). When we walk through the school doors, a few people look at me and whisper to each other. A few friends dap me in the hall. A couple high-five me and I know they are congratulating me on my right hook to Andres' nose.

I say hello to Maria, the school secretary. "You been behaving yourself Gabriel?" She gives me a look over her glasses that tells me that she knows damn well that I haven't been behaving myself.

"Oh, you know me, Maria."

"Yes, Gabriel I do," she chuckles and gives me a wink. I've corrected her a number of times, but she still calls me Gabriel. She says: "You've been Gabriel since you were a snot nosed little ninth grader and you're going to stay Gabriel to me until your butt is graduated." No arguing with Maria.

I report to Zach's office. He's got his feet up on his desk. Always wants us to check out his kicks, I guess. These are pretty cool. Beige canvas Pumas with a multicolor strip along the side.

"Morning Gabe. How's it going man?" He shakes my hand. He's acting like I'm just there to say hello and have a friendly chat. That's his MO. Play it all cool and friendly before dropping into the serious shit. We all see through it but it serves him well.

My denim jacket is open and he sees that I'm wearing the Nirvana T-shirt. "Dude, you listen to Nirvana? I didn't think kids even knew Nirvana."

"It was my dad's."

An awkward silence. Zach breaks it. "Cool. Very cool."

After a little more chitchat, he asks if I'm ready to work things out with Andres. I grit my teeth, think of Mami, and say that I'm totally ready. That I want to put this all behind me. That I want to focus on senior year. He seems genuinely pleased by my bullshit answer. He calls Karina and tells her that I'm here and asks if Andres is there and ready.

"Let's do this Gabe," he says, as if we just got called in off the bench in a basketball game. Dude, it's not gonna be that exciting.

Andres Ramirez /Gabe Meyers Restorative Circle Recap:

1. Andres and Gabe both sulk in
2. Karina introduces Ty, an 11th grade facilitator
3. Ty explains the norms of the restorative process
4. Ty asks if Andres and Gabe both understand and agree to the norms
5. Andres and Gabe both nod
6. Karina tells Andres and Gabe that they need to use their voices
7. Andres and Gabe both grunt "yes"
8. Zach tells them that they both got suspended and need to make things right
9. Andres eventually apologizes for calling Gabe a faggot.
10. Gabe corrects Andres: "It was punk ass faggot."
11. Andres complains: "I said I was sorry man."
12. Gabe apologizes for punching Andres.
13. Andres and Gabe sign a paper saying it's over.
14. Andres and Gabe shake hands.
15. Karina looks happy.
16. Zach looks self-satisfied.
17. Ty looks self-important.
18. Gabe looks sullen.
19. Andres looks pissed.
20. They both leave.

I also have to meet with Trevor and Zach to restore things before I return to Trevor's class. Zach has prepped me and I'm ready to make things right. Trevor comes into Zach's office and says, "Hey Gabe, how's it going?" He holds out his hand and we shake.

"I'm good thanks." It's hard to make eye contact.

"Gabe," Zach says, "Let's start with you telling Trevor what happened, from your perspective."

"I…I got really mad when Andres was saying some stuff to me. I tried to get him to stop but when he kept going, I kinda snapped and just lost it. I know that I should've handled it in a different way and I'm really sorry that I did that in your class." I manage to look at Trevor and he gives me a nod.

Zach asks Trevor to talk about it from his perspective. "Like I told you in my email, I thought everything was okay when you said it was. I've thought about it a lot since the fight, and I'm surprised at how bad it makes me feel. It's the first time I've ever had a fight in my class, and it made me feel like I didn't have control of my own class, that if I had done something different, we wouldn't be here. Also, after you guys were taken out of class, I still had forty-five minutes to teach, and the rest of the day. That was tough. And there's all those videos out there documenting it, with me screaming. I'll be honest, Gabe. It's been hard."

"I'm really sorry."

"Trevor, what do you think needs to happen to make this right, to restore things?" Zach asks.

"First, I think we're off to a good start since it's clear that you've reflected on it, Gabe. That's the first step. I'm ready to have you back in class. It's not the same without you. I miss your cynical comments. I want to hear you complain a little more about how Holden Caulfield is a whiny little punk." We exchange smiles and a chuckle.

"All I ask is that you let me know if there's a problem so we don't have anything like that happen again. Deal?"

"Deal."

"Great," Zach says. "Trevor, I'm going to talk to Gabe for a minute. Thanks so much for coming down to talk."

Trevor stands. He looks at me and says, "Gabe, thanks. I look forward to you being back in class."

"Thanks, Trevor. Me too." I hold out my hand, he shakes it, and he leaves.

# Chapter 8

Not long after the thing with Andres got settled, I really committed myself to getting my shit together, to staying out of trouble, ignoring stupid high school drama. Mami let me pick up a weeknight shift at Dunkin', along with my weekend hours, as long as my grades didn't slip, and I focused on getting into college. Lulu, of course, was overjoyed and determined to hold me to my total commitment to success.

In late October, Lulu told me that she was meeting Billy at the mall and wanted me to come. The two of them had been texting and Face Timing since they had run into each other at the supermarket.

We meet on the second floor, outside of the Apple store. Billy is already there when Lulu and I arrive. He's wearing jeans, yellow Converse, a yellow hoodie with his school's name, Wallace, and a Yankees cap. Lulu gives him a big hug and turns to me. "You guys remember each other, right?"

Billy smiles at me. I'm greeted by that cute gap between his two front teeth. "Of course. Gabriel! Haven't seen you in a minute. How you doin' man?" He shakes my hand firmly and pulls me in for a half hug.

"I'm good. Good to see you. How's it going?"

"It's going great. Happy to be back. Happy to see this one." He pulls Lulu in for a hug.

Lulu breaks in, "I'm starving. Let's go to the food court."

At the food court, Lulu gets a salad and Billy and I both get burgers. Lulu lectures us about how disgusting it is that we are eating the flesh of animals, about how we are not only killing animals, but we are contributing to the death of the planet as well. Lulu could go on all day about why everyone should be a vegan. And over the years she has definitely influenced me to eat less meat. And she got Nic to watch a documentary called Cowspiracy which made him refuse to eat meat anymore. But sometimes I still like a good burger, a real burger, with real dead cow meat. So, sue me.

Billy takes a big bite of his burger and smiles at Lulu. "But it's so yummy."

"Seriously," she growls. "You make me ill." She turns her back to us and eats her salad.

Billy looks at me and mouths, "Oops." We both giggle. Lulu, with her back to us, snaps, "It's not funny."

I say, "Sorry, I promise not to order meat when we are together."

"Well, you shouldn't eat it at all, but I guess not ordering it when you're with me is a start."

"Love you Lulu," Billy says in a little boy voice.

"Love you too. Jerk."

"Gabriel, what are you thinking about for next year? For college?" Billy asks.

"I go by Gabe now, not Gabriel."

"Oh cool. Gotcha."

"I want to study photography. I'm hoping for NYU or RISD, but those are both long shots. And I'd never be able to go if I got accepted unless they gave me a shitload of money, but I'm applying. Lulu and I have been hoping to go to NYU together for the last couple of years."

"That's so cool, Gabe," Billy nods. And smiles.

I'm feeling mad awkward now because Billy has a way of making eye contact—with his crazy beautiful blue eyes—and holding it and it makes me super nervous. I pretend to be exceedingly interested in my remaining fries and ketchup.

Lulu chimes in, "Gabe has an Instagram page of his photography. He has over 12,000 followers, last I checked."

"Really? That's amazing." Billy pulls out his phone. "What's the name of your page?"

"gabemeyersphotography"

Billy looks at his phone, scrolling through my page. I always get nervous when people look at my photos in front of me.

"Wow, these are amazing."

I feel myself blushing. "Thanks man. Appreciate it."

Lulu must sense my discomfort at being the center of Billy's attention, so she interrupts. "Billy's applying to Columbia. How cool would it be if we all ended up in New York?"

"That would be so awesome," Billy says enthusiastically.

I smile and nod. Billy is looking at me. I turn and look at Lulu. She has a huge smile on her face. And at that moment it hits me, I think Lulu is trying to hook me and Billy up. Whoa, I was NOT expecting this.

"So," I say, "Wanna walk around a little?"

We spend the next couple of hours walking around, wandering in and out of stores. Billy and Lulu talk nonstop. I mostly listen and laugh and wonder what it must be like to be so open and free and enthusiastic and positive. They don't push me to talk. They let me be me. Lulu grabs me and kisses me on the cheek. Billy walks in the middle, me on his right, Lulu on his left, one arm over my shoulder, the other over hers. "This is so much fun!" Billy says.

"So much fun," Lulu adds.

"Definitely." I turn my head and smile at them.

# Chapter 9

Later that night, Lulu texts me.

*Lulu: Did you have a good time?*
*Me: Yeah, was fun.*
*Lulu: What did you think of Billy?*
*Me: He was really nice.*
*Lulu: He got really good looking, huh???*
*Me: Yeah, he's definitely good looking.*
*Lulu: He seemed to really like you.*
*Me: ????*
*Lulu: Oh come on Gabe. You guys were clearly into each other.*
*Me: Are you telling me that Billy's gay?*
*Lulu: Yeah, dummy. He told me he's totally out and doesn't care if I told you.*
*Me: Did you tell him I'm gay?*
*Lulu: No! I wouldn't without your permission. But I'm sure he knows. He probably*
*figured it out by the way you got all awkward whenever he smiled at you. LOL.*
*Me: Shut up!*
*Lulu: Just kidding, hon. Well, sorta. You were really adorbs in your awkwardness.*
*Me: Angry emoji.*
*Lulu: He asked me for your number. Can I give it to him?*
*Me: I guess.*

*Lulu: You guess??? He's gorgeous, he's smart, he's funny, and he obviously likes you!*

Suddenly, Lulu appears on FaceTime. I answer. Lulu picks right up where her texts left off, "Seriously Gabe, did you really not get it? Do you really not know when a boy likes you?"

"Um, Lulu, you do realize that I'm new to this, right? It's not like I've had guys falling all over me since 9th grade like you."

"Oh yeah, I guess that's true. But trust me. He's into you. I could tell right away. And as soon as he got home, he texted me to tell me what a great time he had. And he asked for your number. I am so excited. I'm going to send him your number right now."

"Wait!" I yell. "What do I say if he texts me?"

"Oh my God, you are hopeless," she sighs. "Just kidding. Just respond like you would to anyone. Just be yourself."

"Myself is awkward. You know that."

"Your awkwardness is part of your charm," Lulu says.

"Ugh," I respond. "I know you're saying that to help, but it doesn't really. Billy's the opposite of awkward. He's so damn confident. But not in a cocky way."

I hear the front door and the voices of Mami and Nic. Nic comes into the bedroom.

"Listen Lulu, I gotta go. Mami and Nic just got home."

"Hi Lulu!" Nic yells.

I hold up my phone so they can see each other. "Nicky baby! How's it going? How's school?" Lulu asks.

"It's good," Nic says. "I made high honors!"

"I never doubted for a moment that you would. Congrats."

"When are you coming over for dinner Lulu? I haven't seen you in forever."

"Soon, baby, soon," Lulu says.

I'm tired of holding up the phone so I cut off the conversation. "I'll see you tomorrow."

"Hang on," she says before I hang up. "So I can give him your number?"

Damn, I forgot to turn off speaker phone. Nic's head whips around like a dog that spots a squirrel out the window. I turn off the speaker and say to Lulu, "Yes."

"Great! I'll bet he texts you tonight. I'm so excited."

"Bye Lulu." I hang up.

Nic is staring at me, eyes raised in a comical expression.

"What, Nic?"

"Who is this him that she's giving your number to?"

"None of your business."

"Aw, c'mon, tell me."

"I'm not talking to you about guys."

"So it is a guy! Well of course it's a guy because she said *him*. But it's a guy guy, like a guy that you like or something? Like for a date or something?" Believe me, it's a little embarrassing having your twelve-year-old brother interrogate you about a boy that you're interested in.

"I'm not talking to you about this, so stop bugging me."

"You're a terrible big brother," Nic says.

"I know. Now leave me alone. I have to read for English class." I pick up *The Catcher in the Rye* and lie back on my bed and start reading. I can feel Nic's eyes on me, hoping to wear me down. I roll over on my side, so my back faces him. I hide my phone in front of me and turn off the sound so my nosy little brother won't hear a text alert. I try to figure out the symbolism of Holden Caulfield asking the taxi driver where the ducks in Central Park go in the winter, but Billy Sachs has camped out in my brain.

# Chapter 10

Billy did his homework for our first date. When he suggested that we go to the Avon on Thayer Street Friday night to see *The Graduate*, I was pretty surprised. Turns out he asked Lulu what kind of movies I like, and she told him I love old movies, so *The Graduate* it is.

As awkward as I am in regular day to day life, can you imagine my level of awkwardness on a first date? Seriously, there needs to be an instructional manual for first dates. And maybe a separate one for gay first dates. Like, who buys the tickets? Do you each buy your own or does one person buy both? If one person pays, it's like there's already an imbalance in the relationship. But if you each pay for your own, it feels like it's not a date. Just two friends going to the movies. And what about popcorn? Is both sticking your hand into the same tub of popcorn too intimate for a first date? And choosing seats! Do you just go along with sitting where they want or do you stand there and have a whole conversation about why you always sit halfway back on the left side? I sometimes overthink these things.

We manage to work it out. Billy buys the tickets. I get the popcorn (one jumbo tub) and sodas (one for each—sipping from the same straw definitely seems too intimate for a first date.) And we sit on the center left because Billy says he has no preference (weird). Before the movie starts, I kept scanning the theater, worrying that I might see someone I know. But then I realize that the only person that I know who might go to see *The Graduate* at the Avon is my dad, and he's in prison so he for sure isn't here. And then I get all in my head about why I'm worried about people seeing me. I guess even though I'm out at school, no one sees me hanging with a dude in a romantic way. Not that we're getting romantic in the theater. So yup, awkward. Billy sees me scanning the room and jokes, "You looking for a better date?"

I laugh (I hope it's not a giggle), "Nah, I'm good with the one I got."

"Phew," he says as he fake wipes his forehead. "I told my parents we were coming to see this, and they got super excited, talking about how great it is." I wonder if he told his parents it was a date or if they thought he was going to the movies with friends, like Mami did.

"Yeah, it's really good." I tell him about how my dad introduced me to old movies, and about how I took a summer filmmaking class, and we watched a bunch of classic movies, and this was one of them. But I never saw it on a big screen, so I'm glad he thought of it.

"Me too," he smiles. And luckily just then the lights start to go down and I'm saved.

You know how in the movies, whenever people are on a first date and they go to the movies, there's a moment where the guy (usually the guy) slowly inches his hand off of his thigh and moves it toward the girl? And they're both usually staring really hard at the screen but it's obvious that they're not really watching; they're thinking about what's about to happen between them? And finally, he puts his hand on hers and she (usually) takes it and then they relax and watch the movie, and you, watching the movie that they are in, feel all sentimental and shit? Yeah, that didn't happen with me and Billy. We just watched the movie. Together. Side by side. And it was...comfortable. Not awkward. It felt...right.

When the lights come up, we turn to each other for the first time since the lights had gone down. "Thanks for thinking of this," I say. "It was really great to see it on a movie screen."

"You're welcome. Well, actually, you should thank Lulu. If she hadn't told me you like old movies, we would have been at *Zombieland*."

"Our first date would have been our last date! No, just kidding. I love a good zombie movie. Actually, I can find something to like in just about any movie."

Billy suggests that we go for pizza. Coincidence, we both share a favorite pizza place downtown. Over pizza, we talk more about the movie. The main character is this kid, Benjamin, who graduates from college and is lost and has no idea what he wants to do. He ends up having an affair with his girlfriend's mother, who obviously is way older. He's got all these adults expecting him to do great things, all this pressure, and he just feels like he's drowning. And he has a really cool red convertible sports car. I think because his parents give it to him as a graduation present that it's a symbol of all the expectations they put on him. But it's a wicked hot car.

Even though we are only seniors in high school, Billy and I can both relate to the burden of expectations that Benjamin was feeling. Everyone always asking what your plans are for the future, as if you should have your whole damn life mapped out at seventeen. Not wanting to disappoint people but also wanting to do what makes you happy. Billy tells me about how his parents want him to go to Columbia because that's where they met. But Columbia doesn't have an undergrad Journalism program, so he really wants to go to Northwestern in Illinois. But his parents, especially his dad, are really pressuring him. He's worried that he won't even get into Columbia. He tells me about the pressure of having a high achieving older sister who graduated at the top of her class at Columbia and just started Harvard Law. I wonder how he is so open and honest and personal, so comfortable in vulnerability. I listen intently. And then he says, "What about you? What do people want for you? What do you want?"

I think for a moment. "I don't really know. I'm not sure what my mom wants for me beyond graduating high school. I know she wants me to be successful, but I don't think she has a vision of what that means. I want to go away. I know NYU is just a dream. But I want to go away, but then I think about

Nic and leaving him behind. So RISD would be amazing but that's a dream too. Yeah, it's all confusing."

Billy says, "Hang on. Is this your mom?" He has his phone and he's scrolling. He holds the phone up and I see that he's opened my Instagram photography page. I see the photo he's talking about:

***"Solitaria"***
***Black and white.***
*A woman at a kitchen table, alone.*
*Background blurred*
*we only see the woman*
*and the table.*
*Woman in profile*
*hair pulled back in a ponytail.*
*Crow's feet around her eyes*
*Forehead high*
*Nose regal*
*On the table*
*cards laid out in a*
*solitaire*
*pattern.*
*On the top of one pile is*
*the king of hearts.*
*In her hand*
*the card she has drawn*
*poised to put down --*
*the queen of hearts.*

"Yeah, that's my mom. I took that photo a couple of years ago. She and my dad used to play cards with us—Go Fish when we were little, then Crazy Eights, and War, and Rummy. When my dad went away, we stopped playing, but sometimes I would find her late at night, at the kitchen table, playing solitaire."

"It's really an incredible shot. How did you capture this moment? Was it posed?"

"No. I came out to get a glass of water and she was playing solitaire. She looked so beautiful. She didn't look sad, but it made me sad. I asked her if I could take a picture. She made a whole big deal about her hair and no makeup, but I convinced her. I got my camera from my room and told her to just play. I took a bunch of pictures from different angles. I was really surprised to get this shot, with the queen of hearts in her hand and the king ready and waiting for the queen." I'm surprised at how I've opened up to him. When I'm talking about my photographs, it's like I'm a stranger documenting my life from a distance.

"Beautiful," Billy says as he peers into my eyes. I look down and after a moment he says, "What about your dad? Do you know what he wants for you?"

"No."

"You've never talked about it with him?"

"You remember about my father, right?" I ask.

"Yes, I know that he's in prison."

"I don't really...can we talk about something else?"

"Sure," he says. I hate the look of pity that comes over his face. I can feel bad for myself, but I don't want it from other people. "I just thought that it must be hard and maybe you needed someone to talk to."

"Yeah, it is hard but I'm good, I don't need anyone to talk to," I say a little too sharply and I see the discomfort in his eyes.

"Sorry."

"No big deal. It's getting late anyway. I should be heading out."

We get the check and split it down the middle. We walk outside, where there's more awkwardness on the sidewalk. I don't know how to say goodbye in a way that might salvage the mess I just made.

It's gotten chilly. I start to zip up my jacket and the zipper gets stuck. I'm trying to get it unstuck and I make it worse. Billy says, "Let me try." He fiddles with it for a few seconds and says, "Boy, it's really stuck. Wait, wait, I think I got it. There." He slides the zipper up.

I look him in the eyes and he smiles. A smile that's more tentative, less sure, less confident, more questioning. But still the smile that makes me melt. He says, "I really had a good time."

"Me too," I manage to say.

He hesitates for a moment, then says, "Okay if I hug you?" I nod and he moves closer. It's a comforting, a hug that says, "I'm here for you."

"I hope we can do this again." Billy looks at me and I think he really means it. He really does want to see me again, really does want a second date.

"I hope so too."

I want him to ask me if he can kiss me. I want to be able to ask him if I can kiss him. But he doesn't ask me, and I don't ask him.

"Good night, Billy."

"Night, Gabe."

I turn and walk to the bus stop. I want to turn around to see if he's watching me walk away, like in the movies. But I see my bus turn the corner and I run to catch it. I make my way to the back seat—alone.

# Chapter 11

One of my favorite photographs, and one with the most Instagram likes, is a photo of Nic:

*"A Boy and His Cat"*
*Color.*
*A boy lies on his bed,*
*a bed covered with a Star Wars comforter and pillows.*
*His head is on the pillow*
*side by side with Darth Vader.*
*He is reading a book*
*eyes focused on the page. We see the cover—*
*The Giver by Lois Lowry.*
*A fluffy orange Tabby cat is*
*snuggled next to the boy.*
*The cat stares directly at the camera.*
*Her eyes are the same orange as her fur.*

Nic is still awake when I get home. And he starts in on me right away with his nosy little brother routine. "Where are you coming from?"

I try to shut him down, give him the hint with one-word answers. "Movies."

"With who?" He doesn't let up.

"Friend."

"Lulu?"

"Nope."

"Was it a date? With the guy? The one Lulu was talking about?" He's relentless.

"Nic, for Christ's sake just leave me alone. How many times do I have to tell you I don't wanna talk to you about these things? Why are you always so damn nosy all the time, always in my business? God, I can't wait to go to college and have my own space."

Nic doesn't say anything. He takes his book and his blanket and starts to leave the room.

"Nic, wait." He doesn't wait. He walks out of the room.

Anger. Karina tells me that anger can be healthy. But this is not the healthy kind of anger. Getting angry with your little brother because he's excited that you went on a date and yelling at him and telling him you can't wait to get out of here. Getting angry with that date for asking you to open up, for wanting to be there for you. Cutting him off, shutting down, running away. Hurting other people because they care about you. That's not healthy anger. That's just stupid. But it's what I do.

When I slink into the living room, there's just one light on, one of the end tables near the couch. Nic is stretched out on the couch under his blanket. When he sees me, he picks up his book and pretends to be reading. I try to sit on the end of the couch, but his feet are in the way. He doesn't move them. "Nic, move your damn feet. I just wanna sit and talk." He still doesn't move. "C'mon, let's talk."

"I tried to talk but you didn't want to and then you were really mean." He keeps the book in front of his face, but I can hear the tears in his voice.

"I'm really sorry. I shouldn't have talked to you like that. Can you put the book down?"

"I'm reading. I think it's best that you let me read and you can go back into the room and I won't bother you anymore." Man, he's really laying on the guilt, but I notice that he's moved his feet, so I sit. We sit in silence for a minute. Nic's not like me; he doesn't bottle up his emotions, so I know he'll lead the way.

He puts the book down and there's such sadness. His eyes say: I love you and you hurt me. He starts to cry as he speaks. "All I did was ask you a question. Okay, a couple of questions."

"I know, I know. And I acted like a jerk."

"Yeah, a real jerk."

Can't argue with that. Open up. "Okay, so yeah, I went to the movies with the guy that Lulu was talking about. And it was a date."

Nic perks up a little but he just says, "Okay." He's dying to ask all his nosy little brother questions but he's trying to work his guilt angle a little longer.

"Do you want to know how it went?"

"If you want to tell me," he says. "I don't want to be nosy."

"Okay, knock it off you little shit," I tell him. "I apologized, now let's just move on to the inquisition."

"Well, so how did it go?"

"It was nice."

"Nice? What does nice mean?"

"It means nice. We had a good time."

"What did you see?"

"The Graduate. It's an old movie. Really good."

"If it was nice and really good, why did you seem sad when you got home and why did you yell at me when I asked about it?" Damn, the kid's got skills.

If I can't be honest with Nic, the person who probably loves me more than anyone in the world, who can I ever be honest with? "Well, after the movie we went for pizza. We were talking and it was nice...comfortable and easy. We were talking about the future and expectations that people have for us. And he asked me about Dad. I told Billy—that's his name—that I wanted to change the subject. He said okay but then kinda pressed me. I snapped at him a little and said it was getting late and I needed to get going. That made everything awkward, and I think he didn't know how to act after that. I said goodbye and the whole way home on the bus, I was kicking myself about screwing everything up on the first date. So when you asked me…sorry."

"Why didn't you want to talk about Dad?"

"Because I didn't want to cry in front of him on our first date."

"Is that why you never talk about dad with me?"

"Yeah. I'm still really messed up inside about him. I think about him all the time. But I'm so mad at him still. I don't want to be, but I can't get it out of me."

"I really miss him Gabe."

I pull him to me. "I miss him too Nic."

I continue to hold my little brother, my best little brother in the world. He breaks the silence and asks, "You really can't wait to get away from me?"

It's a dagger to my heart.

# Chapter 12

Text to Billy:

*Thanks so much for tonight. It may not have seemed like it, but I had a nice time. Hope you'll give me another chance (prayer hands).*

And he did. But the residue of my behavior on the first date, pushing him away, fleeing when asked me to be vulnerable, lingered. Billy was more reserved, didn't text too much, talked about everyday things like school and clothes and movies and music. Nothing very personal—he didn't share and didn't ask me to. We went out a couple of times just the two of us, but things seemed more comfortable when Lulu came along. I searched for a way to start over, to go back in time to the first date and just answer his question about my dad. But the reality was, is, that I don't know what my dad wants for me. We've never talked about it because we never talk. How do I tell Billy that since my father went to prison, I have never visited him, never spoken to him on the phone, never opened the letters he sends? How do you admit to someone that when your father calls from prison on Thanksgiving or Christmas, you go into your room and leave your mother and little brother to make excuses for you? How do you explain that after three years of counseling, you're still not over your anger and that you haven't told anyone what you're most angry about? That the last thing he said as he stormed out of the house in a rage was that you were the biggest mistake of his life.

# Chapter 13

The smell of Mami frying tostones wakes me and Nic up on Thanksgiving morning. Tostones and eggs are our traditional Thanksgiving breakfast. The big Thanksgiving dinner will be pretty traditional American with a little Puerto Rican twist—the turkey spiced with adobo, mofongo stuffing. There's always two pies — apple for Mami and Nic, pecan for me — and usually for Dad.

It's a lazy day for me and Nic. Mami doesn't let us in the kitchen until dinner is done and we have to do the dishes. We play Pokémon Sword and Shield for a while. It's not too cold out so we go into the backyard and throw the football around. Lulu sends me a Happy Thanksgiving text and, just to ruin dinner for me, reminds me of the horrible conditions on turkey farms. Billy texts "gobble gobble" with a picture of a turkey with his head on it. Nic asks me who I'm texting. When I tell him it's Billy, he says, "Tell him I said Happy Thanksgiving." I tell Billy and he says, "I can't wait to meet Nic...and your mom." I send him a smile emoji and tell him I'll talk to him later.

"Vamos a comer a las 2:00. Your papi will be calling at 1:00," Mami reminds us.

At 1:00, her phone rings. My stomach tightens and my jaw clenches. Mami answers. It's usually at this point that I retreat to my bedroom, but today I stay on the couch, watching a football game. Mami switches between English, Spanish and Spanglish, talks to Dad about work, her boss, how she hears a knocking sound in the car and needs to call Jose to take a look at it. She asks him how he's doing. She says, "uh huh" and "hmm" and "ah si?" I steal a glance. There's happiness and sadness living together in her face. She looks beautiful. She looks weary.

"Nicolás is anxious to talk to you." She passes her phone to Nic. He excitedly tells Dad about every little thing that's happening in his life. Honor roll. His science fair project about cows and methane and global warming. The chess club. He's thinking about joining the track team in the spring. He pauses now and then as Dad asks him questions or probably heaps praise on him. This is the first time I've seen Nic on the phone with Dad. I stare at him, confused and stunned at how comfortable and normal it all seems, as if he's a kid talking to his father on a business trip, not a kid talking to his father in prison on Thanksgiving. How does he handle it all so much better than I do? Is he just a better person than I am, a more forgiving and empathetic human being? Their conversation starts to wind down. Nic is quiet. Listening. He turns and looks at me, his eyes wide and questioning. He doesn't have to say anything. I nod to him. Nic speaks into the phone, "Here he is," and hands the phone to me.

"Hello." It comes out all raspy. I cough.

"Hey Gabe. How's it going son?" This is the first time he's ever called me Gabe. Who told him? Nic? Mami?

"I'm doing good. You?"

"You know, hangin' in there." An uncomfortable pause that I don't know how to fill. "So, how's senior year going?" It sounds forced. He's trying so hard.

"Pretty good so far. Keeping my grades up."

"That's great. I'm really proud of you, son." When I don't respond, he follows up, "You know that, right?"

"Um, yeah...I guess."

"Oh Gabriel." And the emotion in his voice is too much. I can't do it. I can't. I hand the phone to Mami and go into my room.

Nic follows and I turn and snap at him, "Nic, leave me the hell alone! How can I get it through your thick skull that I don't want you around?"

He's about to cry. Then I see his face transform, a face I haven't seen before. "Fuck you, Gabe," he screams through his tears. "You always act like you're the only one who hurts. You think I don't hurt too? I'm always there for you and then you treat me like shit, say really mean things to me. I hate you right now."

"Sorry I'm not perfect like you. Sorry that I can't please everyone like you do. Can't pretend that everything is normal when it's not."

Nic is really sobbing now, loud heaving sobs, snot running out of the nose sobs. "I pretend everything is normal because you're such a jerk and you make Mami so sad. You're the big brother. Dad told me you were gonna be the man of the house now. Why can't you act like it?"

"Fuck you Nic. I didn't ask to be the man of the house."

"No, fuck you Gabe." And then the little shit slaps me across the face!

I grab him tight around the arms so he can't hit me anymore. I've got him in a big bear hug. Mami is in the room now, crying, screaming in Spanish, telling me to let him go, telling me to not hurt him. I loosen my grip around his arms, and now we are hugging each other, sobbing, saying I'm sorry I'm sorry I'm sorry I'm sorry. I tell Mami, "Está bien. We're good. We just need a few minutes alone. Por favor Mami."

She hesitates for a moment. Does she really think I will hurt him? "Estás bien Nicolás?" she asks. Nic responds, "Si Mami. You can leave us."

When we come out, Thanksgiving dinner is on the counter. Mami's eyes are red and puffy. Nic's are too, so I know mine must be also. Mami tells us that we should make a plate and put it in the microwave. When we all have our food heated, we sit at the table. Mami says a prayer in Spanish. We eat in silence.

"Mami," I say breaking the silence, "was I a mistake?"

"A mistake?"

"Was I an accident?"

"Do you mean, did your father and I plan for me to get pregnant? No, we didn't. But Gabriel, an accident is not the same thing as a mistake. When we found out I was pregnant with you, we were surprised. We were young. We were nervous. We came from different worlds. We talked about what to do. But we loved each other. We love each other. You are a product of that love."

"But, that night," I start to say. But she interrupts me.

"I know mijo. I know what he said. People say things when they're angry that they don't mean." And I look at Nic. And he looks at me. And we both know it's true.

*"Thanksgiving Self-portrait"*
*Black and white.*
*Teenage boy*
*Shirtless*
*head in the center of the frame*
*cocked to one side*
*staring directly at the camera.*
*His dark hair covers*
*one of his dark eyes.*
*The other is puffy*
*and*
*swollen.*

# SECTION 2 — DECEMBER

# Chapter 14

In the weeks after Thanksgiving, Billy and I continued to play it real casual. We went out a couple of times, and I slowly began to open up a little more with him. I told him about my big fight with Nic and how I said things that I really regretted. When he asked what the fight was about, I told him it was just about Nic always being nosy, giving me no space. I wasn't ready to tell him about my dad, and the phone call. Then he invited me to his family Christmas party. I must have had a panicked look on my face because he laughed and said, "You don't have to come if you don't want to. No pressure babe." *Babe?* "Lulu is coming. She can protect you."

"I don't need protection, smartass. Yeah, I'll come." Thank God Lulu will be there.

Billy lives on the East Side, up on College Hill. Our Lyft driver pulls over and says, "here we are." Lulu and I get out of the car and we're standing on the edge of a little park; the sign on the wrought iron fence says Prospect Terrace. All of downtown is spread out, twinkling below us. The statehouse is lit up red and green.

We turn and look across the street and see number 67. White Christmas lights sparkle in all the trees in the front and candles burn in all of the windows. Red-bowed wreaths hang on every window and all of the windows are lit with single white candles. It's been snowing lightly for the last couple of hours, so everything is blanketed in a soft layer of fluff. It looks like a scene from a Hallmark movie. A Mercedes pulls up and parks in front. Lulu and I watch as an elegantly dressed couple exits the car and makes their way up the long stone stairway.

"Wow, this place is really beautiful," says Lulu.

"Yeah," I respond.

Lulu hears the nervousness in my voice. "Hey, what's wrong? You seem super tense. It's a party. A Christmas party. At a nice house. On the East Side. It's gonna be fabulous."

"I know, I know," I say. "But I'm really nervous. I'm not comfortable in fancy places and around people I don't know. And I'm really nervous about meeting Billy's parents."

"They're gonna love you!"

"That's easy for you to say. It's different with you. Parents love you. Look at my mother—she thinks you're perfect. All parents do."

"Well," Lulu says, "I do have a certain charm around parents."

"Oh please." We both laugh.

"Okay, we are going in. You got this. They are going to love you almost as much as they are going to love me. You'll see." Lulu kisses me on the cheek, grabs my hand, and pulls me along up the stairs.

She rings the bell. A handsome young man dressed all in black answers. "Good evening," he says. "Please come in. May I take your coats?"

"Why, yes. Thank you very much," Lulu says, handing her coat to the handsome waiter.

When I make no move, Lulu says, "Gabe, give the man your coat."

"Oh, right. Thank you," I say and hand over my coat. Lulu rolls her eyes at me.

A tall, beautiful woman in a red dress with diamond earrings and necklace is walking toward us. She smiles and says, "You must be Billy's friends."

I'm mute so Lulu steps to the plate. "Yes, I'm Lulu and this is Gabe."

"Of course you are. I've been so looking forward to meeting both of you." Mrs. Sachs smiles at both of us, but she seems to look at me a little more closely, which makes me even more nervous. "So nice to meet you Lulu." She hugs

Lulu. "And Gabe. Finally." She hugs me too. Now I'm sweating. I'm probably shaking.

I manage to croak out, "Nice to meet you, Mrs. Sachs."

"Please, call me Patricia," she insists.

"Nice to meet you, Patricia," Lulu says. It's strange, I'm used to calling adults by their first names because we call our teachers and all the adults at school by first name. But for some reason it makes me uncomfortable to call Billy's mom Patricia.

"Please, come in. Honey," she calls across the room. "Come meet Billy's friends." A handsome man in a dark suit and red tie with dark, curly hair like Billy's strides across the room. He walks with the same confidence as Billy. When he gets closer, I see that he has the same blue eyes. He's holding a heavy crystal glass with a couple of ice cubes and brown liquid. Must be Scotch.

"You," he points to Lulu, "must be the beautiful and charming Lulu that Billy talks so much about."

Lulu beams, "Guilty as charged." He hugs her and they both laugh.

"And you," he says, turning to me, "must be the famous Gabe."

Oh God, what has Billy told his parents about me??

"Very nice to meet you, Mr. Sachs," I say as I extend my hand. He shakes my hand with his very firm grasp and says, "Please Gabe, call me Martin. I insist." He beams at me and now I'm feeling like I want to sneak out the door, grab a Lyft and head home and play Uno with Nic, where I won't feel this fish-out-of-water awkwardness.

"Gabe," Mr. Sachs continues, "Is it short for Gabriel? Or Gabriel?" He says it with the Spanish pronunciation.

"Um, yeah. But I sort of prefer Gabe," I stammer.

"Muy bien," he says smiling, "then Gabe it shall be."

I spot Billy across the room. He is laughing with some adults, probably entertaining them with one of his stories. As if he can feel my eyes on him, he looks over at me. Our eyes lock. He smiles. That smile. The lights on the Christmas tree look dim when he smiles. He says something to the people he's standing with and makes his way across the room. The same confident stride as his father minutes before. He hugs Lulu, then me. "I'm so glad you guys are here. I've been stuck entertaining all of my parents' friends for the last half hour." Patricia and Martin laugh.

"Go have fun," Patricia says to the three of us. She and Martin walk away hand in hand.

"Your house is beautiful," says Lulu. "And your parents are super nice."

"Yeah, they're pretty cool. I hope they didn't come on too strong. Sometimes they can be extra with my friends. Like trying to show that they are the coolest parents on the planet. Especially when my dad has had a few drinks, which he definitely has." Billy looks at me. "Um, Gabe. What's up? You look like you're about to face a firing squad. It's a party, dude."

"Do your parents know about me? About us? I just got a weird vibe, like they were checking me out, sizing me up."

"Of course they know about you, about us. They're cool with me dating guys. They've been wanting to meet you. Sorry if they made you uncomfortable. Man, you look crazy tense. Relax," he squeezes my shoulder. "Let's get a drink!"

We head over to the bar and there's a big punch bowl. Gabe says, "There's this Christmas punch my mom makes. Lots of fruit and rum. My parents are cool as long as we don't overdo it." He pours us each a cup.

"One other thing," I say to him. "Your dad asked me about my name. Asked me about Gabe, Gabriel, Gabriel. And he said it the Spanish way. And then he said *muy bien* when I told him I prefer Gabe."

"My dad's half Spanish. His mom, my abuela, is from Spain. I told him about your name and how you changed it."

I'm quiet. Lulu and Billy look at each other. "Now what's wrong?" Lulu asks.

"It's just...I'm just...well, it's like you've told your parents stuff about me."

"Yeah, of course I've told them stuff about you. They're happy that I'm dating, and they kept asking to meet you. I figured a Christmas party was a good time. Other people around so they wouldn't smother you," he laughs. "But don't worry, when they get you alone, watch out."

Gabe, shit's getting a little real here. Is Billy your boyfriend? Are you his boyfriend? Meeting the parents. Drinking their punch. Punch. Have another sip. Or two.

"So, by your reaction, I'm guessing that your mom doesn't know about me..." Billy laughs and snaps me back to the reality of now. Lulu laughs. I cut her a side glance.

"Well, umm...not yet. It's just like...it's a little different with me. She's...well she knows I'm gay, but she still thinks it's a phase."

"A phase?"

"Yeah, she's more traditional or old fashioned than your parents. But she's getting better. I think."

Lulu says, "Gabe's mom will love you, Billy. And you will love her. Has Gabe told you how much she loves me?" We laugh as I roll my eyes.

We're all a little quiet for a minute. Then Lulu breaks the silence. "I'll have another cup of this delicious punch please."

Billy and I both laugh. Our eyes lock. His smile, so bright and warm and loving, reaches in and touches my confused and guarded heart, asking me to open, asking me to give him a chance. He winks and squeezes my hand. I look past him and see Patricia and Martin smiling at us from across the room.

# Chapter 15

Trevor runs a college essay workshop after school twice a week. He assures me that no one is obligated to share their writing. "Some people find that they benefit from sharing their writing and getting feedback from the group. But others like to just listen and take inspiration," he tells me.

I'm a little late to the game and I'm feeling the pressure, since essays and applications are due right after winter break. I definitely need some inspiration because I have a serious case of writer's block; I don't even have a topic yet. Lulu comes with me. There's a pretty good turnout. Trevor's super popular with the students, probably because he's not much older than us. He started teaching my freshman year, straight out of college. His class is really relaxed. He doesn't have a bunch of rules that make no sense. We don't have to ask permission to go to the bathroom. Imagine that. When we're working independently, he lets us listen to music. We all know that if Zach or Miguel, the principal, comes in (or anyone wearing a suit), we turn it off and take the earbuds out. But even though he's relaxed, and the atmosphere is chill, he's pretty demanding. His class has a pretty heavy workload.

Trevor starts us off, "Okay guys, why don't you sit in groups of three. Everyone is at different places, and I think it would be good for you all to talk a little bit with other people. Some of you are almost done with your first drafts, others are just starting, and some are a little stuck on what to even write about. It's cool no matter where you are. We have enough time to get these essays in excellent shape."

Lulu and I grab a table together and Kevin, the star of the wrestling team, comes over and asks if he can work with us. I'm pretty sure he has a big crush on Lulu, so I say, "Sure

Kevin, sit down man." I grin at Lulu and she shoots me a look. But hey, Kevin is cute, has a hot little middleweight wrestler body, and he's not your typical dumb jock. He's a pretty good match for Lulu. At least I think so.

Trevor stops at our table. "Oh, this is a good group," he smiles, and I sense that he's a fan of the Lulu and Kevin pairing too. "I know that Gabe needs some inspiration so it would be good if you two shared what you're writing about and what you're struggling with."

Kevin says, "Sure, Trev. I'll start." He opens a folder. "So, I have rough drafts on two topics. I think I know which one I want to go with, but I'm stuck with the most important part, like the *why* of it. Why it's important. Trevor's comment on here is...well Trev, maybe you can just explain it?"

Trevor takes his paper and looks at the comment. "Yeah, so you chose the prompt that asks you to write about an obstacle you faced. And you describe the obstacle really well, with great details. It's a really compelling story that grabs the reader right away and brings them on the journey with you. But the second part of the prompt is how did it affect you and what did you learn from it. That's the part that you need to explore more. And you need to be really honest with yourself about it. This is what the person reading the essay at the college is really going to be looking for." He hands the paper back to Kevin.

Lulu says, "Do you mind reading it to us? Maybe we have some ideas."

Kevin hesitates and then smiles shyly. "Yeah, okay."

His story is about wrestling, but he's got a really cool angle. I didn't know this, but high school wrestling is coed. Because there are so few girls that wrestle, if they want to wrestle, they have to be on the boys' team. Well, not the boys' team. Just the team, which most of the time is only boys. One day the team showed up for a match and saw that there was a girl on the other team. The boys all started to freak out, wondering who was going to have to wrestle her. Coach came back with his clipboard and the boys all started in, "Coach, they have a girl." "I don't wanna wrestle a girl." "Who has to wrestle the girl?" Coach said, "Listen, she's on their team, she has a right to wrestle." He turned to Kevin and said, "Washington, you got this." The essay is good, building the suspense of the match, Kevin walking out totally confused about what to do. He talks about how he wanted to forfeit but knew that he risked not making the state championships if he did. And he describes how the match was over in ten seconds when he pinned the girl. But Trevor was right — it's missing something.

When Kevin is done reading it, Lulu and I both nod our head and give him a thumbs up. I say, "Kev, that's really awesome. I like how you really made me see you there in the gym."

Lulu cuts to the chase. "So, yeah, I agree with Gabe. You tell the story really well, but what I really want to know is why you wanted to forfeit."

"Cuz she was a girl," replies Kevin, as if that were reason enough.

"So what?" Lulu is a little agitated by his response.

"C'mon Lulu, you don't see why a guy wouldn't want to wrestle a girl?"

"No! She's on the team, so obviously she's practiced and wants to be there, and she deserves the respect of being treated as an athlete."

"That's what Coach said, but..." he trails off, uncomfortable with Lulu confronting him.

Lulu continues, "Were you afraid of losing?"

"Hell no," Kevin replies.

Trevor, who had been listening from a few feet away, jumps in, "First of all, Kevin, thanks for sharing. It takes courage to be vulnerable like that." Lulu and I nod. "Lulu, I would encourage you to give Kevin your feedback in a more neutral tone. It's coming across as a little judgmental I think." I smirk and Lulu kicks me under the table.

"Okay, sorry Kevin. I just think that maybe you could dive deeper to see why you really didn't want to wrestle her."

"No prob, Lu. It's all good." Kevin smiles at her. Yep, definitely has a big crush.

Trevor adds, "Kevin, I think that Lulu is right. For me what is missing is an honest exploration of why you didn't want to wrestle her and how you felt after you beat her so quickly."

"Cool, cool. Imma think on it some more."

"Great. We're almost out of time today," Trevor tells us. "Will you all be here Thursday?" We all nod yes. "Perfect. The three of you can work again together. If Kevin has figured some more out, he can share again. And we'll be sure to get to Lulu and Gabe. Keep working. Good stuff today guys."

I leave feeling even more overwhelmed than when I came. I know that if I'm going to have any chance of getting into NYU, I have to crush this essay. It can't be some lame story about making the honor roll or doing some summer program. I have to dig deep, expose myself. I know I have a killer essay inside. But how do I find the key and let it out?

# Chapter 16

Back in Trevor's room after school on Thursday, Kevin says he's thought a lot about Tuesday and has some new ideas. "If I'm really being honest," he starts, "I was afraid of losing. I mean, I thought that it was pretty unlikely, but I didn't know anything about her, so who knows?"

"And what if you had lost to her?" I ask. "I know you're all-state and everything, but you have lost before, right?"

"Yeah, I don't lose often, but yeah I've lost."

"Were you worried about what the other guys would say?" Lulu asks, with much less judgment in her voice.

"Yeah, of course. Not just the team, although they would have given me a ton of shit about it. It would have spread through school like wildfire. Everyone would be talking shit to me. And then whenever I went to another meet, my opponents would be trash talking about losing to a girl." He looks at Lulu, who is holding her tongue. "Yes, Lulu, I know it's stupid. Hypermasculinity and all that shit, but it's the reality and I'm being honest with myself and you."

"It's cool that you're being honest Kevin," she replies. "It's a systemic societal problem and talking about it honestly from your perspective is helpful. And it will really make your essay so much stronger." She high fives him. Hmm, I think she's starting to feel Kevin.

I interject, "How did you feel when you beat her in ten seconds? Were you happy? Did you do a big jock celebration?"

"No man, I didn't do no big jock celebration. I thought about not going out so aggressive, not trying to end it so fast, but I really did think about her being an athlete, and I would never want anyone to go easy on me. That would feel mad disrespectful. But honestly, I was relieved. I felt a little bad but again, I know that I never want anyone to pity me, so I didn't want to pity her."

I'm super impressed by Kevin's honesty and how he went home and really reflected on it. I can see that Lulu is too. She's smiling and nodding her head.

"Okay man, I need out of the hot seat," Kevin laughs. "Who's next?"

Lulu volunteers. Her essay is about becoming a vegan. She's a really strong writer. You can really hear her voice through the whole essay, but sometimes the voice is a little preachy (no surprise). It's cool to hear about an 11-year-old making this kind of life changing decision, arguing passionately with her parents and her pediatrician. We encourage her to develop that section more.

Now it's my turn. I admit to them that I'm really stuck on what to write about. I thought that I might write about how I discovered photography or the summer student workshop and how nervous I was the day of our photo exhibit. Trevor has made his way back to our table as I'm sharing some of my lame ideas. "How personal are you willing to get?" he asks.

I had been asking myself the same question. "I'm not sure."

"You know, there are thousands and thousands of kids applying to NYU. Like over fifty thousand probably."

"Thanks, Trevor. That's really encouraging. Just the kind of pep talk I need."

"I only say that because I know that you have a unique and powerful story inside of you, and you can bet that kids are digging deep to get into their dream schools. Some of these rich kids have parents who have been gaming the system since their kids were in kindergarten, doing everything they can to make sure they get into these selective schools. Some of these kids are writing essays about their summer spent building an orphanage in Honduras or teaching English to kids in Mexico. You all don't have the opportunity to pad your resumes like that, so you need to tell your honest stories about your lived experiences. You have an incredible story, Gabe. Use it to get what you want, what you deserve."

We're all quiet. I know what story he wants me to tell. He wants me to write about my dad being in prison. Kevin looks uncomfortable, so he probably knows what Trevor wants me to write about. I mean, everyone in the school knows what happened. I tell Trevor that I'll think about it.

As we walk to the bus, Lulu says, "I know it's not something you want to talk about, but can I say something about this without you getting mad?"

"No guarantees Lulu, but you can try."

"The way I see it, writing about your dad serves two purposes. First, it would make an amazing college essay. It would really set you apart from other applicants. Not many kids have that story to tell. It's a big thing to go through and it would help them see why you didn't do so well in 9th grade."

"It feels like I would be asking for pity. I don't want people to pity me."

The bus comes. We make our way to the back.

"You don't have to write it in a way that says *poor me*." She takes out her phone. "Listen, here's the prompt: *Recount a time when you faced a challenge, setback, or failure. How did it affect you, and what did you learn from the experience?* The story of your dad fits it perfectly."

"Yeah, I guess so." Lulu can be pretty convincing. "What's the other purpose?"

"What?" she asks.

"You said writing about my father would serve two purposes. What's the second purpose?"

"Oh right. Well," she hesitates. "You tend to be really guarded with your feelings," she begins. I already don't like where this is heading. "It's like you have this fortress built up around the most difficult parts of your life and no one has the key, except you. And I don't even know if you ever use the key. Writing the essay might help you deal with the emotions that you have bottled up inside."

"You think you know me so well, Lulu." I snort.

"I do Gabe. I'm your best friend. But the only things I know about your father are the things I read in the paper or the things I have heard from other people. I wouldn't even know that you have never visited or spoken to him if Nic hadn't let it slip that time. And remember how mad you got at him? It's like you don't trust me with your feelings."

"I don't need you to fix me. I'm not broken."

"Seriously? I'm not trying to fix you. I know you're not broken. I just want you to talk to me about him." She pulls out her phone and starts texting. This is her way of telling me that she's upset. Lulu is always attentive when you talk to her, and she wants her friends to act the same. She calls it *being present*. She hates it when we're talking and I pull out my phone. She takes it very personally, so this texting that she's doing right now is sending me a message.

"I spoke to him," I tell her softly.

"To whom?" she asks, not looking up from her phone.

"My dad."

She puts her phone down and looks up. "What? When?"

"On Thanksgiving."

"That's great. Well, actually, how was it?"

"It was okay," I say.

"See Gabe, this is what I'm talking about. It was *okay*? What does that even mean? What did you talk about? How did it feel talking to him after so long?"

I reach up and push the stop button on the bus. "Let's get off at the next stop and go to the pedestrian bridge. I don't want to talk about this on the bus."

It's not too cold for December and the sun is still hitting part of the bridge. We find a sun-warmed bench. "I only spoke to him for a few minutes." I tell her how we spoke about school, about how he called me Gabe and how I wondered how he knew. That he told me that he was proud of me. And that when he said, "Oh Gabriel," the pain and sadness in his voice was so overwhelming that I handed the phone back to Mami and went to my room.

"Oh hon." She pulls me in for a hug. Lulu is an all-in hugger. She's a warm blanket on a freezing night hugger. "But you spoke to him, Gabe," she says in my ear. "That's a start, a step."

She's still hugging me. And okay, I'm hugging her back pretty tight now. And not gonna lie, I'm crying now. And suddenly I'm opening up, telling her about my screaming match with Nic, how we both hurled a bunch of *fuck yous* at each other. I pull out of the hug and say, "And Nic slapped me across the face!"

Her mouth drops open and she bursts out laughing. "That is a-maz-ing! Good for him!"

"Hold up, why are you taking his side? That shit hurt. And you're anti-violence!"

"Yes, of course it was wrong. But you have to admit, you can be really mean to him sometimes. And he worships you. You must have really pushed him over the edge for him to smack you."

"I hate how you like my brother and mother better than you like me."

"They're nicer to me. What do you expect?" She puts a hand on each of my cheeks. "I love you, Gabriel Meyers."

"I love you too, Lulu Montez."

We sit quietly for a few minutes. The sun has ducked behind the Superman building, and it's cool in the shade. The light is fading, and it will be December afternoon dark before long.

"So, what about that Kevin?" I ask.

"What about him?"

"His essay is really good. And he really responded to your criticism in a positive way. He seems like a really solid dude."

"Yeah, he does. He's a good guy."

"He's pretty cute," I add.

"Yup," Lulu agrees.

"Looks like he has a pretty hot little body under those clothes."

"Hell yes!" Lulu cries and we burst out laughing.

"It's getting late. We should be heading home. Let's walk."

Before standing up from the bench, Lulu pulls me in and gives me another warm mama bear hug. "Thanks for sharing, hon. I know that wasn't easy for you." She kisses my cheek.

"Thanks for listening." I'm sure she hears the tears in my voice.

"Let's go." She hooks her arm in mine and we walk west, toward the rapidly setting sun.

Lulu is right about the fortress I've built around me, around this part of my life, the most difficult part. Today she managed to do something others haven't been able to, not Mami, not Nic, not Zach or Karina—she found a small hole in the fortress. Or did she make a small hole in it? Or did she push me, convince me, allow me to crack the fortress wall a tiny bit and let a sliver of light in and expose some of my secrets? However it happened, after sharing, there's a small sense of relief, a slight but perceptible lightening of the load I carry. But there are more secrets hidden in there, ones that I guard more closely, ones that will be harder to expose. And the one that I don't think I can ever let out.

# Chapter 17

I pick up a bunch of extra hours during Christmas break. When I am not at Dunkin, I'm dedicated to working furiously on my college essay. Trevor, Lulu and Kevin have inspired me to tell my story. I start, restart, throw it away, erase it, trash it, start again, rinse and repeat. I'm frustrated. But I'm determined. I have a lot of writing, but none of it is working for me. Nic is the witness to my self-torture and bugs me to let him help. "I'm a really good writer. You can ask all of my teachers," he pleads.

To get him to stop bugging me, I promise that if he leaves me alone, once I have a first draft written, I will let him read it. He reluctantly agrees. I think he really believes that he can write my college essay better than I can. Hell, he may be right.

I go back to Trevor's advice: outline the main points you want to make. What do you need to let this total stranger, this college admissions person, know about you for them to say, "hey, let's take a chance on him"?

*Outline:*

- Father in prison and why (when it happened, accident, conviction, etc.)
- How this has been a challenge (anger, family financial struggles, having to be role model for Nic, etc.)
- What have I done to overcome the challenge (counseling, working harder, trying to be better son and brother, etc.)?

This does help me get started. I hate what I write, but at least it's starting to take shape.

Text alert. It's Billy. While I've been focused on my college essay, he's been focused on us getting together.

*Billy: How's it going???????*
*Me: Ugh. It's going.*
*Billy: Sounds like you need some help (wink emoji)*
*Me: SMH*
*Billy: Seriously, you should come over. I can help. I'm here by myself.*
*Me: Um, if you want to help me on my college essay, why does it matter that you're*
*there by yourself?*
*Billy: Jeez, you and your dirty mind. I just meant my parents wouldn't be all in our*
*business. You know how they get.*
*Me: I don't know….*
*Billy: (sends a picture of himself pouting)*
*Me: Well, when you put it that way...okay.*

Billy answers the door with a big smile. *Okay Gabe, you are here to work on your damn college essay!* "Hello there Gabriel." He sees my reaction. "Yo, just kidding. Gabe." I step inside and he closes the door. He hugs me and I hug him back. His curls are a little wet and smell of shampoo. He smells so damn good. I reluctantly pull away and he moves in to kiss me.

"Nope," I stop him. "I'm here to work on this damn essay. Don't lure me over here with the offer of help and then try to rape me when I walk in the door."

"C'mon man, it was a kiss."

"Yeah, I know where that kiss would lead."

"You're no fun," he says as heads into the kitchen and opens the refrigerator. He grabs a couple of cokes and leads me to his room. He has the whole top floor, with his windows looking down on Prospect Terrace and the city below. He tries to act all businesslike now. "Okay, why don't you start by telling me what you're writing about?"

I let out a deep breath. "Well, I'm writing about my dad being in prison and how that has been a challenge."

Eyebrows up. "Wow, that's amazing. That has the potential to be incredible. You feel ready to tell that story?" We haven't known each other for very long, but he knows me. He's seen the fortress.

"I think so. I mean, Trevor says—Trevor is my English teacher and he's helping—he says that the more honest I am, the better chance I have to make them see who I am."

"What's the hardest part of being honest about this, do you think?" Billy is all in. He really wants to help. He really wants to hear my story. And I think I really want to tell him.

"The hardest part is...well, I think it's...there are so many things that I haven't told anyone, and it feels weird to tell these personal, hidden things to a stranger."

"Maybe if you tell some of them to me, it will be easier to write them down."

"Maybe. I'm not sure."

"You know what I really want to know? How did your mom and dad even end up together?"

Yeah, that's where I need to start.

# Chapter 18

Josh Meyers graduated high school in 1998. According to his high school teachers, he was a "smart young man who failed to meet his potential." He passed his classes, some just barely. But he graduated from high school. He reluctantly enrolled in college because that's what was expected. After a year, he dropped out. College wasn't for him. That summer, he pursued his passion—he got a gig teaching surfing. The surfing season in New England is short, but Josh was hooked as soon as he started to learn to surf the summer he was 12 years old. And each summer he got better. When he got the opportunity to teach surfing, he jumped at it.

When the surfing season ended, he worked a bunch of odd jobs, lived with his parents, hung around with his high school friends, drinking a ton of beer, smoking a lot of weed, watching a lot of old movies. Through the long New England winter and late arriving spring, he anxiously awaited warmer weather and warmer water for the surfing season to begin again. After another great summer of teaching surfing, he and one of his instructor buddies, Steve, decided to chase the sun, the warmth and the surf. They ended up in Puerto Rico.

After bumming around the island for a few months surfing, Josh and Steve landed in Rincón on the west coast of Puerto Rico, with beautiful beaches and great surfing. They spent their days in the water and their nights in the bars. When they finally ran low on money, Steve headed back to the Rhode Island, but Josh stayed on and landed a gig teaching surfing, mostly to American tourists.

One day on the beach, Josh saw a beautiful girl in a blue bikini. Long dark hair, tanned skin. She was with a group of friends, but as Josh ended a lesson and walked back to the surf shop with his board, she looked at him and smiled. He smiled back. After he had passed, he turned his head and looked back. She had turned her head too.

Josh looked for her every day that week, but he didn't see her again. Oh well, he thought, she must have been here on vacation. Then, a week later, he saw her again. Same group of friends, same smile as he passed. This time he said, "Hola." She said "hola" back. Her friends were looking at him, so he just smiled awkwardly and kept walking.

A week later he saw her again and realized that she comes every Tuesday. Today she was alone. Time to shoot his shot. As he walked back with his board, he stopped at her towel. "Hola, cómo estás?"

"Estoy bien gracias, y tu?"

"Muy bien." He smiled at her.

"Me llamo Josh."

"Encantada Josh, soy Isabel."

He asked her if he could sit down, join her. She said yes. He asked her if she spoke English. She said, "just a little," so he kept speaking Spanish, which he was getting better and better with. He told her that he noticed that she was here every Tuesday and she told him that it was her day off. She worked cleaning rooms at one of the hotels. Josh asked Isabel if he could take her to dinner one night. Isabel said yes.

Over the next months, they saw each other Tuesdays on the beach and many, many nights at the bars, restaurants, and in Josh's tiny, rented room. When Isabel found out that she was pregnant, she thought about returning to her parents. She was twenty years old, pregnant by a surfer boy from the mainland who would probably deny it was his baby or just pack his bags and head home.

But she loved Josh. And he told her that he loved her too. So, she didn't go home to her parents. She told Josh that she was pregnant. His eyes widened in shock. Then they softened and he smiled and hugged her. He was happy. "Are you scared?" she asked him. "A little," he said. "But I love you."

As Isabel's belly grew, so did their fear and their happiness, their anxiety and their joy, their doubt and their determination. And their love. Their love grew as little Gabriel grew in Isabel's belly.

They talked and talked and talked about the future. Could they raise a baby in Rincón? On Josh's surfing instructor pay and tips? In his tiny little room? Finally, they decided to move to the mainland and start their life as a family there.

On their last day, full of love and hope for the future, they asked a friend to take their final picture in Rincón. In the photo, Josh is standing behind Isabel, his arms wrapped around her, hands on her belly; a small, rounded belly. A belly with the beginning of Gabriel inside. They both look so happy.

# Chapter 19

Billy says, "Very cool. So, your dad was a surfer dude? What about you? Do you know how to surf?"

"Yeah, my dad started me and Nic surfing when we were little. I haven't been on a board since everything went down with my father and the accident and all."

"We should go when it gets nice. I'm not very good, but I got a couple of moves." He winks at me.

"Yeah, yeah, all right, Romeo." We both laugh. I take a sip of my Coke. I feel Billy's eyes on me, and I look up and see his big gap-toothed grin. "What? Why are you staring at me?"

"What, I can't look at my man?"

"Your man? Hmm."

"What's the matter Gabe? You don't wanna be my man?"

I let out a deep breath that I didn't know I had been holding inside. "It's just...well, I didn't know, I didn't realize that you wanted that. I figured you were probably seeing other people."

"Other people?" He laughs as if it's an absurd notion. "Nah babe, there's only you." Billy continues to look at me, those blue eyes trying to peer deep inside me. This time I don't look down, don't break eye contact. "Can I kiss you now?"

I nod my head. He moves closer and we lean into each other. And this time, I don't stop us. I let myself go, give in to the feelings I've been trying to hide for months.

After a couple of minutes, we slowly break apart. Billy holds my head, one hand on each cheek, our faces inches apart. "Thanks for letting me kiss you, babe."

I let out a small chuckle. "Any time. After all, I am your man."

"That's what I'm talkin about!" he says enthusiastically. "Damn, you just made me really happy, man."

"I can see that." I'm laughing and grinning from ear to ear. I marvel at his childlike passion and free flow of emotions, emotions that live right at the surface, emotions that he seems not only willing to share, but almost unable to not share.

"Okay, now that I finally got my kiss, we can move on to the business of the day. So, let's talk college essay."

# Chapter 20

I tell Billy: My dad was tough on me, but I know he loved me, even though he hardly ever said so. He worked construction, long shifts, leaving early in the morning, but he always woke us up for school right before he left, telling us to be good in school. Sometimes he left a note in our lunch bags with a corny dad joke. At night, even though he was tired, he was there for us. Throwing the ball around in the backyard, helping us with our homework, teaching us guitar. On the weekends he took us to soccer and playdates and in the warm weather, to the beach. Always the beach.

I tell Billy: I learned all about 80s and 90s music and old movies from him.

I tell him: Around the time I was starting middle school, he started getting even tougher on me—my grades were never good enough, my chores were never done right, every fight with Nic was my fault. He would compare me and Nic, and in his eyes, Nic did everything better. "Look at Nicolas's report card. Gabriel, maybe he should help you with your homework," he joked, not seeing, or choosing to ignore the hurt in my eyes. At the beach, surfing: "Wow Nicolas, that was a great run. When Gabriel was your age, he was still wiping out on just about every run."

Some nights he came home later than usual. Some nights, late at night, Nic and I could hear him and Mami fighting. He was drinking more. He was working more on the weekends, leaving us.

I tell Billy: They had a huge fight on the night of the accident. They were both screaming at each other as Nic and I cowered in our room, me holding Nic and telling him that everything was going to be okay.

I tell him: All about the accident.

Billy asks me, "What was the fight about?"

And I freeze. I'm breathing heavily. I taste the salty tears running down my face. Billy is holding me, stroking my hair, not saying anything. Not pushing me. Not trying to get me to talk. Just holding me, giving me safety, giving me love, giving me the possibility of finally unloading this burden.

They were fighting because she found out that he was cheating on her.

She found out about him cheating because I told her. That afternoon, my friends and I got off our bus at Kennedy Plaza to make our transfers and we decided to go for ice cream. We took our ice cream to the park and goofed around. I decided to walk home, since it was a nice day. My friends headed back to the bus stop, and I headed north. As I was walking through the park in front of the State House, I saw people on a park bench. They weren't right in front of me, but even from a distance I could see it might be my father. He was with a woman. Not my mother. I got a little closer and saw that it was definitely him. I was about to run over to him, but then I had the thought, who is that woman he's with? I stopped and watched. They were sitting close to each other. Then he put his hand on her cheek. He pulled her closer and kissed her. I walked a little closer to get a better look. That couldn't be my father, because that's not my mother. I'm sure that's not my mother, so that can't be my father. I stood staring, watching them kiss, repeating to myself that it's not him, knowing all the time that it is him. They must have sensed someone looking at them from across the way because they stopped, and both looked at me. My father and I made eye contact. And I bolted. I ran and ran as I heard him screaming, "Gabriel! Gabriel! Come back. Come back."

I sobbed the whole run home. I burst in the front door and Mami saw me. "Qué te pasó mijo?" she screamed. "Gabriel, Gabriel, Qué te pasó? What happened?" And I told her. That I saw daddy kissing a woman in the park.

"What? No, it's not possible. Are you sure?"

"Yes, I'm sure." I was bawling.

Nic came out of our room and said, "What happened?"

"Nothing," I screamed at him. "Get back in the room." He didn't move. "Get back in the damn room!" He ran back and slammed the door.

We heard my father's car pull into the driveway. He walked in and saw the scene, me crying, Mami crying. He knew. "What's going on here?"

"You know what the hell is going on here," Mami hissed at him.

"What did you tell her?" he snarled at me. I just stood there, looking at him. "What the hell did you tell her?"

"I saw you. I saw you." I screamed it at him.

"Gabriel," he said. "You misunderstood."

"I fucking saw you!"

And he snapped. "Don't you ever talk to me like that. Go to your room." When I didn't move, "Get in your room right now before I beat your ass."

In the room, I lied to Nic. I told him I didn't know what was going on, what happened. He asked, "What did you mean when you said, 'I saw you'?" And again, I lied, telling him that I meant that I saw him coming in the house. I put on music, loud enough to drown out the yelling, and I just kept telling Nic that it was all going to be okay, even though I knew it wasn't.

I tell Billy: How Nic finally fell asleep. The fighting had died down. I crept to the door and looked out. My dad was in the living room, sitting on the sofa, eyes closed. The bottle of scotch on the coffee table was almost empty. I closed the bedroom door behind me. He opened his eyes. They looked red and angry.

"What the hell do you want?" His voice slurred.

"I'm sorry." I wondered, could I make things better?

"You're sorry? You're sorry?" he snorted. "You really fucked things up Gabriel. Running home to Mami like a little pussy."

And suddenly Mami was back. She screamed, "Don't blame this on him. This is not his fault."

He stood up and banged his shin on the coffee table. "Shit. Get out of here Isabel. This is between me and my son."

He moved toward her, and I ran between them. "Leave her alone. Don't touch her," I screamed. His slap was hard and unexpected; he had never hit me before. When his hand made contact with my cheek, I lost my balance and fell.

Mami rushed to me and knelt beside me. "Dios mio, Gabriel, are you okay?"

She turned to him and screamed, "Get out!" There was fire in her voice as she hissed, "I hate you. Get out y no vuelvas nunca!"

"Bitch. Getting you pregnant was the biggest mistake of my life." He looked at me as he said it. "You fuckin trapped me." He stumbled to the door and slammed it behind him.

The rest was all in the newspapers.

Wrapped in Billy's arms, my breathing starts to return to normal. The tears are drying. I must look like shit, all snotty and red-eyed. I extricate myself reluctantly from his strong arms. "Be right back. Just going to the bathroom for a sec."

Yeah, I look like shit. I blow my nose and wash my face. I look in the mirror at my red, puffy eyes. No turning back now Gabe. The toothpaste is out of the tube. Deal with your shit, keep dealing with it. Be a man.

Billy puts down his phone when I walk out of the bathroom. His smile is small and soft. "Hey you," he says.

"Hey."

"How you doing?"

"I'm good." I pause and think a moment. "Actually Billy, I am good. I've never told anyone about him smacking me. My mother's the only one who knows. Now you."

"Thanks for sharing that."

I just nod. Sitting back beside him, I take a sip of my coke. My throat is parched. "Hey," he says softly, "are you done with talking about this today or can I ask you something?"

"I'm good. You can ask me what you want."

"You know that people say things and do things they don't mean when they're mad, right? Especially when they're mad and drunk."

"That's what my mother tries to convince me. Sometimes I try to believe it, want to believe it. I want desperately to believe that he didn't mean it. But I came across something online that says: A drunk man's words are a sober man's thoughts. Do you know the Latin phrase, in vino veritas?"

"No, what's that mean?"

"In wine there is truth. I mean, doesn't it seem just too easy to say, that was the booze talking, not me?"

"Yeah, I get that, but you said he loves you. I don't know..." Billy's voice trails off.

"I've tried, but I feel like I can't let him off the hook just because he was drunk. Then I feel bad about that because, shit, he's in jail. It's not like he's been let off the hook. But he hasn't taken responsibility for saying that to me. Or for hitting me."

"Did you ever talk to him about it?"

"No."

"Then how can he take responsibility if you don't talk to him about it?"

"Damn Billy, he's the adult. I'm the kid. I was the kid. It's on him to own his shit. Why should I have to guide him to it?"

"Maybe because if you don't, you won't heal."

"Thank you, Dr. Sachs," I say sarcastically. "How much do I owe you for today's session?" He looks a little hurt. "I'm sorry. Really. Thanks for listening. You're a good listener. I really feel a lot better."

"Good. I'm glad. What about the college essay? You know this story will kill it."

"I think it will, if I can figure out how to tell it."

We hug at the door. This hug feels different—deep, intimate, connected. Wrapped in this new feeling, I head down the stairs. I cross over to Prospect Terrace, where I sit for a while watching the sunset, lost in my thoughts. When I finally get up to leave, I look up at Billy's bedroom window. He's standing at the window, looking down at me. He gives me a little wave. I smile and wave back. Then I head down the hill and cross over to Kennedy Plaza to catch my bus. When I see my bus pulling away right before I get there, I decide to walk. I take the route that I have avoided for the past four years, through the park in front of the State House.

# Chapter 22

"**K**evin asked me out." We're in the cafeteria and Lulu is eating a salad she brought from home. I'm eating pizza and tater tots.

"Really? That's great."

She doesn't look totally convinced. "Yeah, I guess. I mean, I like him and he's really cute. But I don't know if I should be giving my time to some boy when I have so much to concentrate on with school."

"C'mon Lulu. You have to enjoy the last of high school. Nothing you do now is going to change college. You have great grades. It's not like a date is going to ruin your future."

"We'll see."

"He asked you, but you didn't answer him?

"I told him I'd think about it." She nibbles on a raw carrot.

"Oh, I see. Playing hard to get. You think that guys like that, right?" I tease her.

"Well, it's worked for me in the past." We both laugh. "Speaking of hard to get, how's it going with Billy. Have you given in to that lovestruck boy yet?"

"Shut up. He's not lovestruck." She gives me her are-you-serious-right-now look.

"Things are good," I admit. "It's moving along."

"Hmmm, how fast is it moving along?" she asks suggestively.

"Not that fast. You and your dirty mind."

I spot Kevin across the cafeteria. He sees me and I wave to him, gesture him to come on over. Lulu sees me and turns around to see who I'm waving at. When she sees that it's Kevin, she turns back. "Oh Gabe, you think you're funny, don't you? Look at you. Proud of yourself and your little stunt. Well, just wait. You'll pay for this. When you least expect it."

And Kevin is at the table. "Hey Gabe," he fist bumps me. "Hey there Lulu. You don't mind if I sit here?"

"No," Lulu responds. "Of course not. Have a seat."

Kevin surveys the scene and decides to sit on my side of the table, facing Lulu. Good choice, Kev.

Kevin has a big plate of salad from the salad bar. "That's a big healthy lunch," I remark.

He laughs. "Yep, I'm in training. And they don't have much here that I eat. I have to lay off the carbs right now and I don't eat meat anyway."

Lulu perks up. "Really?? You don't eat meat?"

"Nope. You know, the whole my-body-is-my-temple thing."

"So, it's only for health reasons that you don't eat meat?" Lulu follows up.

"Yeah, pretty much. One of my coaches told me how bad it can be for your body, how hard meat is to digest, the hormones they pump into animals. All that stuff."

"Well, it's good that you see the health reasons, but you know there are moral reasons to not eat meat too." Lulu is in lecture mode. Kevin looks a little confused.

I cut in. "Lu, Kev doesn't eat meat. That's the point. Does it really matter why?"

She relents. "I guess you're right. I will reluctantly agree with you and spare Kevin any further lectures. I thank you for not eating meat, Kevin. The animals thank you. And the planet thanks you."

Kevin looks at me, a question mark on his forehead. I shrug. He looks at Lulu. "Um, you're welcome?"

We talk about school, movies, music, work. Kevin works at a different Dunkin than me and we trade stories about crazy customers. Every once in a while, I look over at Lulu. I can see that she's digging Kevin more and more.

"How's wrestling going?" I ask him.

"It's good, man. I'm still undefeated this season. Two more meets. One home, one away. Hopefully I make states."

"When's the home meet?" I can feel Lulu's eyes on me. She knows what I'm doing.

"It's this Friday."

"Great. Hey Lulu, we talked about doing something after school on Friday but we didn't decide what. We should go to Kev's wrestling meet."

"That would be cool," Kevin says, looking at Lulu for confirmation.

"Yeah, that would be cool," Lulu says, and I expect her to shoot me a look or kick me under the table. But she looks like she thinks it really would be cool.

"Great. It's a date," I say and look down and attack the last of my tater tots.

# Chapter 23

A text arrives from Karina as I'm on my way to school. She asks if I'll come to her office before going to my first period class. Damn, now what?

I poke my head into her office. "Morning Karina."

"Gabe." She has just taken a bite of her bagel. "Sorry," she says, covering her chewing mouth. I notice February's motivational poster on the wall behind her. It's a picture of Maya Angelou with the quote: "I've learned that people will forget what you said, people will forget what you did, but people will never forget how you made them feel." I wonder if Maya is right. Will I forget what my dad said? What he did? Will I always remember how he made me feel? I swear that Karina chooses these inspirational posters just to mess with my head.

"You wanted to see me?"

"Yes, thanks for coming in. How's it going?" Oh, this isn't good. What has she heard? Is she setting me up for a counseling session right now?

"Um, it's going good, thanks. Why?"

"Just asking. I actually wanted to ask a favor of you."

"Okay, sure," I say reluctantly.

"We have a new student starting today. He just moved here. He's going to be in Physics with you and I was hoping you could help him out since you're doing so well. He was in Physics in his old school, but he could probably use some help just getting on the right track in a new school."

"Yeah, that's cool." I'm really not feeling helping some new kid when I have all my own shit going on, but Karina's always there for me. And I know how it feels to be the new kid.

"Great." She hesitates a moment. "There's one thing. He just moved here from the Dominican Republic. His English is somewhat limited right now. He's studied English back home, but he'll need a little support."

"Hold up, Karina. You mean you want me to translate for him? In class?"

"I wouldn't ask Gabe, but Kate has a pretty full class there and her Spanish is...well, you've heard her try to speak Spanish." She gives a little giggle and smiles at me.

Yes, Kate's Spanish sucks for sure. But that doesn't mean I'm going to translate. "Karina, you know how I feel about speaking Spanish in school."

"Yes, of course I do. We've talked about that a lot. We've also talked about facing the things that make us uncomfortable. The power in that."

And we have talked a lot about it. I told her about how in middle school, kids started to get mean. There were a lot of kids new to the country who didn't speak English. And a lot of the other kids were horrible to them, calling them names, calling them stupid because they didn't understand. If a teacher forced one of the immigrant kids to read or to answer a question, some of the other kids would laugh or mimic the mistakes that they made. So, I wouldn't speak a word of Spanish. And I could pass because I spoke English and I looked like a white boy. And the name Gabriel, when pronounced the right way, sounds plain old American. No one knew I was half Puerto Rican, and I liked it that way and was determined to keep it that way.

But I'm on a new journey—a journey to own my truth. Karina is giving me an opportunity to broaden the horizons of that journey. She knows what she's doing. There are other students who could translate. But she asked me. Because she wants to push me, wants me to challenge myself. I've opened up about my dad—to Lulu, to Billy, to myself, to my college essay. And I feel better—lighter and calmer. I'm still a bit of a mess, but less of a mess than I've been in a long time.

"What's his name?" I ask.

"Ángel," she replies with the Spanish pronunciation. "But he wants to be called Angel, with the American pronunciation. He thinks it will help him fit in." She smiles knowingly.

I roll my eyes and give her a reluctant smile. "Okay, Karina. I'll do it for you."

"Thanks. I'll introduce you to Angel at lunch." Before I walk out, she stops me. "And Gabe, you're not doing it for me. You're doing it for Angel. And for yourself."

I roll my eyes. "Whatever." She laughs.

# Chapter 24

Last period, I arrive at Kate's class. I see Angel. Karina introduced us in the lunchroom. As we enter, Kate tells us to look for our names on the cards and find our partners. Everyone starts to moan and groan about having to work with someone else and then they moan and groan some more when they see who they have to work with. Karina must have spoken to Kate because I see the card that says ANGEL and GABE. I can see people are looking at Angel. Some of them may have seen him in other classes or in the cafeteria but a lot of them seem like they've never seen him before. Kate starts by introducing him. "For anyone who hasn't met him yet, we have a new student in class. Everyone, this is Angel." Angel gives a little wave. Most everyone acts disinterested, but I know the girls are checking him out for his looks and the boys are checking him out as competition for the girls who are checking him out for his looks. I catch Angel's eye and wave him over to me.

Kate explains that we are starting on a new project called a Rube Goldberg Machine. We will be making a big machine that a ball travels through, sort of like that old school game called Mousetrap. Building this game, we will learn about force, friction, energy, and momentum. It sounds pretty cool.

We listen to Kate's introduction and watch her PowerPoint and the class is super interested. She then gives us the instructions for the first step of our project. I ask Angel, in English, if he understands. He says, "Some of it." I tell him to show me the parts that he wants me to explain. He circles a few sections and I start to explain. There are technical terms that I don't know the Spanish words for, but when I explain them, he gets it. He can talk about some of the concepts in ways that I don't understand. It's not that I don't understand the Spanish. It's that I don't get the concepts yet. He gets all of the concepts because he's studied them before. He's just figuring out how to do it all in English.

I'm trying to keep our Spanish conversation in a hush, on the low, but as we start getting more and more into the concepts, I guess we start to talk louder, and I notice some people looking our way. I figure they're surprised to hear me speaking Spanish. I'm totally into this project, this crazy machine we're going to build, and I'm surprised that I'm feeling really good about my ability to collaborate with Angel, in English and Spanish. I ignore the looks we are getting.

At the end of class, Andres walks over with his friend Daniel. He says to me, "Yo, you speak Spanish?"

"Yeah."

"How do you know Spanish?"

"I'm half Puerto Rican," I tell them.

Daniel and Andres look at each other, wide-eyed, like they can't believe it.

"Word?" Daniel says.

"I thought you was some white boy." Andres looks completely confused.

"My dad's white. My mom's Puerto Rican."

"Damn, the shit we don't know." Andres turns to Angel. "Bienvenidos amigo." They shake. Daniel fist bumps Angel. Then they both fist bump me, turn, and walk out of class.

# Chapter 25

The gym is packed on Friday afternoon. The wrestling team is very popular. We have no football team, our basketball team sucks, and baseball is months away. And the wrestling team is good. State champion worthy good.

I lead Lulu down to the front, but she stops me and says we can't sit in the front because if Kevin sees her, it will make him nervous. With one raised eyebrow, I look at her and say, "Damn Lulu, you think you're so magical that the boy will suddenly lose his ability to wrestle if he feels your presence?" Her non-violent self punches me in the arm, tells me to shut up, and leads me to the fourth row.

"I can't believe I have never been to a wrestling match before," Lulu tells me.

"Actually, the match is the competition between two wrestlers. The whole thing is called a meet. So we are watching the meet," I correct her.

She gives me a baffled look.

"I did some research," I explain. "I didn't want to seem stupid."

"Are you calling me stupid?"

"Lulu, no—"

"Yes, you just called me stupid. You basically said that I was stupid for not knowing the difference between a match and a meet. I can't believe you sometimes."

I try to wiggle my way out of this. "Hey look, there's the team coming in. There's Kevin."

"Wow, he looks super concentrated," Lulu observes.

"Yeah, totally in a zone."

The action begins and our classmate Derek, who is sitting behind us, becomes our private play-by-play announcer. He explains the starting positions and the three two-minute time periods. When one of our guys, Glenn, is on the mat with their guy on top, he busts out and is suddenly on top. Derek tells us, "That's a reversal. Glenn just got two points for that." When Glenn gets the guy on his back, pinned to the mat, our team erupts. But their guy struggles free. "Damn," Derek says, "Glenn almost had the pin. But he gets three points for that. It's called a near pin."

This continues through match after match. Escapes, take downs, penalty points. It's getting very exciting. But Kevin hasn't wrestled yet. "When is Kevin going to wrestle," Lulu turns around to ask Derek.

"I betcha the coaches are keeping Kevin and Ronnie for last. Shit, this is gonna be crazy close. But my money's on Kevin." I've never seen Derek so animated. I'm used to seeing him sitting in the back of math class dozing off.

Derek is right. Kevin and Ronnie are up last. And it all comes down to this match. The visitors are up by five points going into this final match. Derek informs us that this is going to be tough. Kevin could win his match and the team could still lose. "Kevin needs five team points for our team to tie. Six points and they win. It's gonna be hard for either. He'll need to pin Ronnie to get the six points and pinning Ronnie is fucking hard."

Kevin strips off his sweatpants and sweatshirt and now he's standing there in his red singlet. I steal a quick glance at Lulu. She's stealing a quick glance at me too. "What?" I ask her.

"Nothing."

"Nothing?"

"Well, I could tell that he had a good body, even under his regular clothes. But damn," she whispers, "I didn't know he'd look like that."

"Lulu, I can't believe you, of all people, are objectifying Kevin like that. That's wrong, and frankly, it's disgusting."

She glares at me. "You're right, it's horrible. But you know I'm right. And you were thinking the same thing. And shut up."

Kevin's opponent, Ronnie, is a ripped red headed dude with a buzz cut, beard, and full arm sleeve tattoo. He looks as mean as shit. I turn back to Derek. "You said your money is on Kevin?" I ask skeptically.

"Well, Ronnie is tough for sure. I mean, look at the dude. And he and Kev are both undefeated this season. But Ronnie beat Kevin at states last year and Kevin is hellbent on revenge. He looks cool, but he's boiling inside. Ronnie is stronger, but Kev has better technique."

The gym is shaking as the crowd screams for Kevin and Ronnie. They both have a confident strut and an intense gaze as they approach each other to start the match in neutral position. The ref blows his whistle, and the guys grab each other quickly. Ronnie seems to have the early advantage as he wraps himself around Kevin and tries to bring him down. Kevin's feet are planted firmly in the mat, but as Ronnie twists him to his right, his foot slips and suddenly he's on the mat. Take down for Ronnie. Ronnie is working hard to flip Kevin on his back, but Kev is fast and strong and he gets out of Ronnie's grip. Escape for Kevin. The two-minute period seems like ten minutes and when the buzzer sounds, Ronnie is up 2-1.

The second period begins with Kevin on his hands and knees and Ronnie at his side with one arm around Kevin's waist and the other on his elbow. By now, Lulu and I know, with the help of wrestling encyclopedia Derek, that this is the referee's position and Ronnie's in the top position and Kevin in the bottom. The ref blows his whistle and Ronnie is driving his legs into the mat, pushing against Kev with all his force to push him down. Kev is an oak tree, planted firmly, going nowhere. They struggle like this for what seems like minutes, until finally Kevin drops to the ground and scrambles out of Ronnie's grip. They are back on their feet, jockeying for position again. Kevin lunges at Ronnie's feet and Ronnie wraps his arms around Kevin's waist. They are on the ground, one on top then the other on top. Legs wrap around each other, then they break free. Suddenly, Ronnie has Kev on his back. Kev is struggling forcefully, using every ounce of strength he has to keep his back off the mat. Ronnie drives him down; the ref moves in close with his hand raised in the air. Ronnie has Kevin pinned but the buzzer sounds just as the ref is about to bring his hand down to signal a victory for Ronnie.

"Holy shit. That was almost the end. The end of the season for the team." Derek is hyperventilating behind us. I'm feeling the same way.

The final round begins with Ronnie up 8-7. Kevin can still win his individual match on points, but there's no way the team can win without him pinning Ronnie. They begin the final round with Kevin in the top position. Like the first two rounds, the two of them are battling ferociously. No one has the clear advantage as they swap takedowns and reversals. The score is tied at 10-10 with thirty seconds left when Kevin breaks free of Ronnie's grasp and immediately spins around and dives at Ronnie's legs and takes him down. Kevin has Ronnie on his stomach and the struggle continues. Ronnie has massive quads, and he pushes up and almost breaks Kevin's hold, but Kevin grabs him again and spins him around. He has Ronnie on his back now. Kevin is pushing with all his remaining strength and Ronnie is resisting with all of his. The crowd is screaming, the wrestlers are all on their feet, the coaches are screaming instructions that Kevin and Ronnie cannot hear through the noise. Kevin has Ronnie's back on the mat finally. The ref is ready to call the pin. I look at the time clock—three seconds remaining. The ref's hand comes down. Match over. Pin for Kevin. Win for the team.

Kevin is the total hero. His win means that the team is going to states and he is going individually. The gym is rocking. Lulu and I are standing and screaming, as if we are lifelong wrestling fans. I see Kevin break from his teammates and look over to the crowd. He spots me and Lulu—well, he spots Lulu—and waves with an enormous smile. He strides over and the crowd is going wild. People are high fiving him and he's actually pretty humble in the face of all this adoration. No chest thumping, preening, macho shit. Just thanking people and smiling.

He makes his way up the bleachers to me and Lulu. "Thanks for coming guys. It really means a lot to me."

"Dude, you were amazing," I tell him. "I don't know shit about wrestling, but I could tell you are the bomb."

Derek butts in from the rear. "Yeah, he definitely don't know shit about wrestling. But man, you killed it."

"Thanks man." He turns to smile at Lulu. "Did you like it?"

Lulu's smile manages to be shy, and charming, and captivating all at the same time. "Yes, Kevin, I liked it. I definitely liked it."

And the two of them are looking at each other as if they are all alone, instead of in a crowded gym full of sweaty wrestlers and screaming high schoolers. Kevin snaps out of the private moment and says, "I haven't eaten all day because I had to make my weight. I'm starving. Do you want to grab a bite to eat after I shower?"

I'm not sure if he's just talking to Lulu or if he means me too, so I stand there stupid. "What about it, Gabe? Think you can get Lulu to come out for a veggie burger?"

"Yeah Kev. I think I can convince her." I turn to Lulu. "Veggie burger, Lu?"

"Absolutely," she responds to me. But her smile is on Kevin's face.

# Chapter 26

The final paragraph of my college essay was the most difficult to complete. I wrote, shared, revised and revised again. I've done my final revision. I'm as satisfied as I can be. I've been as honest as I can be.

*And the next time that my father calls, I will stay in the room. I won't run, I won't hide, I won't lock myself away in my fortress. I will take the phone. I will follow my little brother's example and speak to my father as if he is on a business trip and not in prison. I will do it for him, for my mother, for my brother. I will do it for myself. I will tell him about school, I will talk about my college essay, this essay, and my hopes and dreams. I will allow him to envision my future and all that it holds. And when he tells me that he is proud of me (which he will) and says, "You know that, Gabriel. Right?" I won't hand the phone back to my mother. I will say, "Yes, Dad, I know you are proud of me. I've always tried to make you proud of me. I love you for being proud of me." And I will try to find a way to make him know that I forgive him and that as difficult as the past three years have been, they have made me stronger, more resilient, and more ready to face my future.*

I click "submit" and my college application is complete.

# Chapter 27

When Lulu asked me if Billy and I wanted to go on a double date with her and Kevin, my first thought, of course, was "are you out of your mind?" That's a whole new level of boyfriend commitment there. But when I really thought about it, I had a pretty good feeling that Billy and Kevin would hit it off. They're both really friendly and chill and both really into sports, so I told her I would ask Billy.

I go to Billy's house after school to help him study for his Physics final. I ring the bell and his mom answers the door. "Gabe! So good to see you sweetie. How have you been?" She hugs me.

"I'm doing well, Patricia. How about you?"

"Oh, you know. Just trying to survive winter, hoping for an early spring. And not too much more snow. Can I get you anything? Soda? Snack?"

"No thanks, I'm good. I appreciate it though."

"Of course. Well, Billy is in his room. Go on up. And Gabe, thanks for helping him study. He's been really stressing over this final. I'm glad to hear that you're so good at Physics."

"Well, I'm not sure how good I am, but I'm happy to help. Actually, Physics is my best subject. I'll get him ready for the final." She smiles at me, and I bound up the stairs. As I approach his room, I hear Post Malone—"Rich and Sad"—playing behind the door. I give a quick knock and walk in. Billy is on his bed in just his boxers. When he sees me, he sits up and greets me with a big smile. He turns down the music. "Hey."

"Hey." I look him up and down. "So, this is how you dress to study for a Physics exam? Boxer shorts? You do know your mother is right down the stairs, right?"

"You're funny. I took my uniform off when I got home from school and then laid down for a bit. I'm going to put my sweats on." He hops out of bed, comes over and gives me a quick little kiss, and then grabs sweats from a pile of clothes in the corner.

"Dude, what's up with that pile of clothes? Are you just pulling shit out of dirty laundry to throw on when I get here? What the—?"

"Nah, it's all clean. My mom makes me do my own laundry. I just washed all of it."

"So why the hell is it in a pile in the corner?"

"Jeez, you sound just like her. I haven't had a chance to put it away."

"Do you know how to fold clothes? Need me to teach you that before I teach you physics?" I stand up and walk to the pile of clothes.

He laughs. "It's a good thing you're so cute or I would beat your ass right now. I know how to fold clothes, smartass, but it's easier to have things right here where I need them. Look, I don't have to go to the closet. I just bend down and, boom, there's my favorite T-shirt." He pulls a faded yellow T-shirt out of the pile and slips it over his head. On the front, in big black letters: LOSER. "So don't go folding my clothes. Sit your ass down and teach me some physics."

I shake my head. "You're really living up to that shirt."

"Har, har. You're wicked funny."

I tell him Lulu's idea about the double date. Billy, of course, loves the idea. No hesitation on his part. "Absolutely!" he says. "Babe, you're letting me into the exclusive inner circle a little more. I love it. Before you know it, I'll be meeting your mom and Nic." He has that shit eating grin on his face. Not gonna lie, that grin gets me every time.

"Baby steps. Okay, now that you're not half naked anymore, let's get down to work on this physics test."

"You don't like me half naked?" he asks suggestively.

"I didn't say that. But your mother is downstairs, and we have work to do."

We spend the next couple of hours immersed in studying. I'm helping him to understand some of the concepts for his test. We're connecting on a different level. This is intellectual, theoretical, practical, scientific. It's taking us in a new direction, allowing us to see aspects of each other that we haven't seen yet. Up until now, I've seen Billy as this really sweet, fun, funny guy. A guy who's caring and emotionally open. But tonight I've seen how smart he is, how curious he is. And how unafraid he is to say that he doesn't understand, that he needs help. I wonder if he's seen new aspects of me. I don't have to wonder long.

"You're brilliant Gabe. I've been struggling in physics this whole semester, and you really helped me to understand this in like two hours. I feel like I can tackle this test. And I need to ace this test or I'm in deep shit with my father."

"Why? It's just one test."

"He's watching my GPA like a hawk. He expects me to graduate first or second in my class."

"First or second? Damn. Where do you stand right now?"

"Second, but barely. Emily Almeida is a solid point ahead of me. Last we checked, Jacob Easton is less than a point behind me. We're practically tied. And he's not taking Physics, so this class is big for me. Thank you for helping me study."

"You got it. Happy to help."

"Can we cuddle for a few minutes before you leave?" He gives me his puppy dog eyes.

"Cuddle? Did you seriously ask me to cuddle?"

"Hey, I'm a sensitive guy, remember? Just lie down for a few minutes. Nothing else. Scout's honor."

"You ain't no scout," I laugh as I hop onto his bed. We just lie there with our arms around each other.

My mind is racing. Billy sees and says, "Hey, what are you thinking about?"

"Well," I start hesitantly. "I'm thinking about two things. First, spring break."

"Yeah? What about it?"

"Mine is the second week of April."

"Mine too," Billy says, softly stroking my hair.

"My uncle and his husband live in Brooklyn, and they invited me down."

"Cool. That should be fun. I love Brooklyn. Well, I've actually only been on the Brooklyn Bridge, but I loved that."

"They said I can bring a friend."

We both say nothing for a moment, then Billy asks, "Is Lulu going with you?"

"Well. I was actually wondering if you might want to go."

Again, no-hesitation, no-pretend Billy says, "Are you kidding me? Of course, I'll go to Brooklyn with you!" He grabs my face and plants a kiss. "This will be so amazing Gabe. I'm so excited. But really, it's okay with them? Do they know about me?"

All I can do is smile at his enthusiasm and marvel at the fact that he's as excited about it as I am.

"Yes, it's okay with them. They told me to bring a friend. They don't know about you. Yet. But I'll tell them."

"Great. We need to start planning. Should we take the train? Yeah, I think the train will be better than the bus. I'll get tickets. When should we leave?"

"Billy, we have time. It's only January. We have months to plan. I still have to talk to my mom about it and you need to talk to your parents."

He's still beaming. Then I see him remember something. "So, you said you were thinking about two things. What's the other thing."

"You know, let's just enjoy this and we'll talk about the second thing later." He looks at me with suspicion in his squinting eyes.

"Okay babe."

"I have to get home. I promised Nic we'd hang out tonight. I've been so busy. He feels like I'm neglecting him, and he knows how to lay on the guilt."

"Aw, you're such a good big brother." He tousles my hair and I push his hand away. "I'll drive you home," he offers.

We head downstairs. I poke my head in to say goodbye to his mom. She's cooking and it smells delicious, all garlic and spices. "Bye Patricia. Nice to see you."

"Oh Gabe, you're leaving? Don't you want to stay for dinner? Nothing fancy, just some pasta."

"It smells delicious, but I need to get home to my brother. But thanks."

"Okay honey," she says as she hugs me goodbye. "See you very soon I hope."

"I'm going to drive Gabe home. I'll be back soon for dinner Mom."

As we walk out, Billy's father is parking his car. Now we're going to get cornered by him. It always takes me forever to get out of his house because his parents are all over me. I guess I should be happy that they seem to like me.

"Gabe!" he says when he sees me. He crushes my hand with his handshake. I smell the alcohol on his breath as he pulls me close. "How's it going young man? Haven't seen you in a while. Doing well in school? Keeping those grades up?"

"Yes sir. I'm doing really well this year."

"That's great to hear. Hopefully this one can get his act together for his final exams," he says, gesturing toward Billy. He says it in a joking tone, but knowing what I know now, he's not joking.

"We just studied for his Physics final," I jump in, trying to rescue Billy. "I think he's going to do really well."

Billy tries to change the subject. "Hey dad, guess what? Gabe's uncle lives in Brooklyn, and he invited him to visit during April vacation and told him he can bring a friend and we both have break the same week."

"That's great, if you pass all of your finals. But, let me talk to your mother before I say yes. I pay a price when I make unilateral decisions." He laughs and I have no idea what he's talking about.

"Dad, I'm almost eighteen. So is Gabe. We're both almost in college."

"I know Billy. It's probably fine with me. I'm sure it will be fine with her too, but I just want to talk to her first. That's how relationships work."

"Okay Dad. I'm going to drive Gabe home. I'll be back soon for dinner."

"Gabe, why don't you join us for dinner. I'm sure Patricia has enough."

"Gee Dad, shouldn't you talk to her first? Isn't that how relationships work?" Billy smirks at his dad.

"What a smart aleck," Martin says and turns to me. "Isn't he a smart aleck? I don't know how you put up with him." Damn, parents are so corny.

I just laugh and Billy saves me. "Okay, we're going. Be right back."

"Bye Martin." He crushes my hand again.

"Come and see us again soon Gabe. And stay for dinner the next time."

"I will. Thanks."

Martin goes into the house, and we get into Billy's shiny yellow Jeep. He pulls out of the driveway and heads west. "Man, I'm sorry about my parents. They mean well, but they do come on strong."

"Why did you have to tell him about Brooklyn with me there? Why didn't you wait until later when it was just the three of you? It made me feel like I was causing family drama."

"First of all, it's not going to be drama. They're going to be fine about it. Well, if I do well on my exams. My mom will have no problem with it. Second of all, sorry, but I was so excited. A week in New York, the two of us. It's gonna be dope. We can do some touristy shit, go to NYU, Columbia. Oh, Brooklyn. We can go to Coney Island. Do they live near Coney Island?"

"I'm not sure actually. I think they're close to the Brooklyn Bridge, and I think that might be far from Coney Island. But hey, you can get anywhere on the subway in New York."

"Have you been to their house?"

"Only once. We went down one Thanksgiving when I was about ten or eleven. We went the night before Thanksgiving and saw them blow up the balloons for the Macy's parade and then Thanksgiving morning we went and saw the parade."

"Get out. That must've been amazing."

"Yeah, it was pretty cool. Nic and I still talk about that trip. Nic will be so pissed when he finds out we're going to visit Andy and Keith."

"Which one is the uncle?"

"Andy. He's my dad's brother. I think he's about three years older than my dad."

I explain to Billy how after the accident, when my father was in the hospital, Andy came up for a few days. Things were a mess, my mother was a mess, Nic and I were confused and of course, I was in total turmoil. I don't think I was really angry at that point. It was more like I had been hit by a car and didn't really know what had happened. Uncle Andy was a rock—calm and in control. He talked to the doctors and explained to us what was going on. He assured us that things would be okay. He brought food, took me and Nic out for pizza. I heard him one night telling Mami that she shouldn't worry about money, that he was going to make sure everything was fine. She cried and he held her. He's only been back to visit one time, about a year later, but he calls to check on us. We're connected on Instagram.

"I haven't told my mom yet about going to New York. But I'm sure she'll be fine with it. I think."

We've reached my house. Billy pulls up to the curb in front.

"Does she know about me yet?" Billy asks.

"She knows your name. She knows you exist. She probably suspects something because Nic's a chismoso. And she hasn't asked a lot of questions about you, which she usually does about new friends."

"When are you going to tell her? We've been going out for almost five months."

"I don't know yet. I told you Billy, she's not as comfortable with it as your parents."

"But you have a gay uncle and she's cool with him and his husband."

"I don't really know how cool she is. She doesn't really talk much about Keith, and she's only really met him a few times."

"Well, you can't hide me forever Gabe."

"Jesus Billy, I'm not hiding you. She knows about you."

"But Gabe, you are hiding me. You're hiding that I'm your boyfriend. If you're pretending that I'm just your friend, that's hiding."

"I can't do this right now Billy."

"What does that mean, you can't do this? Can't talk to me about our relationship?"

"I mean I can't argue with you about my mother. You have your family dynamic and I have mine. They're different. One is not better than the other. They're just different." I'm pretty heated now and my voice is getting louder. "It's really not up to you to decide when I should tell my mother about who I'm seeing."

"Who you're seeing? Oh, okay." He's shaking his head.

"What? Now what, Billy?"

"You make it sound like I'm just some guy that you see sometimes." Now he's getting heated. "I think of you as more than some guy I'm seeing. Maybe I have it wrong."

"Billy, you're really twisting this into something it's not. Just because I haven't told my mother about you yet doesn't mean that I don't care about you. You're acting like a—" I stop myself.

"Like a what?" he shouts.

"Nothing."

"No, like a what?"

"I was gonna say, like a girl. But Lulu would kill me if she heard me say that."

"I'm 'acting like a girl' because I'm emotionally open and honest with you and I tell you how I feel? If that is what your idea of acting like a girl is, then count me in. I'll act like a girl all the time. But if you want to turn our relationship into some twisted stereotype of a heterosexuality with you being the emotionally stunted man afraid to show his feelings, I'm not interested Gabe."

"Okay, got it. You're not interested. I should go then." I reach for the door handle and hesitate.

He lets out a sneering snort of a laugh. "You either didn't listen to what I just said, or you just deliberately twisted my words. So yeah, if you don't even have the balls to work out the difficult shit, then yeah, you should just go."

So I go. And I slam the car door.

I see Mami looking out the window as Billy's Jeep tears away and he speeds off.

# Chapter 28

Mami lets go of the drawn back curtain and steps away from the window. Too late. She knows I saw her looking out. Great. Is a fight with Billy going to lead to a fight with her? I open the front door and she's in the kitchen doing dishes.

"Hola mi amor. Cómo estás?

"Hi Mami. I'm good. How was your day?"

"It was fine. The car is acting up again. I have to bring it back to Jose." She is drying her hands on the dish towel. "Tienes hambre? I made pollo with rice and beans. I can heat some up for you."

"I can do it Mami."

"No mijo. I'll do it. Sit."

Okay, now for sure she is getting ready to ask me about Billy. Otherwise, she would have said what she usually says: "You know where the plates are, and you know how to operate the microwave."

"Where's Nic?"

"He went to Jimmy's after track practice. He's eating there and then Jimmy's father is bringing him home."

"Oh. We were supposed to hang out tonight."

"He didn't forget. He'll be home soon. He told me to make sure you know. He's very excited of course." She strokes my hair. It feels nice.

I dig into my rice and beans. My plan was to put the chicken to the side, but Mami's chicken is so good, I can't resist it. What Lulu doesn't know won't hurt her. Or rather, hurt me. And Nic isn't here to see and rat me out to her.

Mami fixes herself a cup of tea and sits down opposite me. Here we go; she's about to start the inquisition. "Who was that who dropped you off?" Okay, easy enough first question, but I know it will get worse from here.

"It was Billy. I went to his house after school to help him study for his physics test, so he gave me a ride home."

"That was nice of him. And he has a nice Jeep."

"Yeah, it's nice." I'm taking my time eating so I can concentrate on my food instead of looking at her.

"Is everything okay between you and your amigo Billy?"

"Yeah, why?"

"It looked like maybe you were fighting."

"How long were you spying on us," I ask accusingly.

Although I've snapped at her, she calmly replies, "I wasn't spying. I saw a car that I didn't recognize parked in front of the house, so I was looking to see who it was."

"But you looked long enough to see us fighting."

"So, you were fighting? I thought you were, especially when you slammed his car door shut. Y se fue muy rápido." She really has an eye for the details.

"Yes, we were fighting."

"What were you fighting about, mi amor?" Her voice is really tender, the mother voice that brings you back to childhood, the mother voice when you fell down and scraped your knee. The mother voice when you woke in the middle of the night from a bad dream. The mother voice that you sometimes need to hear even when you are almost eighteen, almost a grown man. The mother voice that gives you permission to let it all out.

Through my tears, I say, "We were talking about you."

"Me? Why were you talking about me?" There is no defensiveness in her question.

After a moment of silence, I find my voice. "Billy asked me if I had told you about him, if you knew who he was." I don't know what else to say. Our eyes are locked, mine asking her to help me out. And she does.

"He wanted to know if I knew you were his novio, his boyfriend?" There is only a moment's hesitation between the words "his" and "boyfriend."

I nod my head yes, tears streaming down my face.

She moves to my side of the table and sits in the chair next to me and takes my face in both her hands, wiping my tears with her thumbs. "Oh Gabriel, mi amor. Yes baby, I knew. I knew when I saw how happy you were when you came home from the movies with him. I knew when Nic asked who you were texting, and you said it was Billy. I saw the happiness in your face. I was just waiting for you to tell me, on your own time."

"I'm sorry I didn't tell you sooner."

"I'm sorry I didn't make you feel that you could tell me, but we're talking now. You like this boy a lot, sí?"

"Yes Mami, I do."

"That's a good thing, mijo. So now you need to tell him that your mother knows about him. And that she wants to meet him."

"Really?" Who is this woman?

"Por supuesto. Escucha, Gabriel. We've all struggled the last four years. It's been hard on all of us, but I think it's been the hardest on you. Because you have been so hard on yourself. Mi amor, no es tu culpa. None of it is your fault." When she says this, I break. She wraps me in her arms, and I cry into her neck. "You need to be kinder to yourself. Let go of the guilt you hold onto so tight. You need to allow yourself to be happy. Don't lose Billy."

She holds me until the crying subsides. "Your birthday is coming up. We can have a small dinner and you can invite him."

"Gracias, Mami."

I hear a car pull up. It must be Jimmy's dad dropping off Nic. "I'm going to the bathroom. I'll be right out." In the bathroom, I splash cold water on my face and dry my eyes, and when I come out, Nic is there. When he sees my face, he cocks his head and comes closer to inspect. Of course, he gets too close. "Back up, freak." I push him away laughing.

He says, "You look really happy, but you look like you've been crying. What's up with that?"

"Shut up. I haven't been crying."

"Your eyes are all red. Are you stoned then?"

"No, I'm not stoned. Jesus."

"But you are happy?"

I look at Mami and then I turn back to my little brother. "Yeah Nic, I am happy. And I'm going to be even happier when I beat your ass in Mortal Kombat. Let's do it."

# Chapter 29

In the bottom drawer of my bureau, there is a manilla envelope under my neatly folded sweaters. Inside it are seven smaller envelopes, each one addressed to me. None of the envelopes have been opened. They are all from my father. I take the envelope down to the basement, where I can have privacy.

I open the box with dad's CDs and his discman. I put the headphones on, pop in Nirvana's *Nevermind*, and hit play. The first track comes on, "Smells Like Teen Spirit." As Kurt Cobain growls, I imagine my teenage father playing the shit out of this song.

My hand is inside the large envelope, holding onto the seven smaller envelopes. I've gotten this far before, ready to take them out, but I've never taken the next step. Now I do. I spread them out on the floor and arrange them in order by postmark. One is postmarked October 12, a few weeks after he went to prison. I write #1 on it. Once I have them all numbered, I put them in a pile. I stare at the pile, knowing that I need to do this; I must read them, but I'm afraid. But what am I afraid of? I tell myself that I'm afraid that if the letters are filled with small talk and words of advice that he thinks will make me a man while he's not there to guide me, it will ramp up my resentment and anger that he's never taken responsibility. But if I'm honest with myself, and damn it if this isn't the time to be honest with myself, I have to admit what I'm really afraid of. I'm afraid that it's all in these envelopes—the responsibility, the contrition, the guilt, the apologies—everything that I thought I needed. And if it is all in there, what I thought I needed was there all along, and out of anger and spite, I didn't allow myself to see it.

I take a deep breath and open envelope #1 and pull out the letter. It's one page, with Dad's neat printing, the neat printing I was so used to seeing on the little notes he would leave for me and Nic on the kitchen table every morning when we were little. I flatten out the page:

*Dear Gabriel,*

*How are you son? I have to admit, this is difficult. I can't remember the last time I wrote a letter. I'll bet you've never written one in your whole life, what with email and texting and all. It's also difficult because I don't really know what to say. But here goes. I really messed up. I know that. And I'm sorry. I'm so sorry you and your mom and Nicolas have to go through this.*

*I know we talked about it the night before my sentencing, but I want to say it again. I know it's hard but you need to be the man of the house for the next few years, for your mother, for Nicolas. Sometimes life really tests us to see what we're made of and this is that test for you. I know you can do it, I have so much confidence in you Gabriel. And again I'm sorry that I put this on you*

*and I'll try to make it up to you. I don't know how yet but I'll figure it out. Sorry I'm not better at writing letters but hopefully we will talk on the phone soon and know son that I love you very much.*

*Dad*


I look again at one line: *Sometimes life really tests us to see what we're made of and this is that test for you.* I was fourteen when this happened, when he wrote this. Did I really need to be tested at fourteen? And why was he telling me that? To try to make me strong? Or to avoid responsibility for the fact that he caused all of this? It's hard, reading this, but now that I've started, I can't turn back.

The second and third letters are from December and February, just months after the first one. They're pretty similar. Questions about how I'm doing, bullshit fatherly advice about how to be a man, vague apologies for the "things I did."

Four, five, and six are cards, postmarked mid-March for the past three years. At least he remembered my birthday. Or maybe Mami reminded him. Each of the cards just says: *Dear Gabriel* and *Love, Dad*.

The final envelope is postmarked July of last year. I remember when it arrived. I was surprised because it had been so long. I had put it with the others in my bottom drawer, unread and unopened.

*Dear Gabe,*

*Your mom told me that you are going by Gabe instead of Gabriel now. I totally understand. Grandma and Grandpa always called me Joshua even when everyone else in my life called me Josh. I know your mom is having trouble with it but I think she will come around. I think when*

*Nicolas decided to go by Nic it really made it harder but I told her that it means that he's really looking up to you. You really are his role model you know.*

*I know it's been a real long time since I wrote a letter to you (not as long as your last letter to me...haha). But seriously I've been thinking about it a lot and talking about it a lot. We have a support group in here and we've all become really tight. We meet twice a week with our counselor Ryan and he helps us to talk about the damage we've done and the harm we've*

*caused and how we can fix it. I don't know if there's any way I can fix the harm I caused the Perez family, taking away the mother and little girl. But in our group we talk about how to repair the harm to our own families and I think that if I'm going to do that I have to start with you. Gabe, you were right to tell Mami when you saw me with that woman. I was the one who was wrong and you did what was right. You stood up for Mami and yourself and your brother. You were the man that day, you saw your father doing something that was hurting your family and you spoke up about it. I can't tell you how sorry I am that my stupid actions put you in that situation. You were a kid and shouldn't have to deal with that. I really am so sorry.*

*I hope one day you'll forgive me. I understand that it might take more time and that's okay. You take the time you need and I will be ready to work it out when you are. I love you with all my heart and soul and will never stop trying to have you back in my life.*

*Your loving father.*

It took him three years to realize that he should own it? That he should apologize to me for blaming me that night? He needed counseling and group support to know that a father shouldn't do that to his fourteen-year-old son? That's bullshit. And nothing about calling me a pussy? Nothing about calling my mother a bitch right in front of me. Nothing about smacking me? And nothing about calling me a mistake? The biggest mistake of his life. It's not enough. It's just not.

Back upstairs, Mami is at the kitchen table reading. I drop the letters on the table. "Mami, why did he stop writing? He gave up on me after only three letters in the first four months. After that, no letters for almost three years."

She looks at me through tears and says softly, "I told him to stop. I saw the hard, awful look on your face when the letters arrived. I knew that you didn't read them. I saw them unopened in your dresser so I thought it would be best if he stopped. And honestly, I knew how hard it was for him that you didn't respond. I didn't want him to have five years of writing letters with no response from his son. I didn't think he could take it. I'm sorry, mi amor. I was trying to look out for you, but I also needed to look out for him. I needed him to survive in there, to keep some hope in his heart."

"He shouldn't have listened to you. He should have kept writing. What kind of man gives up on his son like that? I was a kid. There should be a hundred letters in here. And this last one, this one from last summer," I yell, pounding my finger on the letter in front of her, "is bullshit. Screw him."

I gather up the letters and throw them in the garbage can and go out the back door. The February night air is crisp and cold, the black sky is dotted with thousands of bright stars and the moon is almost full. Again, I've taken it out on Mami. Again, I let my anger with daddy spill out all over her. The door creaks open.

"I brought you your coat. Hace frío, mijo." I take it from her but don't put it on.

"Can I sit with you?"

"Yes."

She lowers herself next to me on the stairs. I continue looking at the stars.

"When you were little, you loved the stars. You said you wanted to be un astrónomo. You had your books about the stars and planets, and you would spend hours locating them in the sky and pointing them out to me and daddy. Cual estas mirando?"

I point toward the west. "Sirius. The Dog Star. He's twinkling different colors."

We sit for a few minutes, gazing at the stars, then I ask her, "Have you forgiven him?"

"Yes," she replies.

"How? He cheated on you. On us."

"No es fácil perdonar, lo sé. But I needed to forgive. When you love someone—mijo, it took a lot of work, and many hours talking with Father Daniel, and many prayers, many conversations with God. And many conversations with your father, through letters, on the phone, at the prison. So many tears. He's a good man, your father. He's made mistakes, like we all make mistakes. But I love him, he loves me, and most importantly, he loves you and your brother with all his heart."

She pulls her hand out of her pocket. She is holding a letter. By its length, I know it's the last one. It's stained from the trash can.

"This is a start, Gabriel. This letter doesn't have everything you want or need, but it's a start. It's the opening of a conversation, and this needs to be a conversation, you know. It can't just be him telling you what he feels. He needs to know what you feel. He can't make this right without you. He can't do it on his own. You were a child when it happened, but you're a young man now. You'll be eighteen in a couple of weeks. This needs to be a man-to-man conversation."

And of course, she is right. I just have to figure out how. But for now, I will just rest my head on my mother's shoulder and watch Sirius twinkle as Mami strokes my hair.

# Chapter 30

Billy wasn't as immediately accepting of my apology as I hoped. He ghosted me for a couple of weeks, not answering any of my texts or my calls. At least he didn't block me. I had to call in the big guns and get Lulu to plead my case. Her powers of persuasion are pretty damn impressive, especially when she sets her mind on something. And I know that it's not only that she wants me and Billy to make up; she wants us there for the double date. She's not sure that she really wants to get involved with Kevin at this point, so having us there takes the pressure off, makes it less of a real date. I don't mind being used by Lulu if it means getting Billy to talk to me.

Saturday, I work the morning shift, leave at noon and walk out into the kind of clear and sunny 50-degree late February day in Rhode Island that tricks you into thinking that spring really is right around the corner. Billy agreed to meet me in Prospect Terrace. As I make my way up, I pass the Brown University main campus and watch all the students out on the green, which is still brown, pretending it's spring—picnicking, lying in the sun, reading, studying, playing frisbee. That's me very soon, I think. I don't know yet where I'll be—hopefully NYU, but I'm not banking on it. But I will be in college, and I will be hanging out on a sunny Saturday afternoon with my college friends doing college student stuff.

When I get to the park, I see Billy on a bench in the sun, reading a book. As he hears me approach, he looks up, his face serious. When I smile and give him a little wave, he waves back. Then, unable to hold his stern and serious look, he smiles. "Damn," he says, "my plan was to be all serious to make you feel bad, but I'm not very good at that."

I chuckle and sit next to him on the bench. "Yeah, I can see that. You didn't hold that look for very long. Hey, how did you do on your Physics final?"

"I got an 86," he says with disappointment.

"Billy, 86 on a Physics final is really good. That stuff's not easy. And you studied really hard. You should be proud of yourself."

"Yeah, I know. I did work hard, and I really did my best. But my best doesn't ever seem to be good enough for my father. He acted like 86 was failing, said he was disappointed in me."

"That really sucks. I'm really sorry. But man, you have to be happy with your accomplishments and not worry what he thinks about it."

"Easy for you to say. You don't have a hardass father pushing you to be some perfect version of a son."

I just stare at him. It dawns on him what he said, and he gasps, "Gabe, I'm sorry. Oh shit, what a stupid thing to say."

"It's cool, it's cool."

"No, it's not. I'm really sorry. What I meant was..."

"Billy, it's cool. I know what you meant. Even if my dad was around, you're right. He's not a hardass about school and he doesn't expect me to get perfect grades. Hell, he doesn't seem to expect much from me. I don't have to deal with what you do."

After a moment of quiet, Billy says, "We have to talk about that night, the last time we saw each other."

"Yep."

"We have some work to do if we want this, us, to continue. Do you want it to continue?"

"Absolutely. I want us to continue." Billy listens intently as I apologize and tell him everything. I've decided that I need to be completely honest with him, so I tell him about crying in my mother's arms when she told me that it wasn't my fault, that none of it was my fault, that I needed to stop blaming myself. When I tell him that she knows about him and wants to meet him, his soft smile and happy eyes nearly make me cry, but I press on. His eyes open wide when I tell him that I read my father's letters. I detail what he wrote, what he didn't write, how I feel so confused by it all. I have the final grease-stained letter in my pocket. I read the whole thing to him.

When I finish, we sit in silence for a minute. Billy puts his arm over my shoulder, and at the same moment, we lean our heads to rest on each other's. "Are you happy you read the letters?"

"Yeah, I am. I'm not sure what to do next, but I'm glad I read them."

"Sounds like he's trying to fix things."

"Uh huh. It doesn't feel like enough, but my mother says that it's a start and that I need to help him build on it."

"How do you feel about that?"

"Not gonna lie, I'm still a little pissed about having to be an adult about this. But I think that's the real problem. Ever since this all happened, I had to be an adult before my time. I wanted to just be a kid and because of him I had to grow up. He told me, straight up, at fourteen, I had to be an adult for my mom and Nic, that I had to be a role model for Nic. I didn't want that, didn't ask for it, but I got it. Because of him. So now I have to be an adult to help him fix things. I mean, I'll be eighteen in a month, so I guess it's time anyway."

His fingers are interlaced with mine, our hands one. He raises our hands and brings his lips, soft and warm and gentle, to the back of my hand. "Yep, I guess it's time." The sun and moon share the February sky above us as we gaze at the city below.

# SECTION 3 — MARCH

# Chapter 31

"Where are you going?" Nic asks, getting all up in my business again. I just showered and I'm getting dressed.

"Just grabbing some pizza with Lulu."

"Can I come? Please??"

"Not tonight."

"Why?" he whines.

"Well, it's not just me and Lulu. It's sort of a double date." As soon as it comes out of my mouth, I kick myself.

"Wait a second. You and Billy are double dating with Lulu? Who's Lulu dating?"

"Kevin. You don't know him."

"I can't believe she didn't tell me."

I laugh, "Why would Lulu tell you she had a date? I mean, when would Lulu tell you she had a date?"

"I talked to her two nights ago. She didn't say anything about it." He says it very matter of fact, like it's totally normal that he would be having a conversation with my best friend.

"Hold up, you spoke to Lulu two nights ago? What? Why? What the hell?"

"She calls me every few weeks. You know, just to shoot the shit."

"Shoot the shit?" I'm baffled. "What the hell shit do you have to shoot with Lulu?"

"We talk about school, Netflix, whatever. I think she just likes to check up on me, make sure I'm doing okay. Don't worry, she doesn't give away any of your deep dark secrets."

"Wait, you talk about me to Lulu? You have phone calls with Lulu when you talk about me?" My mind is blown.

"Not much. We have a lot of other interests in common besides you," he says with a smirk. Little shit. "I told her about Sonia. I can't believe she didn't tell me about this Kevin guy."

"Hold up Nic! Who's Sonia?"

"She's a new girl in my class that I like. I didn't tell you about her?"

Now I can't tell if he's trying to mess with me. "No, you never mentioned her. But you told Lulu about her? I don't...I can't...What the hell is going on?"

Nic picks up Señor Gatito, who has been minding his own business curled up on Nic's bed. Señor Gatito dangles from his hands and Nic says, "Señor Gatito, can you believe that Gabe is jealous of me and Lulu?"

"Shut up. I'm not jealous." Okay, maybe I am a little jealous that Nic told Lulu about some girl he likes before he told me. I mean, I'm the father figure here, right? He's supposed to be coming to me for worldly advice and shit. But obviously I've failed because he's turning to Lulu instead.

"Nic, you know you can talk to me about this stuff, right? It's not like I have any answers or anything, but we can talk. You can trust me."

"I know that. Of course, I know I can trust you. I guess I just needed to talk to Lulu because I don't understand girls, and like, she's a girl and stuff."

I take a step back from my jealousy—yeah, I was jealous. But when I take this step back, I see how lucky I am. I have an amazing little brother and an amazing best friend. And the brother and the best friend love each other. And they have a friendship that doesn't revolve around me. They are their own unit; they don't need me to complete it. And that's pretty damn cool.

"And obviously you don't know anything about girls," he adds. Little shit.

Billy finds a parking spot on South Main, and we walk the two blocks to Plant City. It's a huge plant-based food hall with a bunch of vegan restaurants. Lulu loves this place and Kevin has never been. Perfect place for our double date. As Billy and I approach, Lulu and Kevin are already there, hanging outside. We do all the introductions. Lulu looks a little nervous, very atypical.

Lulu suggests the pizza place on the second floor. I'm wondering what vegan pizza is going to be like. Turns out that they make cheese from all kinds of things now. You don't need cows and sheep and goats to make cheese when you can make it from macadamia nuts, cashews and almonds. I'm skeptical, but this is Lulu's night. We order two pizzas -- one has cashew cheese and the other has almond cheese. One has "buffalo chicken" and the other has "pepperoni" but both are made from tofu. And I wonder, if the whole idea of veganism is to not eat animal products, why are we calling things "chicken" and "pepperoni"? But they were both delicious. I would've preferred a real pepperoni pizza with real mozzarella from Caserta, but baby steps.

As expected, Billy and Kevin really hit it off. They're both really laid back and comfortable around other people, so they fall into easy conversation. They also have sports in common. Kevin's wrestling season is just wrapping up and Billy's tennis season is just about to begin. Kevin is going to states for the third year in a row. Billy asks him about wrestling and college.

"Well," Kevin begins, "I've been recruited by a few colleges in Rhode Island and Massachusetts, D-3 schools with good wrestling programs and really good financial aid offers. There's some interest from a couple of D-1 schools far away. The dream is Brown, but that's a real long shot with how selective they are. Half the wrestlers in the country want to go there. We'll see soon. What about you? Will you be playing college tennis?"

"Nah, man. I'm a pretty good high school player but not college material. Well, I could probably play if I went to a state school, but I'd never make the team on the bigger schools I have my eye on. I'm a big fish in a small pond."

"How do you like the pizza?" Lulu asks me.

"Ya know, it's pretty good. I'm dying for some real pepperoni, but this is good."

"Gross. You do know that in addition to being made from dead animals, pepperoni has nitrates, which are really bad for you?"

"Yes, Lulu, I know about nitrates. But a pepperoni pizza every once in a while is not going to kill me."

Billy interrupts, "Oh God, are you two arguing about meat again? Seriously, you're like grandparents, always arguing about the same little things."

"Arguing about meat is not a 'little thing' Billy. It's literally an argument about the survival of the planet."

Billy turns to Kevin. Kevin just shrugs. "Keep me out of this. I'm just over here minding my own business, enjoying my buffalo-not-really-chicken pizza." We all laugh, even Lulu.

After the pizza, we walk across the street to the pedestrian bridge. It's a brisk, clear March night, not super cold. Lulu and Kevin are walking in front of me and Billy, and Kevin closes the space between them and takes Lulu's hand in his. Inspired by Kevin, I do the same and take Billy's hand. Neither of us has gloves on and it feels good to create some warmth for each other. When I take his hand, Billy looks over at me with his eyebrows raised. This is a first for me, holding his hand in public.

"Hmm, Gabe Meyers engaging in PDA."

"Shut up and enjoy it or I'll drop your cold ass hand."

When he lets out a laugh, Lulu turns around and does a double take. "Billy, is Gabe holding your hand? In public?"

"He started it. I was just walking along, and he decided to get all lover boy on me." Now all three of them are laughing.

"Okay, okay. You guys are wicked funny. Kevin, I expect it from these two but now you're joining forces with them?"

"Sorry bro, I gotta do what I gotta do to get in good with Lulu."

"Oh, it's like that?" I say.

"Yeah, it's like that man." He is beaming as he pulls Lulu closer. She doesn't resist.

I pull Billy in closer. He says, "Whoa, don't get carried away there, lover boy." And I laugh with them.

# Chapter 32

I t takes me three days to write.

*Dad,*
*I'm sure you're surprised to get a letter from me after so long.*
*To be honest I'm surprised that I'm writing. I think Mami told*
*you that I never read the letters you wrote to me. I was really*
*mad and didn't know how to deal with it. A few weeks ago I*
*read them all and I've been thinking a lot about what I can say*
*to you. In your last letter you talked about your counselor,*
*Ryan. Mine is Karina. She's the school counselor and she's*
*helped me a lot. In the beginning I didn't know how to deal*
*with my anger and it got me in fights and in a lot of trouble*
*but she taught me how to slow down, take a breath and think*
*before I react. It doesn't always work but it's way better than*
*before. Lately we've been talking a lot about forgiveness.*
*Karina is helping me to understand that forgiving doesn't*
*mean letting someone off the hook, or as she says, excusing*
*their actions. She tells me that forgiving means thinking about*
*what the person did to hurt you and accepting that human*
*beings are flawed. She thinks that if I really want to forgive*
*you, I need to be honest with you. And since I really want to*
*forgive you, I'm going to be honest with you. Because of that*
*night and what you did to make that night happen, you*
*wrecked my teenage years. You told me I had to be the man of*
*the house, that I had to be Nic's role model and I took that*
*seriously but it was a real heavy load to carry and I never felt*
*good enough. I felt that I was always letting everyone down.*
*You made it hard for me to let anyone get close to me because*
*I always thought about how hard it would be to lose another*

*person so it was easier to not let anyone near. And you weren't there to do all the things a dad is supposed to do with their teenage son. You weren't there to continue with my surfing lessons. You weren't there to teach me how to shave. You weren't there to have an awkward talk about sex. You weren't there to teach me how to drive. You weren't there to talk about college and the future. And you weren't there to sit with me by the fire, staring at the stars. But Karina also told me that to forgive, I should look at how I've grown from the experience, even if it was really painful. And I've grown Dad. I learned to shave on my own and it turns out that in the internet age, you don't need an awkward parent conversation to learn about sex. I think I've been a good big brother, a pretty good role model. Nic probably would have been great on his own, but I think I helped him in some ways. I could have been a better son to my mother, but I think I'm getting better every day. I haven't been the best man of the house but I think I've done okay. I've also learned to let people in after pushing them away for so long. I have a boyfriend, his name is Billy, and it took a long time for me to really let him get close. But I got there. I allowed myself to invest in him, knowing that if I lose him, I'll survive and learn from the experience. High school got off to a rough start, but I got it together and I'm doing really well. My college applications are in and I'm just waiting to hear. I know that whatever happens, it was meant to be. In your letter you apologized for blaming me for telling Mami about you and the woman. You told me that it wasn't my fault and that I was right to tell her. But you didn't talk about the rest of that night. So we have a lot to talk about.*
*Gabe*


I seal the envelope, ask Mami for a stamp, and with trembling hands, drop it in the mailbox on the corner.

# Chapter 33

It's not a night for stargazing, but it's a night for sitting by a fire with a blanket wrapped around you and a thermos of hot chocolate. It's a night for a heart to heart with your little brother.

I've created a tent of logs and I'm starting to stuff the newspaper and kindling in. "Hey you lazy bum, don't just sit there on your ass. Get over here and help."

"Finally! All those times I tried to help, and you told me to sit my ass down and let you do it. Acting like the man of the house." I punch Nic's shoulder and we both smirk. I hand him some newspaper.

"Don't crumple it too tight. You want it to get some air, so it catches fire easier. Careful when you put it in. You don't want to knock the logs down." I watch him as he carefully crumples the paper and hesitantly places it under the logs, his face intently focused.

"Good job. You know how to operate this?" I ask, holding up the long lighter.

"Um, I think so. Do you just click it?"

"You have to slide this little safety lever." I show him how to slide the lever with his thumb. "Then you hold it while you pull the trigger. It's like pulling the trigger on a toy gun. Good. Now, catch the paper on all sides." He looks so nervous doing it. I wonder if I looked like that the first time dad showed me.

"Hey, I'm pretty good at this," Nic says.

"Jeez, all you did was set the paper on fire. The logs aren't even burning yet. Give it a minute before you brag about your skills."

And then a log starts burning. We both watch as the flames go up the inside of the log and then begin to circle around. In a minute, the whole log is engulfed in flames, and another is starting.

"Okay kid, you are pretty good at this."

"See? Told ya."

I sit down and wrap myself in a blanket and Nic copies me. I open the thermos and Nic holds his cup for me to pour out the steaming hot chocolate. I fill my own cup, cap the thermos, and relax back in my chair. Nic and I sit, in silence, sipping hot chocolate and getting lost in the flames.

"Did you read it?" I ask. Earlier in the day, I shared my college essay with him and told him we would talk about it by the fire tonight.

"Yes. It's really good. You'll definitely get into college." His voice cracks and I look over. He's not looking at me; he stares straight ahead at the fire. The light from the flames illuminates his tears.

"Hey, what's the matter?"

"I didn't know."

"I know Nic. I didn't want you to know. I didn't want you to know any of it."

"You should've told me."

"I couldn't. I needed to protect you. I needed to do something right, and protecting you was the only thing I could think of that I might be able to do right." I don't know how far to go with this, how much of this complicated land to explore with Nic. He's the same age now as I was when all of this went down but I know that as much as I want to protect him, hiding and lying is not protecting, it's just hiding and lying. "But you're right. I should have told you. But I didn't want you to hate him. I knew that he couldn't take having two sons that hate him."

Nic is still crying, but it's under control, soft and gentle tears now. "Do you still hate him? In your essay you said you forgive him."

"I said that I will tell him that I forgive him. I'm not there yet Nic. I'm trying. But I don't hate him anymore. I wrote him a letter, the first one I've ever written to him."

I tell Nic about the letter. I worry that I've told him too much, that this will all be too intense for him. But I know that he needs to know the truth. I promise him that I won't lie to him anymore, that I won't hide things from him anymore. We sit and stare into the flames. I open the thermos and pour the last of the hot chocolate into his cup.

"Nic, take that stick that's near the firepit and move the logs around, give it some oxygen so it comes back to life."

# Chapter 34

March 24th, my 18th birthday. It falls on a Saturday this year, almost like it's a holiday.

Normally Nic and I have to help Mami clean on Saturday mornings, but as a birthday treat, she lets me sleep in. I hear about the injustice of it all from Nic the rest of the day, as he had to do my share of the cleaning.

Dad will be calling at noon. Mami's phone rings and she chats with him for a minute. Nic wants to talk to him and Mami says, "You can say hello, but he only has a few minutes, and this is Gabriel's day." Nic reluctantly hands me the phone after a short conversation. I take the phone into the bedroom and shut the door.

"Hi Dad."

"Hi Gabe. Happy birthday son. Man, I can't believe you're eighteen."

"Yeah, me either."

"What are you going to do today for the big day?"

"I'm just going to play basketball this afternoon. Then we're having a birthday party tonight here."

"Oh cool. Who's coming?"

"Well, it's Mami and Nic. And then a few friends. Lulu, Kevin, Billy, Francisco, and Mariya."

"Sounds great. I really wish I could be there." He sounds so sad.

After a moment. "I got your letter, Gabe."

"Dad, can we talk about that another time? I think maybe that should be a face-to-face conversation. What do you think?"

"Yes, Gabe, I think you're right." I don't know what to say, and it seems that he doesn't either. Then, finally, "Happy birthday son. I'm so proud of you. And I love you more than you can know." I haven't heard those words in a long time.

"Love you Dad. Talk to you soon." And I disconnect before he hears me crying.

I lost track of time playing basketball, and when I got home Mami and Nic were all over me to hurry and get ready. Mami looks beautiful in a blue dress. She usually wears her hair up, but tonight it's down, curled on the ends, framing her face. I see the young woman on the beach in Puerto Rico in a blue bikini with a baby bump. She sees the look on my face and says, "¿Qué? No me veo bonita?"

"No Mami, you look beautiful."

"And what about me?" Nic asks. He has on dress pants, sneakers, a white shirt, and a Star Wars tie. His hair is gelled and parted on the side. He's cute as hell.

"You look okay. Whatever."

He fake glares at me. "At least I'm not a sweaty stinky mess like you."

I laugh when Mami says, "Yes mijo, you do stink."

"Okay, I'll go shower now."

"Hurry. Your guests will be here in half an hour."

I turn the shower up really hot, not just to wash away the stink, but to try to wash away some of the nervousness I feel about tonight. I can't believe I'm eighteen, and I can't believe my boyfriend is going to meet my mother and brother. How will she react? Will she embarrass me? Will Nic be a goofball? Will they all make fun of me for being awkward and uncomfortable? Wow, I have a lot to be nervous about.

I towel off and grab my outfit. It's all picked out because I've agonized over it for days. I'm wearing black dress pants, a light blue button-down shirt, and black dress shoes. I decided that a tie would be extra. Now I'm not sure, since Nic is wearing a tie. No, no tie. And no gel in my hair. I shaved this morning, and I'm not the five o'clock shadow kind of guy, so I'm looking fresh. Aftershave? Cologne? No, too much ammunition for people to make fun of me.

I'm good to go, so I walk out into the living room. Mami immediately says, "No tie? Look how handsome your brother looks in his little tie."

I take a stand. "No Mami, no tie. It's my eighteenth birthday. I'm a man and I've decided, no tie."

"Okay baby, you're right. It's your night. You wear what you want."

But Nic can't leave well enough alone. "I mean, a tie is always nice on a special occasion," he has to add.

"Nic, you know what?" I ask.

"What?"

"Shut the hell up!"

"Stop it," Mami scolds us. "People are going to arrive soon."

And just then, the doorbell rings. Nic rushes to open the door for Lulu and Kevin. Lulu gives Nic a huge Lulu hug and then says, "Nicky, this is Kevin."

Kevin shakes Nic's hand. "So good to meet you Nic. Lulu's told me so much about you."

"You too Kevin. I was really glad when Lulu told me she was bringing you." Seriously, Lulu talks to Kevin about Nic? Lulu talks to Nic about Kevin?

Lulu hugs Mami and does the whole introduction of Kevin. Mami looks as if the daughter that she never had has just introduced her to Prince Charming. I look on, wondering what it's going to be like when I introduce her to Billy. Nic has dragged Kevin into the living room and is interrogating him about God knows what. Lulu and Mami are still in their love fest when the bell rings again. I answer it and Francisco and Mariya are there. Mariya is holding a bouquet of balloons that say, "Happy 18th Birthday." I invite them in and all I am thinking is, where is Billy?

I send a quick text to him:

*Me: Where r u?*
*Billy: Sorry, had a fight with my dad. Almost there.*

Now I'm even more nervous. If he had a fight with his dad, will he be in a bad mood? I can't comfort him and entertain guests and deal with my mother and Nic all at the same time. As I'm quietly freaking out, I hear a car outside and look out the window. He's parked his Jeep in front, and he is walking up with a bouquet of flowers in one hand and a bag in the other. I open the door before he can knock. I step outside so no one else hears. "Are you okay?"

"Yes, babe, I'm fine. Happy birthday." He smiles and gives me a quick kiss. "I'm really excited to meet your mom and Nic."

"You sure you're okay?"

"I'm great. Let's go in."

And we go in. It's like someone rang a bell, because as soon as we enter, everyone stops and looks at us. I don't know what to do, but Billy smiles and says, "Hi everyone, sorry I'm late." And before I know it, Nic is right in front of us.

"Hi Billy. I'm Nic."

"Of course you are. I've seen so many pictures of you, I would know you anywhere."

"Really?" Nic turns to me. "Really? You showed him pictures of me?"

"Of course, dummy."

"Don't call your brother dummy, Gabriel." Mami is now in front of us.

I take a deep breath. I think everyone else in the room does too. "Mami, this is Billy Sachs. Billy, this is my mother, Isabel."

"So nice to meet you Billy," Mami says.

And then Billy does it. Yep, he speaks to her in Spanish. "Encantado de conocerla, Señora Isabel. Gracias por invitarme." We are in a movie. Everyone in the room stares, mouths wide open in shock.

Mami breaks the shock, "Pero habla español perfectamente. ¿Cómo es eso?"

Lulu drags everyone else into the living room. The three of us are alone in the kitchen. Billy explains that his father's mother is from Spain. When he was little, his abuela lived with them here in Providence and she took him every summer back to Spain with her. Now Mami needs to know the story of Billy's life. She peppers him with questions. Where is his mother from? How did his parents meet? What do his parents do? Does he have siblings? Billy politely answers all of her questions, in perfect Spanish.

Mami turns to me and says, "Gabriel, you didn't tell me that Billy speaks Spanish. He's wonderful." She's beaming. Part of me is pissed off at Billy because him speaking Spanish with her throws a spotlight on my stubborn resistance to Spanish. But another part of me is pretty impressed at the way he handled my mother. Her immediately falling in love with him should take a little pressure off tonight. Then I see the self-satisfied smile on Billy's face, and I'm annoyed again. "Oh yeah, he's wonderful." And I shoot him a look.

"Pero, I have to check on the food. So good to have you here Billy. You two go join the others." And she busies herself at the stove.

I pull Billy into the hallway. "What's up with that?"

"What?"

"Speaking Spanish with her."

"I was just being polite. She seemed to be really happy that I spoke Spanish. I think she likes me, Gabe. She called me wonderful."

"Yeah, yeah. Now she's gonna be up in my case. 'Billy speaks Spanish with me, why won't you?'"

"I'll be honest with you. I don't really get it. You should be proud to speak Spanish. It's your heritage, man."

"Okay, nah. Let's not do this at my birthday party. If you want to speak Spanish to my mother, fine. But I don't want some lecture about what I should and shouldn't do."

"Okay, I'm sorry. Let's just enjoy your night."

"Hey, what did you fight with your dad about?"

"Forget about that. It's nothing." But I can see from his eyes that it's not nothing.

I insist and he finally tells me. He got his progress report from school and his father wasn't happy with his grades because he currently has a B- in Physics and a B in Calculus. He accused him of slacking off and being more focused on me than on his studies. Billy says to me, "But that's bullshit. I worked my ass off, but those classes are hard. You know how hard I worked. You even helped me study. I told him all that and he said, 'Well obviously you're not working hard enough.' I was so pissed off. Then he said he wasn't sure it was a good idea for me to go to New York over spring break, that maybe he should get me a tutor for that week. I was about to explode but my mother saw it and cut me off. She spoke calmly to my dad. 'Honey, let's talk about this before we make any decisions.' Then to me, 'Billy, let me and your father talk about this. I know you've been working really hard. We'll figure it out.' When she said that, I knew things would be okay, because she pretty much always gets her way."

"Man, that sucks. You okay?"

"Yeah, I'm good. He just gets so extra about my grades, and if it was true that I was slacking off I would own it, but I'm not. Some of my friends already have senioritis and really are slacking off, but I'm not. And he was on his second Scotch, maybe his third. So there's that too." He takes a deep breath and let's it out. "Okay, let's kill this discussion and have a party! It's your 18th birthday. You're officially a man today. Any chance we can sneak into someplace private? I need to give you your birthday kiss." That smile.

"Dude, my mother is here. And my little brother. And my best friend."

"Your point?"

"Hah, let's see how the night plays out. Let's go to the living room. Warning, as soon as we get there, Nic is going to corner you. Don't say anything to him that he can use against me. You do, I will cut you off!"

As soon as we enter, on cue, Nic rushes over. "Where have you been? I haven't had a chance to talk to Billy at all."

Billy laughs. "You're right Nic. We need to talk. Let's find a nice quiet spot." He winks at me and grins. This boy.

I join the others, and Kevin, Mariya, and Francisco are hatin on Lulu's choice of music. She's complaining, "I'm done with y'all. This is The Smiths. This is Morrissey. The greatest band of all time. And you won't even listen, you don't even hear the lyrics. He's singing about people who don't even care about us and how we waste our time on them. He sings the truth!" I have to side with Lulu on this one, this song freakin speaks to me. It's a super happy sounding song, but it's all about being miserable even when you find something that's supposed to make you happy. Okay, maybe they're right that it's depressing, but it's a killer song for depressed teenagers.

Mami calls everyone to come and grab some food. We dig into her totally meatless, totally carb-filled buffet of lasagna, arroz con gandules, mac and cheese. There's a bowl of salad that only Lulu and Kevin take, and some sort of vegan sausage for Lulu. Everyone oohs and aahs over how delicious everything is and Mami accepts the compliments like the queen that she is.

Finally, the lights are turned out and Lulu and Nic come in from the kitchen. Nic is carefully carrying a birthday cake, with eighteen lit candles. They sing Happy Birthday and clap when it's finished, but then Mami says, "Now in Spanish." She starts them off with Cumpleaños Feliz. Everyone knows all of the words except for Kevin, but he mouths along with it. I blow out the candle and make a wish, which I will keep private.

Then it's time for presents. Nic is super excited. "Open mine first," he cries, shoving his gift in my face. I tear it open and it's a t-shirt. On the front is a picture of him and me, a selfie we took last summer sitting in the lifeguard's chair at the beach. I hold it up and everyone says, as a chorus, "awwww." Nic says to me, "Do you like it?"

"I love it. It's awesome."

"Put it on," he says.

"Nic," I laugh, "I'm not going to change my shirt in the middle of the living room during a party."

Lulu takes Nic's side of course and scolds me, "Gabe, just put it on over your shirt."

I do as I'm told, and everyone claps. "Satisfied Nic?"

"Wait," he says. "I need a picture of us together with you wearing a shirt with a picture of us together." Everyone laughs as we pose together, and they all take a picture of us.

"Thanks buddy. You're not bad for a pain in the ass little brother." Nic beams. I hug him as Mami and Lulu scold me for calling him a pain in the ass.

Mariya and Francisco give me gift cards for the Avon Cinema. Next, I open Lulu's. It's a hoodie, gray with purple NYU on the front. Applause, uh-huh, that's what's up, yes! I look at it and say, "I hope you didn't jinx it Lulu."

"No way, you got this," she responds.

Next, my mind is blown. Billy hands me his gift, which is obviously a book. When I unwrap it, I'm shocked to see the photography book he has gotten me -- Robert Mapplethorpe Polaroids. Billy had gone with me and Lulu to a Polaroid exhibit at RISD. I loved the exhibit and talked about how much I wanted to get a Polaroid. Billy remembered. And got me this amazing book.

But that's not what blew my mind. Yeah, I was shocked by the gift, but what blew my mind was when I opened the final gift. Mami handed it to me saying, "This is from me and your father." A Polaroid camera. Polaroid Originals One Step. How? How does Billy coordinate his gift with Mami's? Then I look at Lulu. We lock eyes. She smiles and I know. This all runs through Lulu.

I pop the film cartridge in the camera. I arrange them all, all of these people I love, these people I live for. I move them around, position them, until the composition is perfect. I look through the lens. Click.

*"18th Birthday"*
**Black and white Polaroid.**
*A beautiful woman, hair hanging loose*
*sits next to a young boy on a sofa.*
*Standing behind the sofa*
*five teenagers.*
*In the center*
*a tall, handsome boy with curls,*
*his right arm draped across the shoulder of a girl*
*with long wavy hair,*
*her head leaning against*
*the smiling boy on her right.*
*On the other side is a couple*
*holding balloons that say*
*Happy Birthday.*
*All of them are facing the camera directly*
*smiling.*

# Chapter 35

After everyone is gone, I go to the kitchen. Mami takes a sip of wine and continues loading the dishwasher. When I ask if she needs help, she responds, "No mijo, it's still your birthday. You get the night off." She smiles and says, "He's a nice boy. Y muy guapo." This is new territory for me and I'm not sure how to handle it when your mother tells you that your boyfriend is handsome. I'm not trying to have a conversation with my mother about Billy's exceptional physical attributes.

"You seemed to really like him. And you seem okay with it. Are you really okay with it? With me being gay? Having a boyfriend?"

She places the bottle of wine and her glass on the table. She gets another glass from the cupboard. "Sit down Gabriel. Here, have some wine," she says as she pours.

"Really Mami?"

"Of course. In Puerto Rico, we don't treat drinking like we do here. Teenagers can have a little wine with their parents and it's normal. You're eighteen today, you're a man. But you're still not legal here for drinking, so be careful."

"I will." I look at my mother, so beautiful. And she seems lighter, happier, than she has in a long time. Maybe it's the wine, but I don't think so.

"You know, mi amor, I admit that it hasn't been easy for me to get to where I am with this. It took a lot of thinking, and reading, and talking, and praying. I had never even thought about this possibility. I always imagined you bringing home a beautiful girl. I imagined grandchildren. And I know, you can still give me grandchildren, but it's just going to be different than I had always dreamed so I had to figure out how to change this vision I had for so long. I spent many hours on the phone with your Uncle Andy. And he told me something that I never knew, that your father never told me. When Andy told his parents, when he told your grandma and grandpa that he was gay, they kicked him out. He was eighteen and your father was fifteen. Andy and Josh were very close, like you and Nic. Andy ran off to New York and Josh was heartbroken. Andy couldn't come home, and your father was too young to go to New York on his own, so they didn't see each other for more than a year. Andy came back to visit and stayed with friends and they were able to reunite, without their parents knowing. Brothers had to sneak around to see each other. Imagine. Your father wanted to tell them, to tell them that they couldn't stop him from seeing his own brother, but Andy told him not to. He didn't want them to know he was back, didn't want your father to have more fights with his parents. I couldn't believe that your father had not told me this. The next time I went to the prison, we spoke about you and Billy, and I asked him about it."

I interrupt, "You talked to dad about me?"

"Of course. Just because he's in prison, doesn't mean he's not your father. And I needed to talk to him—for me. And for you."

He told her about his parents and Andy. When Nana and Poppa told Andy to leave, told him he was no son of theirs, Uncle Andy and my dad cried together as Andy packed his things. They hugged when he left, and Andy told him that it would be okay, that their parents would change their mind, that he'd be back soon and everything would be back to normal. But he wasn't back soon, and it didn't go back to normal. By the time my father graduated from high school, he and his parents barely talked. He couldn't wait to go to college and get away from them. And he did for a while but ended up living back there when he dropped out of college. He talked to Andy all the time, but the family was broken. No holidays together, no birthdays.

My grandparents live in Florida. I've only seen them four or five times in my life, a few times when they were in

Providence and twice when we went to Disney. They send money to me and Nic on our birthdays, Christmas, and Easter but that's about it. It's funny, I never really questioned why they weren't more a part of our lives. I guess I just thought it was because they lived in Florida. But now it's starting to make sense.

After some years, Uncle Andy and my grandparents got to a point where they at least spoke again, but then he met Keith and they didn't want to meet him, so Andy stopped seeing them. They talk on Thanksgiving, a quick call to say hello, but that's it. And dad has never really forgiven them for kicking Andy out, for depriving him of his brother at a time when he needed him.

There is so much I don't know. My parents have had lifetimes of experience, and I will never know half of what they have lived. I won't ever really know how they became the parents that I know, the people that I know. I know none of their pain, none of their heartache.

"The thing that parents want most of all, mi amor, the thing that your father and I want most of all, is for our children to be happy. We know that we've made it difficult for you to be happy for a while. When I spoke to your father and told him about you, and about Billy, he said to me, 'Isabel, is he happy?' And I said, 'Yes honey, he's very happy.' And when I said that, we both had tears in our eyes."

And at this moment, Mami and I both have tears in our eyes.

# Chapter 36

This month's poster on Karina's wall depicts a sun setting behind the mountains. In bold white letters: YOUR TRACK RECORD FOR SURVIVING DIFFICULT DAYS IS 100%. Okay, true enough, but is survival really the goal?

This time, I made the appointment with Karina. Usually she calls me in when there's been a problem or a teacher has told her about me seeming depressed, or disturbed, or insane or whatever they tell her about me. Her, "Hey Gabe, how's it going?" is friendly and casual but it doesn't hide that this is unusual, and she is concerned about this change of events.

"It's going good Karina. You?"

"Oh, I'm fine. Busy time of year with all the college acceptances and all."

"Sorry, I don't want to take your time if you're busy."

"Oh no, I didn't mean that I don't have time, Gabe. I've blocked off this time in my calendar for you. I was surprised when I got your email. Pleasantly surprised. I feel like I'm always dragging you in here. I like having you come on your own free will," she laughs. I laugh a little awkwardly, so Karina forges on. "What brings you here? Everything okay?"

"Yeah, well for the most part everything is okay. There have been some really good things happening lately and I'm trying to do what you told me, to celebrate the good when it comes, but my mind keeps twisting the good things until I convince myself that they're going to fall apart, or end, or blow up. Then I start focusing on the bad and there's a lot happening right now, and my brain feels like it's going to explode. Everything is jumbled up and rattling around in there and I need help to get things to settle into place."

"Okay. How about we start with a couple of deep breaths?" I know, it sounds super corny and when she first tried to get me to do it, I resisted like crazy, but that shit helps, so I take a couple of breaths along with Karina. "Good, I would really like to hear about the good things that have been happening lately for you. Not how you've twisted them, but just how they are, just describe these good things for me."

I start with Billy, about the fight and the aftermath, how I've been more emotionally open and honest with him and how the relationship is really developing. Our trip to New York is coming up in a couple of weeks and we've been planning all of the things that we want to do, and Andy and Keith are taking us to see *Hamilton* on Broadway. My birthday was on Saturday and my mother finally met Billy and it went really well. My mother loves him, my little brother loves him, my friends love him.

"That's great. It sounds like things are really going well with Billy."

I nod.

"So, what's keeping you from being able to celebrate that? You said that you twist the good things. How are you twisting it?"

"Oh God, I don't even know where to begin. Okay, so, I start thinking about the end of high school being three months away and we may both end up being far away and he'll want to date other guys, or girls, or whatever, when he's away at college. So why am I investing myself in something that's just going to end soon anyway?"

"Is this feeling based on conversations you and Billy have had? Have you talked about seeing other people when you're in college?"

"No, we haven't talked about it." She doesn't say anything. I know this is her ploy, just look at me, give me a hugely awkward pause, so I can admit how ridiculous I am. "I know. I know what you're not saying to me. I'm worrying about the future, and I can't control the future." She nods. I continue, "But I can control not getting hurt in the future. Can't I?"

"By not enjoying the present?"

"It's not about not enjoying the present. It's about protecting myself in the present, not putting myself in a position to get hurt in the future."

"I would argue that that is the absolute definition of not enjoying the present."

My elbows are on her desk, my forehead resting in the palms of my hands, my thumbs massaging my temples.

"Can we go back to something you said earlier? You were talking about the party and how your mother loved Billy. That's really big. Did you present him as your friend or your boyfriend?"

"Boyfriend."

"Gabe, I hope you can step back and realize that this is a really big deal. You introduced your boyfriend to your mother. At eighteen. To your mother who thought you were going through a phase. And she loves him."

"Well, as soon as I introduced them, he spoke to her in Spanish."

"Oh boy," Karina says, and we both laugh.

"And at the end of the party, when everyone was gone, my mother and I spoke." I tell Karina about the whole conversation, about my grandparents and Uncle Andy, about my father crying when my mother told him I was happy. I tell her that I spoke to him on the phone for my birthday and that I said 'love you dad' before I hung up.

"How are you feeling about all of this with your father?"

"I'm so confused. I don't know why my mother has been able to forgive him, but I haven't. He cheated on her, not on me."

"I'm not sure that's true, Gabe. Maybe, when someone cheats on their spouse, they're also cheating on their kids. But is it really the cheating that you can't forgive him for?"

And that's not it. Sure, that was always a part of it. It will be hard for me to ever forget the sight of my father kissing another woman in a park. But for me, it's always been about me. About the smack. About the words, even more about the words. That I was a mistake, the biggest one of his life.

"Gabe, you said that when he called you on your birthday, he started to talk about the letter, but you stopped him and said you thought it would be better for that to be a face-to-face conversation. Can that conversation wait until he gets out?"

My chest is tight as I prepare to say what I never thought I would say. "I'm going to see him at the prison."

# Chapter 37

Waiting for college acceptance letters is torture. I feel like I'm a contestant on a reality tv show, waiting to know if I can move on or if I'm being kicked off the island, if I'll be validated or told I'm worthless. News is about to trickle in during the last week of March, with April 1st being the big day when most letters arrive. The first email arrives and—I'm not validated but I'm also not worthless. After five minutes staring at the subject line, Rhode Island School of Design Application, I finally click on it and open the attachment:

*Dear Gabriel Meyers,*
*Thank you for your interest in Rhode Island School of Design. We have completed our application review process and after careful consideration, I regret to inform you that we are unable to offer you a position at this time, but we would like to offer you a place on our waitlist. My colleagues and I would like to acknowledge the strength of your application and ensure you that you will be given thorough consideration should space become available.*

At first, I think that this is not bad. At least they saw enough in my application to put me on the waitlist, at least there is some hope. But then I start to feel that maybe it's worse; maybe it's better to know one way or the other, get the rejection over with, rip the damn band aid off.

I FaceTime Billy, Lulu, and Kevin to let them know about my RISD waitlisting and to find out what they've heard. They try to be positive and encouraging, but we all know that waitlist is not exactly great news. Lulu hasn't heard anything today, but Kevin heard that he got a wrestling scholarship at the University of Wisconsin. He says they have a good wrestling team, but it's Wisconsin. He's still hoping for Brown, even though it's a longshot. And Billy? I can tell he's holding out. "Billy, you heard something, didn't you?" Lulu says. Leave it to Lulu, read the scene and pull no punches.

"Yes. I heard from Northwestern." I swear that Lulu, Kevin, and I all gasp and scream, "And?" in unison.

"I got accepted," Billy says, without the enthusiasm you would expect from someone who got accepted at their number one.

"That's amazing," Lulu gushes.

"Way to go, bro," Kevin adds.

I'm looking at his face on my phone and it's not the face of an aspiring journalist who's just been accepted at one of the best schools for journalism in the country. "Hey Billy, you don't really seem excited. You okay?"

Billy lets out a long sigh. "I know it's good news, but I can't get my mind off of Columbia. If I don't get accepted, my dad will think I screwed up and if I do get accepted, he'll expect me to go there. I don't know which is worse."

And not gonna lie here, Billy's got me lowkey pissed off with this. I got waitlisted by one of my top choices while he got accepted by his number one, and he's acting like it's the end of the world. His private-school-worried-about-what-daddy-will-think-thing is not what I need right now, so I keep quiet and let Lulu and Kevin console him.

"Two more days until April 1st," Lulu says. "And let's all remember, whatever happens is meant to happen. And we have each other and always will. Love you guys."

Lulu and I made a pact. We are going to wait until both of us have our emails from NYU and we will open them at the same time. On April 1st, all the seniors are buzzing. The teachers have resigned themselves to the fact that we are going to be checking our phones all day long. There are spontaneous celebrations as people receive good news and comfort/crying sessions as people receive bad news.

At lunch, Lulu looks nervous. "Nothing yet?" I ask. She shakes her head.

"Me neither. Hey, how about we try to forget about it until tonight? By then we should have something. You could come over. Rice and beans and emails that determine our future."

"You sure we should do this? What if we get different results?"

"Lu, hopefully we get the same results, but if we get different results, one of us will celebrate the other and one will comfort the other. Like best friends should."

Sweet kiss on my cheek, sweet Lulu kiss. "Love you Gabe."

That night, she comes over. By this time, we both have emails from NYU and we both haven't opened them. We have somehow managed to wait for hours, to not cheat, to do this as best friends, whatever the outcome. Because to wait is worth it. To share this moment is worth the wait.

Nic and Mami are there of course. I kind of forgot that they live with me and that I wouldn't be able to do this without them knowing. Lulu and I decide that we will sit down and share some rice and beans and salad, that we will talk about Mami's day at work and Nic's day at school, and then after a proper dinner, we will look at our emails.

We make it through two or three bites when Nic says, "This is crazy. Open the emails! I need to know who I'm going to be visiting at NYU next year."

Mami corrects him, "No mijo, you are not going to visit anyone at NYU. Not next year. Not the year after. Maybe when you are sixteen."

Lulu and I both laugh as Nic protests. Lulu looks at me. We both nod and take out our phones. I scroll through my email and find the one from NYU. When I look up, Lulu is looking at me. "One, two, three."

I finish reading the first paragraph and I know my future. I hide my emotions and raise my head. Mami and Nic are staring intently at both me and Lulu. Lulu and I lock eyes, neither betraying our emotions.

"Waitlist," Lulu says, draining the excitement from the room. I don't know how to respond, and no one says anything. They are all just looking at me.

"I got in." I say it quietly, without the excitement I expected to feel. I now wish that Lulu and I hadn't done this together.

But Lulu screams, "Oh my God! That's so great." She's hugging me, Nic is jumping up and down, and Mami is in tears.

"But Lulu, it's supposed to be us. Together."

"Hey, I'm on the waitlist. Don't count me out. You haven't gotten rid of me yet. I will bug the heck out of them, and you know I can be very persistent."

"I hadn't really noticed that about you." She rolls her eyes at me while Nic hoots.

Mami goes into the kitchen and returns with a cake, white icing with blue letters: Congratulations! "I had confidence that we would be celebrating tonight."

As we are all eating cake and Nic is talking excitedly about New York and visiting, I'm thinking about me and Lulu. She has a higher GPA than me, more extracurricular activities. I messed up my freshman year and it shows on my transcript. How do I deserve this over her? Do I even want to go without her?

She plops down next to me on the sofa and puts her arm around me. "Hey you, I know what you're thinking." Of course she does. "You deserve this Gabe. You worked so hard in the face of some really difficult crap. You need to accept that you deserve this. Remember what Trevor said, all these rich kids with padded resumes wrote about whatever it would take to get in. You opened your soul, put it all out there. If anyone deserves this, it's you." She kisses my cheek. "And seriously, I have not given up on NYU. I've still got a chance, and if it doesn't happen, it's for a reason. I'll be sad, sure. But eventually, at some point, something amazing will happen in my life and I will realize, this is why I didn't get in. I'm where I am supposed to be."

# Chapter 38

For weeks, since he found out that Billy and I were going to New York to stay with Uncle Andy and Keith, Nic has been relentless, begging and angling to go with us. Finally, Uncle Andy called and told him that this trip is his present to me for my eighteenth birthday and that he will get the same when he turns eighteen. He'll get to bring a friend, or girlfriend, or boyfriend or whatever, and they will see a Broadway show and go wherever they want to visit. It will be his special birthday present. Nic seems to have finally, reluctantly, accepted that Billy and I are going alone.

Billy and I are leaving in the morning. I'm packing, neatly rolling my t-shirts, stuffing my socks inside my shoes, while Nic lies on his bed teasing Señor Gatito with a piece of string. Nic wants to know every plan we have, and he has made me a list of all the places where he wants me to take selfies. I tell him that we are not planning everything out, we are just taking it day by day.

"What? Not planning? You? Not planning? You plan your outfit for the next day before you go to bed. How can you not plan your trip?"

"I know, I know, but Billy wants to be spontaneous. He doesn't want everything mapped out, so I'm going to give it a try."

Nic objects to this idea. "It's New York City, Gabe. You need a plan. There's so much to do, you need to narrow it down. I can't believe I have to tell you this."

"Yeah, okay. You don't have to tell me this. Believe me, I know. But you know what? You can do that on your trip when you turn eighteen. I'll do it my way."

"Whatever."

I continue packing, he continues teasing Señor Gatito. Then he drops this bomb. "Are you and Billy gonna sleep in the same bed?"

"What?"

"Well, I think I remember that Uncle Andy and Keith have two bedrooms. Remember? Mami and Daddy slept in the bedroom and you and I slept on the couch. Is one of you going to sleep on the couch?"

"I'm not sure, Nic. I don't really know where we're sleeping." Damn, this kid. I'm trying to play it cool, fold clothes and put them in the suitcase.

"Why are you blushing?"

"Shut up. I'm not blushing Nic."

"Yeah, right."

"I'm not talking to you about where Billy and I are sleeping. I'm just not."

"Okay, that means you're sleeping together. Does Mami know?"

"Hold up, that's not what I said. Don't put words in my mouth and don't go talking to Mami about this and making her think about it. Jeez Nic."

"If you and Billy are having sex, it doesn't bother me."

"Nic, really, stop. I'm not talking to you about this."

"But when you found out that I was talking to Lulu about the girl I liked, Sonia, you said, and I quote, 'You know you can talk to me about these things, right Nic?' And now when I want to talk to you, you tell me to shut up."

I'm ready to explode, but I take a deep breath and try to get into role model mode. "So yes, I meant it when I said you can talk to me about these things. But I meant that you can talk in a general way, you know...like ask questions about sex and masturbation and relationships and stuff. I didn't really mean that you could ask me questions about my sex life."

"Hmm," he grunts.

"What?"

"So you have a sex life. That's good. I'm happy for you. Señor Gatito, aren't you happy that Gabe has a sex life?"

I throw a pillow at his head. He screams and Señor Gatito lets out a loud meow and ducks under the bed.

# Chapter 39

As we get off the train at Penn Station, Billy orders a Lyft to take us to Brooklyn. Rain is coming down in buckets and outside of the station, people are pushing and shoving; everyone is huddled under the awnings for cover. There are so many taxis and cars, all laying on their horns. It's a total assault on the senses—a confusing, exciting, exhilarating assault.

We got off to a bad start that morning. I got to the train station to meet Billy. I spotted his bright yellow jacket and then my jaw dropped. He cut his hair. All the beautiful curls—gone. He has a fade with it super short on the top. And the top is bleached. When he saw the look on my face, my utter disbelief, he started laughing and walked to where I had frozen in my tracks.

Now I was looking at it up close and I said, "What the hell did you do?"

The smile melted from his face. "What, you don't like it?"

"No. And you didn't even ask me."

"Ask you? Ask you if I could change my hair? I didn't know I needed your permission to change my hair. I'll keep that in mind next time." He shook his head and turned to pick up his bag.

"I didn't mean that you had to ask me. I just meant that you didn't even mention it to me and then I show up here and I'm caught by surprise."

"And you don't like it. I get it Gabe. Let's go downstairs. The train is due in ten minutes."

I followed him down the escalator and we were quiet while we waited. I kept looking at the sign to see how long it would be, and when it said the train would be arriving, I stared down the tunnel. I noticed a young woman staring at us. Well, staring at Billy. Finally, the loud whistle echoed through the tunnel and blasted into the ears of the waiting passengers.

"Should we go to the front or the back?" I asked Billy.

"Whichever. You decide." Oh boy, this could be a long ride.

The train wasn't too full of people who got on in Boston, so we were able to get two seats together. I made sure they were facing in the direction we were going. I hate riding backwards on a train. "Do you want the aisle or the window?" Asking Billy, I realized how many things we didn't know about each other. I know that Nic always has to have the window so he can point out every interesting thing he sees outside. Lulu prefers the aisle because she's a people watcher. She likes to make up stories about people who walk down the aisle: where they are going, why they are going there, who will meet them when they get off the train at their final destination.

Billy grunted, "You pick." So I threw my bag on the overhead rack and took the window seat. Billy plopped himself down in the aisle seat, put his red Beats on his ears and cranked up his music. Yep, this could be a long ride. And a shitty vacation. Way to go, Gabe.

Not gonna lie, his hair looked really cool like this. It was a total change, and it was fire. I was surprised, sure, but I think there was also a flash of panic that it would bring even more attention to us than usual. People stare at Billy. He's that kind of attractive that makes people turn their heads. When we first started going out, I thought people were looking at us because they saw a gay couple. It made me paranoid that people were judging us or that someone was going to beef with us. Then I realized that they were really looking at Billy, and when they would look at me, I figured they were thinking, "How the hell did he land that guy?" I know. I know.

I nudged him with my shoulder, and he turned and looked at me but didn't say anything. He faced forward and I nudged him again. "What?" It was soft, more hurt than angry.

"I want to talk. Can we talk?"

He pulled his Beats down from his ears to his neck. I could still hear The Weeknd, but at least Billy was giving me a chance to speak. "I'm sorry, Billy. I had no right to imply that you need to ask my permission to do anything."

"That's not what I'm mad about. That's just stupid. We both know that we don't need permission from each other to do anything. I'm mad, or whatever I'm feeling—mad, sad, insecure—because you said you didn't like it. I was excited to do something bold for our trip to New York and I thought you would think it was dope and then I just felt stupid and ugly."

"Ugly?" I asked in disbelief. "You? Ugly?"

"Yes."

"I'm really sorry Billy. It looks great. It is totally dope and you look so great like this. Seriously, haven't you seen the people checking you out, in the station and on the train?"

"No."

"Really? There was a woman near us on the platform who couldn't keep her eyes off you. She was practically drooling. I thought I was gonna have to fight her." He didn't laugh at my attempt to lighten the mood.

"I don't pay attention to people looking at me."

"What do you mean?"

"I stopped paying attention."

"When? I don't understand."

"This is something I don't really talk about much. It's uncomfortable because I don't want to sound conceited."

"I've never heard you sound conceited, Billy."

He took a deep breath. "Ever since I was little, people have commented on my looks. Family members, family friends, total strangers. 'Wow, what a handsome young man.' 'You get more and more handsome every time I see you.' 'Boy, this one will have to beat the girls off with a stick.' People would say how "exotic" I look. I figured that adults just talked like that to all kids because they had nothing else to say to us. Then I noticed that my mother started to break in when people commented on my looks, steering the conversation to things that I do well. 'You should see how well Billy is doing in school.' 'Billy's been practicing tennis really hard.'

"When I was twelve or thirteen, I became really self-conscious because people were always staring at me. I became withdrawn, and my parents tried to figure out what was wrong with me. I admitted that I felt that people were always staring at me. I didn't know what was wrong with me, why they were staring. I remember my mom and dad looking at each other, a look of understanding, like they knew this was coming. They assured me that there was nothing wrong with me and they explained that they believed that people were looking at me because I'm beautiful. My mother said, 'Billy, beauty is very hard to define. What one person finds beautiful, another person may not. But there are some people, who for some unknown reason, many people look at and find beautiful. And they get stared at, not because there is something wrong with them, but because people see so much right in them.'

"They went on to talk about the difference between outer beauty and inner beauty and how they valued my inner beauty—my kindness, my compassion, my openness. So, I started to put blinders on, to block out the stares, to look straight ahead, to focus on my inner beauty. But I've been doing it for so long now, I no longer have blinders on; I just don't really pay any attention to the stares."

I searched for what to say next and my silence prompted Billy to say, "I guess I sound really conceited, huh? Talking about how beautiful people think I am?"

"No, Billy. Not at all. That was as far from conceited as you could possibly get. I'm curious. And if you don't want to answer, just tell me. What do you see when you look in the mirror? Do you see the beautiful person that people stare at?"

He thought a moment before responding. "Beauty is subjective, right? Or is beauty objective? I guess I'm not sure. But I guess I recognize what people see as beautiful; I get what people are looking at. But I don't see what they see, or maybe I don't focus on what they focus on. I see this zit on the side of my nose. I see one ear lower than the other. I see this small scar near my left eye from when I fell off my bike when I was seven and had to have stitches. I see the gap between my two front teeth."

I squeezed his hand. "Again, I'm really sorry."

"Don't be. It's really messed up. Because I think that I really did it—chopped off my curls and bleached my hair—to try to disrupt the beauty narrative. And it worked, so I should be happy. But then when you didn't think I looked good, I got pissed. I really need to process that."

"Hold up, for the record, I think it looks really good. And if I am allowed to objectify you, I think you look beautiful. Is it okay if I objectify you?"

His rolled his eyes, then the grin appeared. "Yes babe, you, and only you, are allowed to objectify me."

"Great, then I am just going to stare at your beauty for the rest of the ride to New York."

Billy laughed, "Get the hell out of my face." He gave me a quick kiss, grabbed my hand in his, put his Beats and The Weeknd back on, and settled in for the rest of the trip.

# Chapter 40

The Lyft driver takes the Manhattan Bridge to Brooklyn and pulls to the curb in front of Andy and Keith's building in Clinton Hill. On the ground floor is Uncle Andy's restaurant, Americana, and their apartment is above it. The rain has let up and people are on the sidewalk in front of the restaurant, umbrellas in hand, waiting for tables. The restaurant is packed.

I ring the bell and the buzzer sounds. When we reach the first-floor landing, Keith is standing in the open door, a huge smile on his face. "Gabe!" He pulls me in for a hug. "You're all grown up." He releases me and steps over to Billy. "Welcome to Brooklyn, Billy. I'm Keith. It's so good to meet you."

Billy shakes his hand and replies, "So good to meet you, Keith. Thanks so much for having me."

"Of course. Andy is down in the restaurant for a bit. Saturday brunch is insane. Why anyone goes out to brunch in New York is beyond me. Hang your coats up in the closet there. How was the train ride?"

"It was good," Billy answers. "After our fight, we both had a good nap." He grins and laughs.

"Oh boy, a fight on the train. I think that I've had a fight or two on a train with a Meyers man myself." He winks at me. Oh great, two minutes in and Keith and Billy are going to be allies against the Meyers men. Billy and Keith are amused; I roll my eyes.

"Let me show you to your room. You guys can shower or nap or whatever you need. I made some lunch and Andy will hopefully join us in a little while. He's so excited that you're here. He tried to take the day off, but that's nearly impossible when you live above your restaurant."

Keith leads us down a hallway, shows us the bedroom and bathroom, and leaves us to get settled. I realize at that moment that I never had the discussion with Billy about our sleeping arrangements, even after Nic interrogated me about it. But apparently Keith and Andy are just assuming that we are sharing a bed. I contemplate saying something about it to Billy, but he's just acting like this is totally normal, like we're some couple who always sleeps together, settling into the guest room. I decide not to complicate things, to try to go with the flow, even though going with the flow is not in my nature.

I begin unpacking my suitcase and putting my clothes in the dresser drawer. Billy says, "Look. The rain stopped and it looks like the sun is trying to break through. I'm so excited to be here, Gabe. Keith seems really great." Obviously my face has not gotten the message that we are going with the flow, because Billy takes one look at me and says, "What's wrong? What's spinning around in that brain of yours?"

"It's stupid. It's just that we never talked about sleeping arrangements. And the reality hit me that we're going to be sleeping together. And we've never slept together."

"Are you not comfortable sleeping together?"

"I don't know. I mean, I've never slept with anyone before. And there's sleeping together and there's sleeping together."

"We can just sleep, like sleep in the same bed. We don't have to do anything more than what we've already done, or we don't have to do anything more than sleep. Let's just be honest with each other about what we want and what we're ready for. How about we just enjoy our first day in Brooklyn and then we'll figure it out tonight?"

"Sounds good." Relax Gabe. He's right. You'll figure it out...together.

Keith has lunch ready when we come out of the bedroom. He and Billy fall into an easy conversation. When Billy reveals that he's on the tennis team, Keith lights up. "We should play while you're here. I played in college, took some time off, and started playing again a few years back."

"That would be great! But I didn't bring any of my gear."

"You can use one of my racquets. And the club has tennis shoes to rent. We can get you all set up. I'll book a court for tomorrow unless you two already have plans."

Billy looks at me questioningly. "No plans; you guys should play."

"Perfect. I'll book it. That will give Gabe and Andy a chance to catch up on their own."

And as if on cue, the door opens and Andy walks in. Whenever I see him, I'm stunned at how much he and my father look alike. I stand up and he's right in front of me. "Gabriel. Sorry, Gabe. I'm so happy you're here." Our hug is long, filled with the shared loss of the past three years.

When we separate, I turn to see that Billy and Keith look almost embarrassed, as if they had just spied on a private moment. I break the tension, "This is Billy. Billy, this is Andy."

They say, "Good to meet you," in unison as they shake.

"I can only stay for a minute because all hell is breaking loose downstairs, but I promise that I will be all yours tonight. I made a reservation at a friend's place, and I told my manager that she should only contact me if the restaurant is burning to the ground." He shovels a few spoons of pasta salad in his mouth and rushes out as quickly as he came in.

"My life," Keith sighs as Andy closes the door. "I'm the mistress. The restaurant is his husband." Billy and I giggle, but it's a little uncomfortable. And a little personal. "I'm just kidding boys. It's all good. Actually, it's great. While he toils away on a Saturday afternoon, I get to go to the gym, do some shopping, meet a friend for coffee." He smiles, and I think he means it.

"I'm going to let you boys have the afternoon to yourself. Make yourselves comfortable. The weather is clearing and looks like a beautiful afternoon. Thanks for bringing the sun with you. If you want to go out and explore, I'm sure you can find your way around the big bad city. Here's a set of keys. This is for the downstairs door, and this is the apartment key. You have my number. Just text or call if you need anything."

Billy and I decide that we'll keep it local for this afternoon, explore this part of Brooklyn. We wind our way through the brownstone lined streets and come to Fort Greene Park. The cherry blossoms on the hill are beginning to bloom. Families are picnicking, the tennis courts are packed. We stop for a bit and watch a spirited soccer match, friendly but competitive, between Jamaicans and Central Americans. We climb the hill and descend the north side and make our way to the Brooklyn Bridge. The beautiful April Saturday has brought out throngs of tourists. The crisp air is filled with the mingled music of Spanish, French, Italian, German, and languages that we do not recognize. It seems like the whole world has decided to have a peaceful, friendly, joyful meeting on the Bridge.

***"Saturday on the Bridge with Billy"***
***iPhone selfie, unfiltered***
*Background -- two stone arches,*
*thousands of thick, woven cables*
*descend in all directions.*
*Foreground -- two young men;*
*the one on the left has shoulder*
*length, shaggy hair. The one on the*
*right, short hair, dark and buzzed on*
*the sides, bleached with dark roots*
*on the top. Both smile directly into*
*the camera, full happy smiles.*

# Chapter 41

Billy comes out of the bathroom looking as handsome as all get out, in a light blue button-down shirt with a red tie. There's something about these dressy clothes combined with a bleach blond fade that works; it probably shouldn't, but boy does it work. "Well, look at you."

"I clean up nice, huh?" he asks with his crooked grin.

"Yeah, not bad."

"You don't look bad yourself mister. And you smell pretty delicious too." He's got a frisky look that I shut down real quick.

"They're waiting for us. Let's not make us be late."

Billy gives me his you're-no-fun eye roll.

"Oh, and you cannot live out of your suitcase the whole time, with clothes spilling out of it. Clothes on the floor and thrown over the chair. There's a dresser, there's a closet."

Another eye roll and then he turns and walks out of the room. I follow him and we join Andy and Keith to head to dinner.

Andy's friend's restaurant is in lower Manhattan, just over the bridge in Tribeca. Billy and I both look at each other when we walk in. It's a total New York scene, like out of a movie. Everyone is dressed in cool fits and there are so many good-looking people. Billy turns to me and says, "Damn, this is amazing." He's excited and comfortable and I already feel totally out of place.

A statuesque Black woman approaches us as we wait by the door. She has close cropped, bleached hair. Her short dress is gray but shimmers silver in the light. She wears huge silver hoop earrings and a silver stud in her nose. When she sees Andy and Keith, her face lights up the room. "Finally! They gave you a night off," she says as she kisses them each on both cheeks.

Keith says, "You know how hard it is to get him to take a night off."

"Oh, believe me I know," she responds.

"I can't make it happen," Keith continues. "You can thank these two," he says, pointing to me and Billy.

Andy says, "Jalinda, this is my nephew Gabe and his boyfriend Billy. They're seniors in high school, down for spring break."

Jalinda smiles brightly as she says, "Enchanted to meet you both," and gives us both the double-cheek kiss. She looks up at Billy's hair and says, "Boy, that hair is fierce on you." Billy turns to me with a smug look that says—see? What do you know?

Jalinda instructs one of the waiters to bring us to our table, and we make our way through the packed room to a table in the back corner with a view of the whole restaurant. Andy tells me and Billy to sit in the back chairs so we are facing the action.

"How do you know Jalinda?" Billy asks.

Andy explains, "Jalinda worked for me for about ten years. She managed the front of the house and as you can see, she's pretty magnetic. She was a really big part of making our little Brooklyn bistro a destination. We had really good food, but she helped draw the crowds. She had dreams of opening a place in Manhattan, and I considered it…"

Keith interrupts, "Okay, I'm about to be the bad guy in this story so let me tell it. When Andy said that he was thinking about opening a restaurant in Manhattan with Jalinda, I was not on board. He was already so consumed with the Brooklyn place, that I knew we would never see each other."

"He is not the bad guy. He was absolutely right. I had no real desire to open another restaurant. And it was Jalinda's dream, not mine, so when word got out that she wanted to open a place in Manhattan, potential partners came out of the woodwork. Since opening night, two years ago, this has been the hottest restaurant in New York City." Andy says this with pride, as if one of his children has gone off and made a better life, accomplished even more than the parent.

"How did you even end up owning a restaurant?" I ask. It has suddenly occurred to me that I know so little about Uncle Andy's life. I know he has Keith. I know they live in Brooklyn. I know he owns a restaurant. But I don't know how any of that came about.

Andy explains that he moved to New York when he was eighteen, wanting an adventure. I don't think he knows that I know about his parents kicking him out when they found out he was gay. Like so many young people who move to New York, he got a job in a restaurant. He was a busboy in an Italian restaurant, where he worked his way up to waiter. After a few years, he moved on to a French restaurant. French restaurants were more expensive, and the tips were great.

The restaurant scene in Brooklyn was really hot, so he and one of his friends decided to open a place of their own. They found a little place in Fort Greene, only ten tables. It was slow going at first, but they persisted and became a popular neighborhood spot.

That's when Keith came into the picture. A young lawyer, working for a civil rights non-profit, living in Fort Greene, a few doors down from the restaurant. He became a regular, eating a couple of nights a week at the tiny bar. More than a couple of nights a week when he started pursuing Andy.

"He was a tough fish to reel in," Keith says. "Here I was, eating at that damn bar practically every night, spending half my damn salary, and this fool thought it was because of the food. I mean, the food was good, but I had an appetite for something else." Billy and I crack up.

Keith eventually reeled Andy in, and the restaurant continued to be a hit. So much so that they moved to this bigger place in Clinton Hill. Then the apartment upstairs became available, and they moved in.

The sun streams through the small space on the side of the window shade and lands on my face. I roll over to hug Billy, but he's not there. The bathroom door opens, and he comes out wearing shorts and his Jason Collins Nets 98 jersey. I look at him with a confused blink. "Keith and I are playing tennis, remember? I don't have my tennis clothes. This will have to do." He gestures to his outfit.

"You look cute. Come back to bed."

He lets out a laugh. "Get outta here with that. The one time I've got something to do, you're all cuddly all of a sudden. Nope. And don't sleep the whole morning away. You need to be up and ready to go when I get back. Today is Coney Island, baby!"

I roll over and go back to sleep.

When I stumble out, Andy is at the kitchen table drinking coffee and reading the paper. "Hey. Morning. How'd you sleep?"

"Good." He's staring at the Smashing Pumpkins t-shirt I slept in. A slight smile appears on his face. It just as quickly disappears.

"Looks like you need coffee. There's a fresh pot. Milk in the fridge, sugar on the counter. There are bagels also." He goes back to the paper and lets me do my thing on my own. I'm glad he's not a big morning conversationalist.

I fix coffee, toast and butter a bagel and sit down. I scroll through Instagram and Tiktok, read a few Twitter threads. Finally I'm awake. "Thanks for last night Uncle Andy. That was great."

"I'm glad you had fun. And I'm glad that I had the excuse to get out for the night. I really needed that." He folds the paper and sets it down. "Billy seems great."

"Yeah, he is great. I'm lucky."

"And so is he." I don't say anything. Just sip my coffee. "I hope he returns my husband in one piece after kicking his ass on the tennis court."

"He told me that Keith played college tennis, so he's not sure he's going to kick Keith's ass."

He's filling his cup. "More coffee?"

"Thanks." I hold my cup out for him.

"You okay? Your mind seems far away."

"Yeah, I'm good. I'm just..." I trail off, not sure how to continue, or if I should continue. But I need to talk about this and if I'm going to talk about this to anyone, it seems like Andy is the best candidate. "Well, the thing is...sorry, I'm not good at talking about awkward things." Andy doesn't say anything. Just nods, waits, ready to listen. "Billy and I haven't had sex yet. And we've been together for almost six months. I mean, I guess we've sorta had sex. We've done stuff, but we haven't gone too far. You know?"

"Do you see that as a problem?"

"I don't know if it's a problem. I'm confused. I want to...well, I want to go further, I want to do more. And Billy definitely wants to, but I keep stopping us when we get close to it. Last night we slept together, like real sleeping, for the first time, and I stopped us."

"Oh God, Keith and I talked about sleeping arrangements and whether we should have one of you sleep on the sofa, but then we thought that since you're both eighteen it would be fine to just have you in the same room, sharing a bed. I should have asked you first. I'm sorry."

"No, don't be sorry. It was nice to sleep in the same bed with Billy."

"And you know it's okay to set boundaries on what you do, right?"

"I know that, and Billy's not really pressuring me. I mean, it's obvious that he really wants to do more, but he's not pushing me. I think last night was frustrating for him though."

"Please, promise me that when you decide to go further, you'll be safe."

"Of course, we'll be safe. Billy's parents gave him condoms. My counselor at school gave me condoms. We're prepared."

"Good."

After a pause, I say, "I really want to, but I'm afraid that it will bring us too close." There. I said it. Admitted it.

"And you don't want to get too close because...?"

"Because it will hurt more when it's over."

He gives himself a minute to think about this before responding. "You're probably right Gabe. It can really hurt when you get close and it ends, but you can't be planning for the end before it's really started. You need to give your heart the opportunity to be broken. When your heart is broken, it means that it was whole and full and alive. And broken hearts mend. They get better. They get stronger. They love better and love stronger."

Andy stops talking. He sits quietly, drinking his coffee, allowing his words to set in, words that sound grounded in experience. Who is this person that Andy loved? Who broke his heart? Who made his heart stronger and better?

"So, the Smashing Pumpkins?" he asks, nodding his head toward my t-shirt.

"I found it in the basement in a box of dad's old clothes. I figured he wouldn't mind me wearing it."

"No, I suspect that Josh would be very happy to see you wearing it. Want to hear the story behind that shirt?"

"You know the story behind this shirt?"

"Yep. I bought it."

"Get out."

"I'm guessing I was about twenty and your father would have been about seventeen. I had been living in New York for a couple of years and I came home. I wasn't getting along with my parents at the time, so I stayed with friends." When I nod, he asks, "Do you know about what happened with me and my parents?"

"Yes, my mom told me."

"Good," he replies. "Well, I didn't want my parents to know I was back in town, so I told Josh not to tell them. I surprised him for his birthday with tickets to that concert. It was at the Fleet Center in Boston. We were both big alt-rock fans and your father loved Billy Corgan. He was the lead singer. Or is. I think the band may be back together."

Andy looks happy and sad at the same time as he tells me about that night. "We met near the train station and got stoned before catching our train to Boston." He sees my raised eyebrows. "Yeah, I know. Getting my little brother high. But hey, I was still a kid too and he was seventeen and I knew that he had been getting stoned for a couple of years. I probably shouldn't be telling you this part. Oh well, too late."

He tells me about the train ride, walking around Boston high, and the concert. How much they loved the concert, how happy my father was. And the t-shirt, part of his seventeenth birthday gift. It was a special night, a reunion, their first time hanging out since Nana and Poppa kicked Andy out for being gay, since the night they had cried together, and Andy had told dad that everything would be okay. Andy says, "I remember it like it was yesterday. Your dad and I, our arms over each other's shoulders, singing along to all the songs." He's floated back in time; he's twenty years old with his baby brother beside him.

We smile across the table at each other, smiles that hope to take the place of tears. He reaches across and takes my hand in his. "He's a great little brother, your father. And a good man. I know you have complicated feelings about him right now. Believe me, I understand. It took me many years to resolve some of the issues with your Nana and Poppa. And many of the issues were never resolved and probably never will be. But as I've gotten older, I've learned that I can't give up valuable space in my head and my heart to anger and resentment and bitterness. That space is precious, and I need it for love and joy and understanding and empathy. Take the time you need, Gabe. But I really want you to believe me when I tell you that your dad, my little brother, is worth whatever effort it might take." His voice cracks when he says, "my little brother."

The door opens and Keith and Billy enter, laughing. It startles me out of this moment of emotion, and I pull myself back from the verge of tears. Andy's face, at the sight of his husband, his love, his sweaty and smelly love, shows me the power of a heart that's been tested. Andy loves Keith better and stronger because he's allowed his heart to break and mend.

"So?" Andy asks them.

Billy lets out a sigh. "The old man beat me 9-7 in a third set tiebreak."

"What?" Andy and I scream at the same time.

"Oh, glad to hear you had so much confidence in me honey," Keith says to Andy.

"Yeah, he's got game, man. I'm beat up. Ran me like a fool." Billy takes a sip of my coffee.

"Damn Billy, you stink. Get your butt in the shower."

Andy agrees. "You too Keith. You're both stinking up the place."

Keith and Billy protest but they know they can't deny that they stink. I rise and cross to Andy, who is still sitting. I bend down and hug him, whisper thank you in his ear, and follow Billy into our room.

# Chapter 42

Okay, so I had heard that the Coney Island Cyclone was the OG roller coaster, that it was scarier than it looks, that it's the oldest roller coaster in the country but after almost a hundred years, still one of the best. Billy and I stand in line on a cool late morning in April. The line isn't long. We check out the Cyclone from the ground. Doesn't look very high, doesn't look too steep. Billy and I argue about whether we want the front car or the back car. He wants the front car because he thinks it's more exciting to feel like you're plunging headfirst down a mountain, facing your fears head on. As the physics geek, I want the back car because I know that when the first cars go over the apex and head down, the acceleration and gravity combine to make the back car go even faster. In the back car, you don't see what's coming, it's the element of surprise. So we agree that we will ride twice, once in the front and once in the back.

We get the front car for our first ride. Damn, these cars are small. My legs are scrunched in, and the safety bar is digging into my waist. The seat is not very padded, and my bony ass is not comfortable. And we're off. We make a quick turn and begin to climb. Oh, this climb is steeper than it looks from the ground. And they were right. This is a wooden roller coaster. And this wood looks chipped and rotting. How the hell is this wreck still standing? All I can concentrate on is the sorry state of the wood and some of the screws that seem to be protruding. Holy shit. The car jerks and jerks as we slowly climb. It makes a click, click, click sound and when I look up, I only see sky. We are almost at the top, at the apex of this long, slow climb. I'm clutching the safety bar and I turn, and Billy already has his arms in the air. Oh, he's that guy, the arms-in-the-air-on-the-roller-coaster-guy. I guess I should have figured. As I say, "Holy shit," Billy says, "This is frigging awesome."

The first drop is dramatic and sudden and seconds later we are already climbing the next hill. Before you know it, we are speeding down the second hill and around a turn. I'm jerked to the side, smashing into Billy, and my knees smack into the front. In spite of the pain, I'm exhilarated. With every drop, there's a sense of weightlessness, a sense of not caring about anything else in the world but this moment, this descent, this plunge. I'm frightened and free at the same moment.

We pull around the final turn and the cars stop. Everyone piles out and we exit. Billy says excitedly, "Should we get right back in line so we can ride the back car?"

I want to tell him that once was enough. That he was right—that the front car is the way to go. That we don't need to wait in line for another ride. But I think about what Karina and Zach always talk about, how we have to change our perspective, experience things in different ways. Do what scares us.

We ride again, in the back car this time. When the safety bar clamps down, Billy says, "This time, you have to put your hands in the air, babe. It's such an amazing feeling."

"Get out of here with that, Billy."

"C'mon. I'll hold your hand."

"You can hold my hand on the bar."

"You can do it. It's a total rush."

The cars jerk and we start again. Billy has his left hand over my right hand, which is clenching the safety bar with an iron grip. We begin the climb and Billy says, "Just let go Gabe. Just take my hand. You can do this. Trust me."

The slow climb continues. I'm breathing rapidly, looking up at the sky, knowing that we are going to be plunging down in a few seconds. I release my grip on the bar and grab Billy's hand. I'm practically crushing his bones. "Okay, I'm gonna raise our hands in the air." And he does. The front car has just reached the apex. Billy has his other hand in the air. "C'mon, put the other hand in the air. Let's do this together."

It takes every ounce of courage that I have to let go of the bar and to open myself up to a new experience—a scary but exciting experience. The front car begins its descent, and my physics calculations are correct; it is faster, and there is a sense of not knowing what's coming. I normally prefer the known, prefer to see what's coming, but there is something to be said for hanging there in midair, knowing that something exciting and scary is on the way. Billy and I are both screaming, along with everyone else. And he was right. It's a total rush with my hands in the air, a sense of freedom, almost like flying. When we are slowing down, Billy says excitedly, "You did it! You did it man. How'd it feel?"

"It felt amazing, Billy. It felt amazing."

After the Cyclone, we eat hot dogs at Nathan's. Although these hot dogs rock, I can't really enjoy them because I hear Lulu's nagging voice in my head. I take a picture of Billy stuffing a dog in his mouth. I'm about to post it when Billy stops me. Oh yeah, we do not need Lulu lecturing us on social media for all the world to see.

We sit on a bench on the boardwalk. The sun tries to peek through the clouds. It's warming up a little. Small waves lap at the shore. It's a good day.

We both check our phones. I'm scrolling through TikTok when Billy says, "Shit, email from Columbia."

"Really? Wow. Do you want to open it now?"

"I think so. I need to get it over with." He takes a breath and hands me his phone. "You read it. Just rip the Band-Aid off."

I click on the email and read the first sentences. "Billy, you got in! You got accepted at Columbia."

"Really? Oh my God. I can't believe it. I really thought they were going to reject me."

"Congratulations. That's so great. Your parents are going to be so excited."

"Yes. I think I'll wait to tell them. I'll tell them when we get back." I can see that he wants to be excited. Getting into Columbia is a big deal, and it must be a relief, knowing the pressure he has felt from his father. But his heart is set on Northwestern. It would almost be easier if Columbia had rejected him.

He stands, grabs my hand, and says, "Let's get some cotton candy."

***"Cotton Candy"***
***Black & white and Color***
*Coney Island Boardwalk.*
*A young man*
*leans against the boardwalk railing,*
*roller coaster*
*in the background.*
*In one hand*
*a full cotton candy.*
*The other*
*holds a hunk of the cotton candy,*
*close to his mouth.*
*The entire photo is*
*black*
*and white,*
*except for*
*the pink cotton candy.*

# Chapter 43

We cram so much into the next few days. On our last full day, we have a tour of NYU and eat sandwiches in Washington Square Park, packed on a beautiful April day with every kind of person imaginable. Lulu would love it—so many stories to create about all of these strangers. Billy says, "This is gonna be you next year. Hanging in this park after class. The Village will be your campus. Pretty cool."

"I still have to wait on financial aid. If they don't give me a ton of money, I won't be here next year." I'm trying to imagine myself here. Another scary but exciting experience, like riding the Cyclone with my hands in the air, but for four years instead of two minutes.

We walk west a couple of blocks and head down Christopher Street. We see a small crowd of people at a little park and realize that we have stumbled on the Stonewall Monument. We get closer, read the signs about the history of the park, and then listen in as a park ranger gives a tour. She explains the statues and the history of the Stonewall Inn, as she paints a picture of those nights in June of 1969 when Stonewall patrons and neighborhood people finally rose up against the police harassment. Billy takes my hand as we listen to her talk about the bravery of these gay men and lesbians, fifty years ago, and the legacy they left future generations. They said enough is enough, and they got beaten for it, arrested for it, shamed in the news for it. But they kept fighting. Because of them, I can be out at school and out to my family. I can be out at work, and I can get married. And I can hold hands with my boyfriend in public. I turn to Billy and give him a soft kiss on the lips. Because I can.

Next, we hop on the 1 train and head to Columbia. The train is packed, people jammed in like sardines, midday on a Tuesday afternoon. Where the hell are all these people going in the middle of the day on a Tuesday?

When the train pulls into the 116th Street Station, Billy says, "This is our stop." We emerge from underground, and we are right at the campus. It's beautiful, with expansive lawns surrounded by old stone and brick buildings. Where NYU seems like a bunch of buildings scattered around a neighborhood, Columbia seems like a college campus in the middle of a huge city.

"It's beautiful, huh Billy?"

"Yeah, really pretty. This is gonna be great. And only 16 subway stops from you."

"What?"

"I counted. It's only 16 stops on the 1 train from the Village to here."

I'm not really sure what to say to this. We continue walking the campus. Finally I say, "Billy, I love that you counted the subway stops, and I would love for us to be in the same city for college, if I can even afford to go to NYU. But you don't really want to go to Columbia. It feels like you're trying to convince yourself to do something you don't want to do."

"Columbia is a great school. And it's in New York City. I can be really happy here, I think."

"You know you need to tell your dad that you really want to go to Northwestern, right?"

"Yes, I know."

# Chapter 44

Nic and Mami want to hear all about the trip. Nic is still a little mad that he didn't get to go, but he's also super excited to hear about it all. I tell them all about NYU and Columbia and the Cyclone and all of Coney Island. Nic can't believe that I rode with my hands in the air. "No way! You are way too chicken to do that. I'm gonna text Billy." He pulls out his phone.

"Do not text Billy, Nic! Why the hell do you even have his number? Just stop it. Trust me, I rode the Cyclone with my hands in the air. Jeez."

Mami wants to know all about Andy's restaurant. I tell her about the last night, when we ate there. Andy was working, but he made sure that Keith, Billy, and I were well fed and well taken care of. He worked the room, talking to everyone.

I show them all the pictures. Mami loves the cherry blossoms at the Brooklyn Botanical Gardens. Nic loves the Coney Island Freak Show pictures. And the group pictures of me, Billy, Andy, and Keith. And the selfies of me and Billy. And the dozens of pictures of Billy. The final pictures are from the last morning, before Billy and I caught our train home. I got up early and snuck out, careful not to wake anyone. I walked down to Dumbo, the area of Brooklyn along the river where you can look at the Brooklyn Bridge from down below. I got there just as the sun was rising. Looking from below, facing east, I see the city wake up.

*"The Sun Also Rises"*
*Color, wide-angle lens*
*The sun rises behind the Manhattan skyline.*
*Wispy clouds turn orange*

*yellow*
*and red*
*on a background of bright blue.*
*In front of the skyline*
*the Brooklyn Bridge*
*grows out of the rolling waters of the*
*East River*
*majestic arches reaching skyward,*
*tethered to earth by thousands of tightly*
*wound cables.*
*The water of the East River*
*is orange, yellow, and red*
*the mirror image*
*of the sky above.*

# Chapter 45

I had put off telling Mami that I wanted to visit Dad in prison. Turns out I didn't need to tell her, didn't need to plan a visit. Mami got the call while she was at work. My father's parole had been granted; he was coming home. She told us that night at dinner. She cried and Nic hugged her and asked a thousand questions. When? How did you find out? Did you talk to him? Will we go pick him up?

It hit me like a wave. I didn't even know that it was a possibility at this point, so I hadn't prepared myself. When Mami asked me why I didn't seem happy, I replied, "Of course I'm happy. I'm just shocked right now. This came out of nowhere. Yes, I'm happy. I just need a little time to process." I hug Mami and tell them I am going outside to stargaze.

Lulu answers on the second ring. "Hey Gabe, what's up?"

"My dad's parole came through. He's getting out in the next couple of weeks."

"Oh my God, that's amazing. I'm so happy for you."

"Thanks."

"Are you okay? How are you feeling?"

I'm feeling so many emotions right now. I want to feel happier than I do. I know I should be super happy—happy for him, happy for the family. I guess I am happy, but other emotions are stronger. I'm nervous and stressed; I'm resentful. Things are pretty good in my life right now. Everything is coming into focus and I'm figuring out the composition, how things are arranged, how they fit together, work together. I'm doing well in school, and I'll graduate in a little over a month. I've got college acceptances; I have a boyfriend. I'm going to have two photos in the end of year student exhibit. I'm getting along really well with Mami and Nic and I've been taking the role model/man of the house thing seriously. I feel like him coming home is going to disrupt everything. And I'm still angry and we're going to have to deal with all of that. And of course, I feel really guilty for not feeling happier.

"I feel horrible that I don't feel happy."

"Gabe, it's a lot to take in. You just found out, so you'll need some time to work through all your feelings. It's okay to feel negative emotions. He's been gone for almost four years, and you've gone through a lot. So much has changed. I think it's normal to feel nervous and unsure."

"Yeah, I guess you're right." I need to change the subject. "How are you? How did it go meeting Kevin's parents?"

"Well, they loved me of course."

I groan, "Yes, of course. I know, all parents love you. Conceited much?"

"I can't help it. It's true. Anyway, it was nice. They were really sweet with me. Kevin was really nervous even though I told him about my way with parents. But I'm not sure what we're even doing. I mean, I like him a lot but he's probably going to college in Wisconsin, and I don't want to be that girl in college who has a long-distance boyfriend from high school. We haven't really talked about it yet. What about you? Have you and Billy talked about that?"

"When we were in New York, he was talking about Columbia. I know that's where his parents want him to go, but it felt like he was using being close to me as a way to convince himself. But I think he should go to Northwestern."

"I should hear from NYU this week. I spoke to someone at admissions and I'm pretty high on the waitlist, so I'm feeling pretty good. Nervous, but a little confident."

"I should hear from RISD this week also about the waitlist."

"Well, you're already in at NYU so it doesn't really matter all that much."

"I don't think NYU is a done deal for me. For one, there's the money. I haven't heard about financial aid yet. I want to see what happens with RISD."

Lulu is uncharacteristically quiet.

"What's wrong Lu?"

"Nothing."

"I can hear from your silence that something is wrong."

"I was just thinking about how NYU has been our dream."

"I know. I'm just keeping my options open until I know what all my options are. Let's wait and see what happens in the next week."

"You're right."

"Okay, I have to go back in and check on Nic. He seemed really happy, but I need to see how he's really feeling."

"He's so lucky to have you as a big brother, Gabe. And it'll work out with your dad. You'll figure it out."

Of course, Lulu is correct. I will figure it out. It's what we do, right? We're on an endless cycle of figuring it out. Just as we figure one thing out, a more complex and perplexing problem comes along. It won't be easy, but I can figure it out. I think.

# Chapter 46

Nic's on his phone playing Trivia Crack when I walk in the room. I start to talk to him, and he says, "Wait, wait, what's the capital of North Dakota?"

"Bismarck," I tell him.

"Are you sure it's not Pierre?"

"Pierre is South Dakota. Trust me."

"Yes! Got it."

It looks like he's about to start another round. He doesn't look up from his phone. "Wait Nic, put your phone down. I wanna talk to you." He stays staring at his phone. "Nic. C'mon man." When he doesn't look up or put the phone down, I grab it out of his hands.

"Hey! What the hell? Give me my phone back."

"We need to talk."

"I don't want to talk. I want to play Trivia."

"What's wrong?"

He stares at the ceiling, taking a couple of deep breaths, before saying, "Why can't you be happy that dad's coming home? He's finally coming home, and you act like you want him to stay in prison."

"Nic, I don't want him to stay in prison. I am happy that he's coming home."

"You didn't act like it."

"Okay, I told you that I'm not going to hide things from you anymore, so I'll be honest with you. I'm nervous and stressed about him coming home. I'm used to things the way they are now with me, you, and Mami. Things are pretty good for me and I'm in my last months of high school. It's going to be like a stranger moving into the house."

"He's dad, not a stranger."

"I know that, but it's been three and a half years. We've changed, and I'm sure prison has changed him. It's not going to be like it was before, Nic. Not at first. Probably not ever."

This hurts him. He wants to believe we will go back to the way things were before. His face brings a lump to my throat. I try not to cry as I tell him, "I just want you to be prepared. This might be hard. Harder than you think, or harder than you want to believe."

"I know. I know. But will you promise me something? Please?"

I begin to tell him that I will promise him anything, but I catch myself. I know I can't promise him something I can't deliver. "What Nic? What do you want me to promise?"

"Promise me you'll try. Promise me you'll try to forgive him. Promise me you'll try to stop hating him."

I move to his bed and sit beside him and hug him. He hugs me back. We hug hard and I say, "I promise. I promise that I will try."

# Chapter 47

I submitted a portfolio of twenty photos to the Citywide High School Arts Exhibit, and they notified me that I was accepted and that I can exhibit two photos in the show.

"I can't decide which two to pick."

Trevor is looking intently at my portfolio, dissecting each photo with his eyes. He gives an occasional murmur—hmmm, nice, okay, wow. "Gabe, these are really good. Even though they're all very different, I see a definite style emerging. They have an off-center, off-angle sort of vibe that's really interesting. Thanks for sharing them with me."

"Thanks. I really appreciate that. It's almost harder to choose two than to just choose one. With one, people just get to see a sample, one shot. But with two, I have the opportunity to show more of who I am as a photographer."

"Well, if you could only pick one, do you know which one you would pick?"

"I'm pretty sure I would pick this one." I point to the black and white photo of my mom, at the table, the one called "Solitaria." The one that Billy commented on the night we met, when he first checked out my Instagram account.

Trevor agrees. "Great choice. I think that even if I didn't know your mom, if I didn't know her story, I would understand everything from this photo. The sadness, the loneliness, the king on the table and the queen in her hand. There's so much going on here with so little in the photo."

I'm always amazed when people look at one of my photos and see what I saw at the moment I took it. I remember that night so clearly, walking out of my room late at night and seeing her there playing cards all by herself at the kitchen table. I remembered all of our family card games and saw the loneliness on her face. I knew that even though my father did so much to hurt her, she was still lonely and missing him.

"Of course," I say, "I'd have to ask her for permission to use this one. If other people see it the same way you did, it would really be putting her on display."

"Have you ever shown it to her?"

"No."

He pauses. "She might really like it."

"Maybe."

"Well, if you did choose that one, how would you decide on a second one?"

I've definitely thought about this. "I have two thoughts on that. One is that I choose another one that's similar, to show my style, my vibe. Or I choose one that's different to show my versatility. See, this is why it's hard to have two instead of just one."

"Yes, it is a dilemma. But either one will work. I think that if you choose another one that has real meaning and emotional connection for you like that one does, it'll be really powerful. Try to imagine that big space, with all of this artwork displayed. Imagine people approaching and seeing: GABE MEYERS. What do you want them to see? What do you want them to walk away thinking? What do you want them to say to their friends?"

And now I'm actually imagining the scene that Trevor has painted for me. This scene that will be happening soon. This exhibit is a big deal. Crowds of people turn out for it. My friends will all be there. My teachers. My family, maybe even my father. Strangers, art makers, art lovers.

"I'm going to give this some more thought. Thanks so much Trevor. I mean, you just scared the shit out of me, but thanks for helping me to imagine this night."

"You got it man. You'll be a huge hit."

I close my portfolio and get ready to take off. Trevor stops me, "Hey, have you decided what's next? You'll need to make your college commitment soon. Have you said yes to NYU?"

"Actually, I haven't told anyone this yet, but I think I have made a decision."

"That's great. What's the big decision?"

"RISD moved me off of the waitlist. They gave me good financial aid. And their photography program is amazing. I think I'm going to say yes to RISD."

"Wow, congratulations Gabe. RISD seems like a great choice for you. I thought sure you were going to NYU, since you and Lulu talked about it so much."

"It's a tough choice. But you know, I was in New York over break, and it was great. It's amazing and exciting and my uncle lives there. But it felt overwhelming. I had a hard time imagining myself living there right now."

"I get that. It's New York. There's no place like it in the world, but it's really intense. My sister lives in Brooklyn and I visit a lot. I have a great time, but after a week I'm usually ready to leave."

"Also," I say, "I have some unfinished business here in Providence. I don't want to leave until it's taken care of. I don't want to feel like I'm running away."

Trevor just shakes his head knowingly.

"I take it you heard that my dad is getting out on parole soon."

"Yes, I did hear that. I'm happy to hear that. How are you feeling?"

"I'm feeling good. I know it's going to be challenging, but I'm up for the challenge."

Trevor laughs gently, smiles, and shakes his head.

"What?" I say, defensively.

"I just can't believe how much you've changed. I sit here having this conversation with you, this incredible adult conversation, and then I flash back to ninth grade when I asked you to take out your book and you said, 'Fuck off.' I was a first-year teacher. Man, you almost made me quit that day. But I'm so glad I stuck it out, because I get to see this amazing transformation. And you did it all against pretty difficult odds. Respect, man."

"Respect to you Trevor, because you sat there during our restorative meeting and I told you I was sorry for saying f— off, and I pretended that I meant it, and you pretended to believe that I meant it." We both laugh thinking about the meeting. "But seriously, even though you knew my apology wasn't sincere, when I came back to class, and every day in your class since then, you treated me like it was a thing of the past, like it never happened."

Trevor smiles and nods. "When I was a teenager, I hated it when adults told me they were proud of me. So hate me if you want, Gabe. I'm proud of you, man."

"Thanks Trevor." I definitely don't hate it.

"Lulu told me that she got off the waitlist at NYU and that she's accepted. Did you tell her yet that you decided not to go to NYU?"

"Not yet. Haven't found the right time."

"There's no right time. But she's your best friend. She'll support whatever decision you make."

"Fingers crossed," I say as I zip up my portfolio.

# Chapter 48

It's May 1st, National College Decision Day, but our class worked with our administrators to figure out a way to honor everyone in our class, not just those of us who are going to college next year. We decided on NEXT STEPS DAY. The whole school is in the auditorium in the afternoon. The seniors are excited and nervous because our next steps are going to be announced to the whole school. The underclassmen are probably just excited because they get to miss last period class.

Miguel, Zach, and Karina are up on the stage. The underclassmen are all seated, and the seniors are all waiting outside. The front rows are blocked off, saved for us. The music is blaring, and when Cardi B. and Bad Bunny come on with "I Like It," everyone goes crazy.

Finally, the music fades and Miguel steps up to the microphone. "Okay everyone, welcome! We are so excited to have the whole school here to celebrate our seniors on Next Steps Day! Graduating high school is a huge milestone in life, a turning point, and the choice of what comes next is a big decision. It's a personal decision. Some people make it on their own, some make it by consulting with family, friends, teachers, and mentors. But it's just the first of many decisions you will make in your adult lives. So today we are here to celebrate these first decisions. Let's give a big round of applause for our senior class on their Next Steps Day."

The auditorium erupts as we all file in. A lot of us are wearing our college sweatshirts and t-shirts. Andres and a few others are in their URI shirts, Angel has on a Providence College sweatshirt, and Mariya is wearing her Navy shirt. Some are in CCRI shirts, and some are just in regular clothes.

Derek comes out in his red Target uniform shirt with his fists in the air and people start chanting, "Tar-get, Tar-get, Tar-get." It's that kind of moment when I really appreciate my school, appreciate how diverse we are and how supportive we are of each other.

Karina and Zach come to the mic together to call each of our names and to announce our Next Steps. Jimmy Davis gets the same loud cheers for joining his father's construction company as Kevin gets for going to the University of Wisconsin on a wrestling scholarship. The crowd goes equally crazy for Lulu going to NYU as they do for Tara going to automotive tech. And they definitely seem to support Derek's managerial position at Target over me studying photography at RISD. But the whole thing is way less corny than I expected it to be. It's actually exciting and affirming and all of us seniors are smiling, hugging and high fiving.

Miguel finally dismisses the assembly, and the underclassmen all rush out as if they have just been released from jail. Some of the seniors hang around and a few of the teachers stay and talk to us. Kevin, Lulu, and I find each other. We're all wearing our college sweatshirts. It feels like a beginning and an end at the same time.

"That was way better than I thought it would be," I say. "I thought that shit would be mad corny, but it was cool."

Kevin says, "When they started chanting 'Tar-get, Tar-get' I just about lost it!"

We're all laughing about Derek and the power of Target when Trevor walks up. "That was so great. I can't begin to tell you how it feels to look at the students that I had as freshmen, in my very first year teaching, going off to college. My mind is blown."

"Aw, Trevor," we all say in unison. Then Lulu says, "Are you crying Trevor."

Trevor replies, "I'm not crying, you're crying," and we all roar.

"So Trev," Kevin starts, "Any advice about college and dorm life? Is it all partying and drinking and sex?"

Trevor hesitates, smirks, and says, "No, Kevin. No partying, no drinking, no sex. It's study, study, study."

The three of us groan: yeah right, that's bull, uh-huh sure.

It's a perfect spring afternoon, crystal clear blue, as we jump in Kevin's car. We are going to swing over to the East Side to pick up Billy and then head down to Misquamicut beach. Lulu rides shotgun and she plugs in her iPhone and blasts The Smiths, "There is a Light that Never Goes Out."

I text Billy when we are almost there.

The lawn and sidewalk in front of Billy's school is teeming with students. You can tell all of the seniors from the other kids, because they are all wearing their college sweatshirts for commitment day. I see a couple of Harvards, a Yale, Miami, Brown, Villanova. Billy sees us and waves, daps his friends and bounds over cheerfully in his Northwestern sweatshirt.

He hops in the backseat and says, "Hey babe," and gives me a gap-tooth smile and a kiss. Kevin looks in the rearview and jokes, "Dudes, gross. Not in my car."

Billy says, "Don't be jealous, Kev. There's plenty of me to go around."

Kevin replies, "Man, don't flatter yourself. If I had to, it would most def be Gabe over you."

"Oh my god," Lulu breaks in. "You are such boys with your sophomoric humor."

"How can we be sophomoric, Lu?" I tease. "We're all seniors."

Lulu groans as Kevin and Billy say, "Good one Gabe."

"Okay," Lulu says, taking control. "Kevin, let's get moving. Drive! And Billy, tell us everything. How did it go with your parents? How was commitment day?"

Kevin pulls away and we head south, and Billy tells us about his talk with his parents last night and the big ceremony today. Billy's older sister came down from Cambridge to be there and give him moral support when he told his parents that he was choosing Northwestern over Columbia. His dad was in a really good mood because his sister had been so busy with

Harvard Law School that she hadn't been down to visit since Christmas. His dad had a Scotch before dinner and opened a bottle of red wine with dinner, so Billy hoped that the big sister/alcohol combo would work in his favor. Or the alcohol could make his father belligerent. He wasn't sure what to expect.

But it worked in his favor, although he realizes now that maybe he was putting way too much pressure on himself over this decision. His father was definitely surprised at first, and there was a moment when no one said anything and his dad had a look of disappointment on his face. But his mom broke the silence. "Honey, that's wonderful. Of course, we're going to miss you being so far away, but I know that Northwestern is really your dream, so we're very happy for you."

Patricia looked at Martin, and Billy knew that his parents had talked about this possibility and that his mother had prepared his father to accept it.

"Yes, son," his father said, as though he was about to recite lines that he had memorized. "We are very happy. I know that Columbia was always my dream and not yours. And you've done the hard work that we asked of you. Just a few more weeks to push so you can hang onto your salutatorian spot, or maybe even grab the valedictorian spot from Emily Almeida."

His sister came to his rescue, told his father that his class rank really wasn't that important, and insisted that they open a bottle of champagne to celebrate.

"We had the commitment ceremony this afternoon, and they make a big deal of it. Buffet lunch for staff, students, and parents. When they announced my name and Northwestern, I came onto the stage and everyone was clapping and yelling, and I looked out and saw my dad. He was clapping and smiling and really looked happy." Billy looks happy and relieved.

We spread our blankets out on the soft sand and all stretch out. Billy is lying on his back, his eyes closed, soaking up the early May sun. I lay my head on his chest and stare out at the ocean as I listen to his heartbeat. Billy plays with my hair. The waves are calm, softly lapping at the shore.

Kevin is sitting behind Lulu, his legs wrapped around her. She leans back against him and he rests his chin on her shoulder. They, like me, stare at the ocean, hypnotized by the sun shimmering on the water, and the gentle waves breaking. The tide is coming in, and I'm transfixed watching the water slowly creep closer to us.

"Damn, ya'll," Kevin says softly. "This is beautiful. And this was a big day. We all just committed. We made big decisions."

"We're adults now, man," replies Billy.

"Oh please," Lulu laughs, "there is nothing adult about you Billy. Don't play yourself."

"There are parts of me that are very grown up. Right Gabe?"

I lift my head, look at him, and say, "Don't even." They all laugh.

I lay my head back down and we slip into our comfortable silence again. After a minute, Lulu says, "Gabe, do you want to talk about tomorrow? If you don't, it's okay, but we're all here for you if you do."

It's been hanging over the whole day. I've tried to push it to the back of my mind, but it claws its way to the front whenever I try. It's stronger than me. We've known for weeks that my father would be coming home, but we didn't know when. They gave us the news two days ago. He will be home tomorrow.

I sit up. Billy is now free to prop himself up on his elbows. "I don't know if there's anything to really talk about yet. I'm way nervous because I have no idea what it's going to be like. It's been almost three and a half years. I was just starting high school when he went in, and here I am about to graduate. I'm a completely different person. It's possible he is too."

"How are your mom and Nic feeling about it?" Lulu asks.

All three of them are looking at me now. "My mom is happy but she's really edgy. She's been cleaning like crazy, nagging me and Nic to help. She's bought enough food to feed an army, as if he hasn't eaten for years."

"Well, he hasn't eaten your mother's delicious cooking," says Billy.

"True that," I respond.

"And what about Nic?" Lulu continues.

"He's really excited. Well, he was excited but now I think he's excited and nervous because he thinks I'm likely to mess everything up. He knows me pretty well."

None of them say anything. None of them tell me that I'm not going to mess everything up, and I'm glad that they don't. I don't want them feeding me shit that's not true.

"Anyway," I say. "I want to try to put it out of my head for a while. Let's play frisbee."

We all get up and spread out along the beach. I roll up my jeans and walk to the edge of the incoming tide. The frigid water washes over my feet and ankles as the sun warms my face. I toss the frisbee to Lulu, who tosses it to Kevin, who tosses it to Billy. The sun lights Billy from behind and he glows as he gives me a big smile and shouts, "Ready babe? Go long!"

He hurls the frisbee, a perfect toss, floating it far down the beach. I sprint as fast as I can and as it descends, I leap and snatch it before it hits the sand. I roll and come to a stop. I sit up, with the frisbee held above my head in victory.

I watch the three of them cheering and laughing and I begin to think about how little time we have left before we all go our separate ways—before Lulu is in New York City, before Kevin is in Wisconsin, before Billy is 986.5 miles away in Evanston, Illinois.

Not the time to worry about the future, Gabe. If there was ever a time to live in the absolute present, it is today, right now, on a perfect May afternoon on the beach with your crew.

I stand up, dust the sand off my jeans, run a few steps back their way and launch the frisbee toward Billy and the sun descending behind him.

# Chapter 49

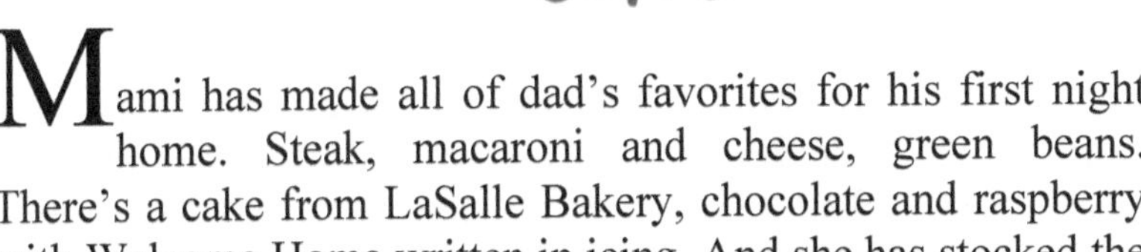

Mami has made all of dad's favorites for his first night home. Steak, macaroni and cheese, green beans. There's a cake from LaSalle Bakery, chocolate and raspberry with Welcome Home written in icing. And she has stocked the fridge with his favorite beer. It's a beautiful May evening, so we are eating at the picnic table in the backyard.

Nic and I both took the day off from school so we could go with Mami to pick him up. We sat in the car outside of the gate, just waiting, Mami in the driver's seat, me in the front passenger seat, Nic in the back. None of us said anything while we waited; we looked at our phones, looked up, looked down at our phones, and looked up again. Finally, Nic shouted, "There he is!" I looked up and saw him walking toward us. Nic and Mami jumped out of the car and ran toward him. Soon they were all hugging and crying.

I stepped out of the car and stood waiting. The three of them began walking back to the car. As he got nearer, we locked eyes. He looked so much older. He probably thought the same thing as he looked at me. Suddenly he was right in front of me, holding out his hand. I took it, we shook hands, and he pulled me in for a hug. "Gabriel, I'm so happy to see you, son." His voice shook as he whispered in my ear.

"I'm happy to see you too, Dad. And it's Gabe now, remember?"

"Oh right. We'll need to talk about that at some point. With Nicolas too. Your mom told me about him wanting to be called Nic now." He shook his head, as if it's silly that we decided what we want to be called.

"Okay," he said. "Let's get out of here." We all walked to the car, and I began to open the front passenger door, my spot, shotgun, where I always sit. Dad stopped me before I climbed in. "Son, you sit in the back with your brother so I can ride up front with your mom." He walked to the passenger side.

"Aren't you driving?" I asked.

A pause. "My license is still suspended. That's one of the details I have to work out with the parole officer. Hopefully I can get it back soon." He tried to say it in a matter-of-fact way, as if it was no big deal, but there was an aggravated edge to his voice. I don't know if he was aggravated with himself or aggravated with the situation. Or maybe he was aggravated with me for asking, making an already awkward situation more tense. I reluctantly moved and hopped in the back seat next to Nic.

As we drove home, Mami talked about all the food she had made and Nic told dad all about school. We talked about RISD and me staying in Providence. He asked me about my trip to New York and Andy and Keith. The tension began to ease, like a knot slowly coming untied.

The steak looks too delicious to pass up. Dad is teasing Nic about not eating meat and I worry for a moment that Nic will give in, break his principles to please Dad, but he stands his ground. "Dad, if you saw this documentary, you would never eat meat again."

"I doubt that," he replies. "And after that disgusting excuse for meat they served us inside, I'm gonna enjoy this delicious steak your Mami made for me without you telling me how disgusting it is or how I'm killing the planet." He turns to me. "It's a delicious steak, right Gabriel?" Is he calling me Gabriel on purpose or by accident? Let it slide for now, Gabe.

I admit that, yes, it's a delicious steak.

Nic jumps in. "Gabe is a halfass vegetarian. He pretends to not eat meat because of Lulu but he cheats all the time." Dad laughs.

"Shut up, Nic," I say to him, more aggressively than the situation calls for.

Mami tries to calm it down before it takes off. She senses that I've been tense all day and she knows that it won't take much for me to go off. "Okay you two. No fighting. Everyone just eat what you want and not worry about what the other is eating."

I take another bite of my steak, but Nic has ruined it for me. I push it aside and dig into the mac and cheese. I'm a little pissed at Nic—not for ruining the steak, but for ganging up on me with Dad, and for making it look so easy to welcome him back into the family as if nothing ever happened.

Next comes the chocolate cake, his favorite, to welcome him home. I watch him intently as he eats it; he savors every bite as if it is the first time he has ever tasted chocolate or the last time he will ever have cake. He looks like he could cry. He finally speaks. "Thank you mi amor for this beautiful dinner." He leans over and kisses Mami. "And my boys." He looks at Nic, at me, back at Nic. "How happy I am to be home."

We move to the firepit and Nic announces, "I'm going to make the fire."

Dad says, "Really? You know how to build a fire?"

"Yep, Gabe taught me," he says proudly.

"All right then," Dad says.

Nic begins to lean the logs against each other, building a teepee like I taught him. Dad says, "You have them too close together. There needs to be more space between them so you can put in the kindling and newspaper."

Nic adjusts the logs. When he moves one of them, a few of them fall. "Shit," he says and Mami chastises him for cursing.

He gets the logs back in place and begins to crumple up the newspaper. When Dad tells him to not crumple it up so tight, he says impatiently, "I know what I'm doing, dad."

"Okay, just make sure you leave enough space so there's room for it to breathe."

"Jesus, just let him do it," I snap. "He knows what he's doing. I taught him. He can do it on his own."

"Well, it doesn't look like you taught him right. He's gonna smother it with too much paper and not enough air."

I snap and yell at him, "Well, I taught him to do it just the way you taught me, so if I taught him wrong, then it's your fault. It means that you taught me wrong."

Mami pleads with us, "Stop it please. Everyone stop fighting."

"Well, what he's doing right there," he points to Nic and the firepit, "is not what I taught you."

"Yes it is!" I turn to Nic and say, "Nic, that looks great. Go ahead and light it." He picks up the lighter.

Dad says, "No Nicolas, don't light it yet. Take that last piece of newspaper out to give it more air."

Nic stands there with the lighter in his hand, frozen. How do you ask your little brother to choose? Listen to you? Or listen to your father? I remember my promise to Nic. I promised to try. I give in and say through clenched teeth, "You know Nic, dad's right. Maybe there is a little too much paper in there. If you take out that last piece, it'll probably burn better."

I take out my phone and text Billy:

*Me: meet me in Prospect Terrace?*
*Billy: now?*
*Me: yes, be there in 15*
*Billy: you okay?*
*Me: yes. meet me?*
*Billy: I'll be there waiting*

Nic starts lighting the paper. He does it just how I taught him, moving around and lighting it on each side so that it will burn evenly. Once I see that he's got it going, I stand up and say, "I'm going out."

Mami says, "Qué?"

Nic says, "Where are you going?"

"I'm meeting Billy," I tell them.

"It's 10:00," my father informs me.

"Yeah?"

"It's a little late to be going out," he tells me.

"I'm eighteen. I can decide when it's late." I stare him down.

"Gabriel," Mami pleads. "It's late and we're all together. Please stay."

"Let him go," my father tells her.

I stand and turn and walk away from the fire. I try not to, but I turn around. Mami is looking at me with tears in her eyes. Nic is staring at me and the words YOU PROMISED are written on his face. My father is not looking at me. His back is to me as he stares at the fire and drinks his beer.

Billy is just coming down the steps of his house as I get out of the Lyft right at the edge of the park. It's a moody May night; I feel a few drops of rain and notice that the perfectly clear night has become slightly overcast and fog is rolling through downtown. The smile on Billy's face when he sees me is exactly what I needed to see. He pulls me in for a hug and says in my ear, "Hey you. How are you doing?"

"I'm better now that I see you."

We sit on a bench overlooking the city — the same bench we sat on the last time we were here. There's a fine mist in the air; my face feels damp and cool, and I feel calmer. Billy takes my hand in his and asks, "What happened?"

I give him the whole rundown, about how things went from awkward to almost normal to messy, how my emotions went from nervous to annoyed to happy to proud to hopeful to resentful to angry, all in a day. "It was like the Cyclone, but not as fun."

He laughs. "I'm glad to see you have a sense of humor about it. How are you feeling now that you stepped away from it?"

"Stupid. Guilty. Like I ruined everything my mother prepared. Like I disappointed Nic. Again. Like I was selfish on my father's first night home."

"Maybe you're being a little hard on yourself? He did provoke you a bit. You all have to adjust to this new situation after all this time."

"Yeah, he did kind of provoke me. And he keeps calling me Gabriel."

"Okay, I gotta give him a break on that. You were Gabriel for fourteen years, so it'll take time for him to make that change."

"Shut up. I hate when you're right. You know what? Let's just stop talking about all of this and make out instead."

The excited puppy expression on his face lasts just a few seconds. Then he says, "Wait, this is a test, right? I'm supposed to say that talking about your problems is more important than making out. Right? I'm so confused right now. I don't know what to do."

"Oh man, will you just shut up and kiss me already?"

"Yes sir," he says, and for the next half hour, I forget all about my family.

# Chapter 50

It's Billy's final tennis match of his high school career. Kevin, Lulu, and I head over to Wallace as soon as we get out of school, and we pick up Nic on the way. Their team doesn't have a chance of making the playoffs, but they are playing their rivals and Billy is playing against a guy called Benedict. Nic says, "Billy and Benedict have played twice this year, and they each won once. Benedict beat him pretty bad last time." Lulu, Kevin, and I all look at Nic. "What?" he says. "I did my homework."

Billy is amped for this match, determined to go out on top. He's been putting in extra hours on the court all week. He's talking to his coach, listening attentively, nodding his head, his eyes intense. The coach says something and Billy laughs, they high five, Billy heads onto the court. He is standing on one side of the net, Benedict on the other, and the umpire explains the rules and tosses the coin. Benedict wins the toss and chooses to serve.

The first set is pretty lopsided. Benedict is serving really well, putting Billy on the defensive right from the start. Billy's serve is shaky, even though he's been hitting hundreds of practice serves a day for the last week. He double faults a few times, his placement is off, and he begins hitting soft serves that Benedict just gobbles up and nails for winners. The crowd is shouting encouragement—C'mon Billy, you can do this. Great shot Billy. You got this, Billy—but before we know it the score is 2-5 with Billy serving at 30-40. He misses his first serve and Kevin and I turn to each other, both of us nervous about the second serve. Billy tosses the ball up for his serve but catches it because it was a bad toss. He says sorry to Benedict and begins again, bouncing the ball six, seven, eight times, tosses it, bends into his service motion and reaches his racquet high. I hold my breath as I watch the ball leave his strings, hit the net cord, bounce into the air for a few seconds, and drop to the court—on his side. Double fault, first set to Benedict, 6-2.

Billy skulks off the court and tosses his racquet. His teammates are there offering encouragement, but his coach pulls him aside for a one-on-one. He holds Billy by his shoulders and looks him straight in the eyes as he gives him his pep talk. Billy's nodding and the ump calls time. Coach pats Billy on the back. Billy picks up his racquet and jogs back on court. All of the negative energy from the end of the first set is gone, and Billy's back to his usual positive self, bouncing in place as he prepares to receive serve to start the second set.

Billy turns the tide in the second set. He serves much better, no double faults, and I can see he is pumped with confidence. It's a long set with lots of long points. Billy wins it 6-4 and they are going to a third set.

The third set is a tiebreak, first to ten points wins. Benedict and Billy both hold serve and are at 6-7, with Benedict serving the next two points. He starts with a double fault, and they are tied at 7. Billy is now standing inside the baseline for the next serve, trying to apply the pressure. It works; Benedict misses his first serve and Billy moves into the court even further to receive the second serve. Benedict hits a weak, nervous second serve and Billy crushes a forehand down the line for a winner. Billy serves at 8-7, a strong first serve out wide and Benedict barely gets his racquet on it and pops it up. Billy moves in to take the weak return out of the air and smashes it. But it lands wide. Benedict's team and fans cheer as we all moan. Tied at 8, Billy hits a kick serve out wide to Benedict's forehand. Benedict slices it back deep to Billy's forehand. They trade crosscourt forehands, each trying to make the angle wider. Finally, Billy changes direction and hits it down the line and rushes the net. Benedict scrambles and stabs the ball with his backhand. It's just sitting there in the air and I hold my breath, praying that Billy doesn't miss. He hits the smash and wins the point. Our side erupts. Billy will now serve at 9-8, one point to win the match and end his high school career in glory.

I'm squeezing Lulu's hand as Billy walks to the line to serve. I'm wondering if he's totally in the moment or if he's thinking about the fact that this could be the final point of his high school tennis career. He takes a deep breath. The crowd is hear-a-pin-drop quiet. I see a calmness come over him—I think I see a slight smile on his face. He bounces the ball three times, just three times, and reaches up for the biggest serve of his past four years. The loud pop of the ball coming off of his strings echoes through the quiet crowd. It's a body serve that Benedict manages to block back, but the ball lands short and Billy moves in. He blasts a forehand for a winner, and as our side screams, he heads to the net to shake Benedict's hand. Billy takes in the applause and scans the bleachers until he sees me. I'm on my feet clapping as he gives me a big smile.

After all the matches finish and the crowd disperses, Lulu, Kevin, Nic, and I make our way down to congratulate Billy. He's with a few of his teammates, seniors who are also celebrating their last high school wins. Billy introduces us all and one of the guys, Ansel, says, "Hold up, you're Gabe? The boyfriend Gabe? We didn't think you really existed, man."

I laugh. "What?"

Another guy, Justin, says, "All this time we thought Billy had an imaginary boyfriend. You know, like kids have imaginary friends? He talked about you all the time but he never brought you around, so we thought you weren't real." Everyone is laughing now, including Billy.

My phone vibrates and I slide it out of my front pocket. A text from dad asking when I'll be home. I immediately get defensive; rather than answer, I reply, *"Why?"* He tells me that he has a surprise. I tell him I'll be home around 6:00.

Things have been hit and miss since the fire incident and me storming off in the night. We're both trying, but there's a tension between us, and it seems like we're trying for the sake of Mami and Nic, instead of for us. He got mad when I sat at the head of the table at dinner and didn't want to move and let him sit there. When I said sarcastically, "I thought the head of the table was for the man of the house," he stared at me, his jaw clenched, on the edge of saying something back to me, something I probably deserved. But he didn't speak, just stared, so I got up and said, "My bad," and moved. Mami and Nic sat in stunned silence, waiting for the eruption that never came.

One night I grabbed a beer from the fridge and was heading out to the backyard. He stopped me and said, "Whoa, what are you doing?"

"I'm going out back to call Lulu." I kept walking.

"Hold it, Gabriel."

I stopped. "It's Gabe, remember?"

"Right. So, hold it Gabe."

"What?"

"You're not old enough to be drinking beer."

"Seriously?"

"Yes, seriously. The drinking age is twenty-one."

I laugh. "How you gonna stand there and tell me I can't drink a beer at eighteen when you were getting stoned off your ass at fifteen? Don't even." And I walk out back.

He's yelling, "Get back in here," and Mami's saying, "Josh, let it go, let it go." I guess he decides to listen to her because I hear no more shouting and he doesn't follow me.

I don't even like beer, and I know I just did it to get a reaction from him, but I feel like I won again. Then I feel bad that I'm making this a competition, creating games to try to win.

But it hasn't been all bad. One day I got an Instagram notification that JoshDad started following me. I clicked on JoshDad—zero posts, zero followers, one following. Then I got a ton of notifications. JoshDad was liking all of my photos. I had to turn off notifications because he was liking every single one, thousands of them. It seems like a little thing, but I got a lump in the throat with that. Later that night I was folding laundry. "Gabe, your photos are amazing. They're really incredible."

"Oh, are you JoshDad, my Instagram stalker?" I joked.

"Hah, guilty as charged. What gave it away?"

"The fact that you have no posts, no followers, you're only following me, and you liked every one of my posts." We both laugh. "Thanks, Dad," I say, and we smile at each other, a breakthrough. A small one, but a breakthrough.

Billy is going out with the team to celebrate, so we say our goodbyes. Kevin and Lulu drop off me and Nic, both of us wondering what the surprise is. We say our goodbyes and walk up and see Dad's ten-year old gray pickup in the driveway. He totaled his car in the accident and when he was arrested, they suspended his license, so his truck has been parked in the garage since then, coated in four years of dust. But here it is, sparkling in the early evening light.

He comes out the side door and stands on the top stair. I stop, look at the truck, look at him, look at the truck. "What's going on?"

He walks down the steps and joins me and Nic in the driveway. "Well son, my truck has been sitting in the garage. My parole officer said it'll be a while before a judge allows me to get my license back. So I had Jose fix her up and take her to the car wash to get her ready for you."

Nic says, "Holy shit, you're giving him your truck for real?"

My jaw drops. "Really? Are you really giving me your truck?"

"Okay, hold on. There are some conditions. If you agree to the conditions, then yes, I am giving you my truck."

I eye him suspiciously. I knew this was too good to be true. He's trying to buy my forgiveness, using his truck as a bribe. I say hesitantly, "What are the conditions?"

"Your mother and I pay for the registration and the insurance for now, you pay for the gas and any repairs. It's in very good shape, but when it needs an oil change, new tires, any of that stuff, you have to pay. That's part of owning a vehicle."

Not bad. "Okay, what else?"

"No drinking and driving. No getting high and driving. No texting while driving. No friends riding in the back. I know we can't really enforce those things, but if you get pulled over for any of that, or God forbid, get in an accident because of it, you no longer have this truck. And I don't need a lecture about all the things that I did as a teenager."

Or as an adult, I think. I say, "Of course. I understand."

"Your mother and I spoke about curfew. We agreed that for the rest of the school year it should be 10:00 on school nights. Unless you're working a late shift or if you ask us permission first. Your mother is petrified of you being out driving late at night, so you just have to be in contact with us."

"Yeah, not a problem. I'll let you know where I am."

"Finally, and this one might be a little harder, I'm starting back to work next week on the construction crew. I'll need a ride to work until I get my license back. I can get a ride home from one of the guys, but I can't ask them to pick me up in the morning. Your mother doesn't have time to drop me off and get to work on time, so I'll need you to drop me off before school. You'll have to get your ass out of bed so we can be out the door by 6:15 every day."

My eyes bulge out of my head. "Out the door at 6:15?"

"Yep. That's the final part of our deal. You agree to all of the conditions, the truck is yours."

Getting up that early every morning won't be easy, but I figure it's a small price to pay for the freedom of having my own ride. "Okay, dad. I agree to all the conditions."

He holds out his hand and says, "Remember, if we shake on this, you are giving me your word. A man is as good as his word."

I put my hand in his and shake. "You have my word."

"This is so cool!" Nic gushes.

I have a truck.

# Chapter 51

Karina's poster of the month shows four rocks, one piled on top of the other. YESTERDAY IS HEAVY. PUT IT DOWN.

I point to the poster and ask, "Did you put that one up just for me?"

She turns and looks at the poster. "Ah, no. This one is for everyone. Believe me Gabe, you are not the only one holding on to things from the past. I thought I was putting it up for the students, but then I realized that I probably also put it up to remind myself to let things go."

"You mean you have problems too, Karina? I thought you had it all figured out."

"Funny. I would love to be able to tell you that you'll get through your teenage years and then it will all be easy. But I hope that all the work you've done in this office over the past four years, and you've done a lot, will at least give you the tools to manage what's coming—the bumps in the road, the potholes, the collisions, the breakdowns." She smiles at me and says, "I hope you appreciate the driving metaphor now that you have your own truck."

"Yeah, I do. I'll definitely tell Trevor too. You know how he loves a good metaphor."

"Oh, yes he does." After a short pause, she gets down to business. "There's a lot going on right now. For everyone, but especially for you. How are you doing?"

"Well," I start, "the good and the bad are still all tangled up, but I guess that's normal, huh? I'm excited about RISD but a little sad and jealous that all of my friends are going away to college. I'm happy that I'll be around for Nic, but I don't want to keep living at home and I don't think my financial aid is enough for me to live in the dorm. Things are going really well with Billy, but I don't know about a long-distance relationship. And my dad." I pause to try to organize my thoughts about him, but I really can't. "There are times when I'm happy that he's home. Sometimes we get along, have good talks and I think it'll be normal soon. Then one of us will do something to piss the other one off and I start wishing he wasn't home. And I know that's horrible. We're both trying, but there's still a lot getting in the way."

"Do you think you've forgiven him yet, Gabe?"

"No."

"What do you think it will take for you to forgive him?"

"I don't know. I really don't know."

Karina is silent; her mind seems to have left our conversation as her head is turned and she stares off into the distance. After an uncomfortable minute, she turns back and looks me in the eye. "Forgiveness is everything, Gabe."

Her intensity surprises me into silence. She continues, "I had a tumultuous relationship with my parents. I was the immigrant kid, becoming too "American" for my parents' liking. Things didn't go well for us, and it took me a long time and a lot of work to forgive them and repair things." She turns and looks at the poster on the wall behind her. "I told you I put this poster up for myself as well as for you. I carried those rocks around for years, a backpack full of rocks just weighing me down, keeping me from getting where I wanted to go. When I finally started forgiving, it was like I was emptying that backpack, one rock at a time."

"And it's all good with your parents now?"

"Well, we understand each other better now. They don't agree with a lot of the choices I've made, but they know that my life is my life. Gabe, it seems that parent problems don't go away when you reach adulthood. I guess you just hopefully learn to deal with them in a more mature way. And by them, I mean both the problems and your parents."

"Oh great, and here I was thinking that all my problems were going to magically disappear soon." We both chuckle. "I know I have to talk to him. Whenever I think about it, I get mad that he's not making the move to talk everything out. Shouldn't he take that on? Why should it be me?"

"I imagine that he has a lot of emotions swirling around also. He may feel guilty. He may feel confused. He probably feels really sad that he missed four years of his sons' lives."

"He may feel angry too. What if he hasn't forgiven me? I know he said in his letter that it wasn't my fault, but what if he's still holding on to it?"

"I guess that's possible. That's something that hopefully will come out when you talk. Gabe, do you want me to find someone for you and your dad to talk to together?"

"Like a family counselor or shrink? I don't know. Gotta think about that. Not sure how he would feel about it either."

"Well, you think about it and let me know. I can also talk to your dad about it."

"Okay, thanks Karina. I should get to class." I stand up and pick up my backpack and turn toward the door. "By the way, another good metaphor—the backpack and the rocks and all."

"Ah, I guess I'm feeling metaphorical today." She smiles and says, "Have a good day, Gabe. Be kind to yourself."

# Chapter 52

**M**y phone alarm wakes me out of a dream, and I'm confused because it's not all that light out. I pick it up and I'm even more confused when I see that it's 5:30. What the hell? How did I set my alarm wrong? I turn it off and roll over to go back to sleep when dad sticks his head in and says quietly, so he won't wake Nic, "Don't go back to sleep. We leave in forty-five minutes." Oh damn, I have to drive him to his first day on the job. The deal, the damn truck deal. Why the hell did I agree to these terms?

I drag myself out of bed, throw on sweats, and stumble to the kitchen. Dad is at the table drinking coffee and reading the paper. He looks up and says, "Jesus, you look like crap. I guess this is early for you, huh?" He chuckles. He's enjoying this, seeing me in zombie morning mode.

"Really funny," I say as I pour a cup of coffee and spoon in six sugars.

He has a smug, satisfied grin on his face. "Your mom said she'd be out of the bathroom in five minutes. We need to be out the door and in the truck at 6:15."

"Yes, sir," I reply as I grab a granola bar and my coffee and head back to my room to get my clothes ready. Nic would sleep through a fire or an earthquake, so I don't have to worry about waking him up.

Mami's out of the bathroom so I take a quick shower and brush my teeth. I don't bother to shave, and I'll wear a baseball cap so I don't have to worry about my hair. By the time I'm dressed and ready, it's 6:10. I can't give him any excuse to nag, especially at this hour. I meet him in the kitchen, backpack strapped on. "You ready?" I ask.

He looks at his watch. "Hmm. You're ready on time." That smirk again, telling me that he didn't think I could do it, that he didn't believe in me. I bite my tongue, say nothing, and walk out and get in the truck.

He stops for a moment when he sees me in the driver's seat, a perplexed look on his face, and that's when I realize how weird this all is and how difficult it must be for him. I wonder if he is regretting his decision to give me the truck and have me drive him to work. He's never even seen me drive, never been a passenger while I drive, didn't teach me to drive. We are venturing down a new, unfamiliar, potentially hazardous road, and I'm suddenly nervous.

He situates himself uncomfortably in the passenger seat, buckles his seatbelt, and proceeds to tell me how to get to the highway. I inform him that I know how to get to the highway, and I back out of the driveway. The tension radiates off of his body and fills the truck. He looks nervously at the end of the driveway as I'm about to pull out. "Okay, you're good on this side," he almost barks and I back out and head down the block.

We ride in silence, and I see his footstep on his imaginary passenger side brake every time we roll up to a stop sign or red light. Finally, I say, "Can you stop doing that? You're making me nervous."

"Doing what?"

"Putting your foot on the imaginary brake, as if you think I'm about to fly through every damn intersection without stopping."

He's quiet for a few seconds and I prepare myself for his wiseass comment, but he says, "Sorry, didn't realize I was doing that."

At the next stop, I take a right to go to the highway and he says, "Why are you turning here?"

"This is how I go to the highway."

"What? This is not the best way to go. You're taking us out of the way, and I'll be late for my first day back to work."

I pull over to the curb and put the truck in park. "What the hell are you doing?" he asks.

I'm on the edge of an eruption, either an eruption of tears or an eruption of curses. Or an eruption of tears and curses. I take a deep breath, reminding myself that this is hard for him too, and say calmly. "I know how to drive. I know how to get to the highway. But you're making me so nervous."

He lets out a long breath and says, "Okay, I'm sorry. This is all new for me and I need to adjust. Let's just start up again. You take your way to the highway, get off at exit 17. Then I'll tell you where to go." He waits a few seconds and asks, "Are you okay now? You good to drive the rest of the way?"

"Well, you can't drive, so I guess I have to be." I know that I've landed a good punch, so I put the truck in gear and take off. We both say nothing until I get off at exit 17. Then he directs me to the drop-off spot. Before he gets out, he says, "Gabe."

"Yeah?" I reply, looking straight ahead.

"Hey, look at me, will you?" It's a request, not a command. I turn to him.

"I'm sorry, son. Thanks for the ride. Drive safe, have a good day at school. Let's talk more tonight."

I nod. "Okay. You too. Have a good day at work."

He opens the door and steps out. He says, "I love you," and closes the door right away, not waiting to hear if I say it back to him.

There's a group of three guys, all dressed in fluorescent yellow construction shirts. As he walks toward them, they are all smiling and calling out to him, but the truck windows are closed so I don't hear what they say. When he gets to them, they shake his hand, hug him, pat his back.

As I drive off and head to school, I feel happy that he has these friends welcoming him back with open arms.

I get back on the highway and head north for two exits, making it to school with just enough time to make it to first period. I slog through the morning, trying to concentrate on schoolwork, but I'm still annoyed at dad for his constant reminders that he thinks I'm an idiot. And although it felt satisfying when I landed the jab about him not being able to drive, now it's eating at me. His first day back to work, and that's how I send him off. He closed the door so fast that he didn't get to hear me say, "I love you too."

I construct an alternate ending to the scene in my head and play it back over and over. In this revised scene, instead of him walking away and me driving off, I roll the passenger side window down. I yell, "Hey dad." He stops in his tracks and turns back to the truck. His face is still stony, stoic, serious. Hurt and wounded. I motion him to come back and he sticks his head through the open window. "What is it, son?" His voice betrays no anger, just a hint of defeat.

"You closed the door before you could hear me respond." He cocks his head at me questioningly. "You didn't hear me say 'I love you too Dad' before you walked away."

He smiles softly and says, "Hey, come out and meet the guys for a second."

I walk with him to the guys, and they all welcome him back with handshakes, hugs, and pats on the back. He introduces me to them, and I shake all of their hands. He embarrasses me when he starts bragging about my grades, graduation, RISD, and my photography. The guys are suitably impressed, and dad is the proud papa, all puffed up over having created such a perfect child. I tell them that it was nice to meet them and that I have to rush to school. Dad gives me a hug, and I drive to school knowing that I am the son of a proud father.

But we don't get to construct alternate endings for things that have already happened, so I have to live with the original, the one of guilt, anger, and confusion. I stew in those emotions through the morning, trying, not so successfully, to concentrate on my schoolwork. The teachers are not going easy on us at the end of senior year, and I know I could just coast and still pass all my classes, but I vowed that I would do really well this year and I'm going to stick to it to the end.

Lulu and Kevin cheer me up at lunch with plans of graduation parties. We're trying to balance our family celebrations, trying to figure out if there's a way we can be at each other's parties. We're going to do a big bash at the beach with Billy and some of his Wallace friends. It helps get my mind off of dad.

When I look at the board in Physics class, I think it's a joke. Kate has posted the final exam study groups and I locate mine: Gabe, Angel, Andres. Is she out of her damn mind? I walk to the front of the room where Kate is looking through some papers. I approach her calmly and use all of the skills Karina has equipped me with over the last few years. "Hi Kate, can I speak to you for a minute?"

"Sure Gabe, how can I help you?"

"I don't think I can really work with this study group. I'd like to request a change."

"Sorry, we're really pressed for time to get ready for the final. I don't have time to rearrange groups."

"I think you know, I have history with one of those guys."

"Gabe, in life you can't always choose who you work with. You're adults. You'll work it out."

Ninth and tenth grade Gabe would lose his shit on her, but twelfth grade Gabe thinks about the consequences. I definitely can't get in trouble in the last month of high school, so I mumble okay, sign out and take the hall pass. I'm trying to decide who is more likely to intervene and get me out of this group—Karina or Zach. I have a feeling that Karina will spin it as an opportunity to practice forgiveness, and I won't have any argument against her. She's too persuasive. If I go to Zach and present it as me being worried about getting into another fight with Andres, he might decide that it's better for everyone not to take a chance on messing up this close to the finish line. He'll ask Kate to change us. Zach it is.

I check in the office and Maria tells me Zach is not in. I text him and he tells me he is on the second floor. I find him on hall patrol in his zebra striped Converse high tops. "Hey, what's up man?" he asks when he sees me. There's a hint of concern in the question, so I know that he sees that I'm in a mood.

I explain to him about Kate, and the grouping with Andres, and how she wouldn't change us, and how I'm worried that we'll get in a fight. Zach's not buying my story; maybe I should have gone to Karina.

"Okay, listen. That was at the beginning of the year, and you worked it out in a restorative circle. You both apologized, shook hands, and moved on. If Kate put you together in a group, it's for a reason. And if she says she can't change it, I'm going to respect her decision. I can't even tell you all the people I've had to work with in my life that I didn't like. Finals are in a week and a half. Time to suck it up and be the adult that you are."

There's really nothing left to say because I can see he's not going to give in, so screw it, I'll just deal with it for a week and a half. I don't have to talk about anything other than physics. I don't have to be nice or pretend to like him. It's all business.

When I walk back in, Kate looks up from the group she's been working with, looks at me, looks at the clock, looks back at me and makes a gesture with her hands that basically says, "Where the hell have you been?"

"I wasn't feeling well. I went to the bathroom to splash water on my face," I lie. She looks at my dry face, my dry hair, raises her eyebrows in doubt, and moves on to the next group. I sit down with Andres and Angel and say, "Sorry, had to go to the bathroom."

"No problem," Andres says. He hands me a packet of papers and explains that we need to review all of this for the final. It's a ton of stuff, a year's worth of physics.

Angel says, "Shit, I don't know how I can pass this exam." Yeah, his English is coming along pretty quickly.

I flip through the packet to figure out what makes sense. I don't like the order Kate has it in, so I start taking the pages apart and reordering them. Angel and Andres look at me like I'm crazy. "Okay, take all the pages apart," I instruct them.

"Then I'll tell you what order to put them in. We'll work through them from easiest to hardest."

Kate approaches as we are all ripping our packets apart. She laughs, "What's going on here?"

"Not gonna lie Kate, I don't think you put all of this in the right order for studying, so I'm rearranging it."

"Go for it. Whatever works best for you." She looks at Andres and Angel. "You guys are in good hands. Gabe knows what he's doing." She moves on.

"Yo, what's your grade in this class?" Andres asks.

"Right now, A-minus."

"Damn," they both say in unison.

"I'm failing. This shit is mad hard. I have to pass this final if I'm going to pass the class and graduate," Andres says.

"Me too," says Angel. And for emphasis, he adds, "Fuck."

Andres says, "Damn man, you could barely say hello in English when you got here, now you're all *fuck* and *shit*." We all laugh.

Now I know why Kate put us together. And probably why Zach wouldn't intervene. I'm supposed to get these two to pass their final so they can graduate. I consider this idea for a few seconds and say, with conviction, "Okay, let's do this. Put your papers in this order: Newton's Laws of Motion, Velocity and Acceleration, Wave Properties, Electricity and Magnetism." We get down to work.

# Chapter 53

I remember that when I dropped Dad off this morning, as he got out of the truck after the tension-filled drive, he said, "Let's talk more tonight." It's time.

I'm working the four to eight shift at Dunkin. On my break at six, I text him: *Home by 8:30. Nice nite for a fire. Just me n u.*" He texts me back a thumbs up emoji. The rest of my shift, I'm thinking about what I will say to him. I decide I'm going to wait for him to talk, to see what he has to say.

At 8:20, I walk in the side door and they are all in the living room watching television. Mami says, "Are you hungry, mi amor? There's arroz con gandules in the fridge. Y pizza tambien."

"Thanks, Mami. I ate at work."

Dad stands up and says, "Gabe and I are going to have a fire and talk."

Nic jumps up. "Oh good."

"You know what, Nic?" Dad says. "Tonight it's going to be just me and Gabe, okay?"

"What? Why? I want a fire too," he complains.

"Buddy," I say, "we can have another fire this weekend. Dad and I have a few things to talk about, alone. Okay?"

I see the moment when he realizes that dad and I are finally going to have the talk. His face is happy, hopeful, nervous. "Okay. Sure. Thanks." He sits down next to Mami on the couch and watches me and dad head out back.

I go directly to the shed and begin bringing out the wood and kindling before he can do it. Dad just sits and watches as I get to work, doing everything he taught me, but with my own modifications. I fan the flames as the newspaper all goes up and the logs are beginning to catch fire. Dad says, "Looking good. Be right back," and heads into the house.

When he comes back out, the fire is going strong and I am sitting. He has a six-pack in his hand, and he hands me one. I hesitate for a moment, take it from his hand, and twist it open as he opens his. I take a sip and relax back in my chair and stare at the flames. I look up and the crescent moon hangs low in the sky. I remember how when I was little, dad would tell me that if I looked really close, I could see the man in the moon, his face smiling in the curve of the crescent. I look for it now, hoping that I can convince myself that I see him, like I convinced myself when I was little. But the man in the moon is not there.

Dad's question breaks the silence. "How's everything going with Billy?" Not how I expected this to start, but I'm happy to ease into the real stuff.

"It's going good," I respond. I'm about to ask him if he's okay with me being gay, with me having a boyfriend, but I stop myself. I don't need him to be okay with it. So I just continue, "He's going off to Northwestern, so I don't know if there's much of a future, but for now it's good."

He nods his head. After a pause, "I'd like to meet him." Another pause. "Only if you want that."

"Yeah. He wants to meet you too."

We continue to sip our beers in silence. I try to distract myself by locating the bluish white star Vega.

"Gabriel, how do I make things right with you? I'm trying to get things back to normal, but you're angry. And you have a right to be. But I need your help."

"I don't think it's my job to tell you what to do to make things right, dad. You're the one who fucked everything up. Why do you expect me to tell you how to fix it?"

"I don't expect you to tell me how to fix it. And I know I fucked up. I'm trying to fix it. I've been thinking about how to fix it for the last four years."

"Okay, well let's start with you coming home and acting like we haven't been figuring out how to go on without you.

You tell me that I didn't teach Nic the right way to make a fire, you kick me out of the chair I've been sitting in for the last three years, you tell me that I don't know how to drive, you act like you can just walk back in and be the man of the house and take my place. You sat here, at this fire, almost four years ago, and you told me that I had to be the man of the house, that I had to step up and take care of Nic and Mami. And I did it. I was there for them. I went to school and worked and helped around the house and still had time for Nic. I did what I was supposed to do. And it was fucking hard. But I did it." I'm spitting out anger-filled words while tears stream down my cheeks.

"I'm sorry that I burdened you with that. It was too much. You shouldn't have had all that placed on your shoulders. You should have been able to be a teenage kid. I never should have said that to you. I'm really sorry."

"Why did you do it?" I've now turned to face him, to look him in the eye.

"Why did I do what?"

"All of it. Why did you cheat on us? I've thought about this a lot. Going with that woman, you didn't just cheat on Mami. You cheated on me and Nic too. Why? Why weren't we enough for you?"

I've landed a punch in the gut and I'm glad. "Son, there is no possible excuse for what I did, none at all. You and Nicolas are everything to me. Of course you were enough for me."

Now I am going to lay it all out there. He wanted me to be the man of the house, I am going to be the man. "What do you remember about that night? I want to hear your version of that night, the night I have been living with for the last four years."

I don't think he was expecting this. He takes a few deep breaths and says, "I've relived that night over and over, in my head, in group therapy." I just stare at him and wait for him to continue. "I was in the park by the State House, and I felt someone looking at me. I looked up and saw you."

"What's her name?"

His eyes widen and he is silent, but I'm not letting him off the hook.

"What's her name?" I repeat.

"Suzannah," he replies.

"What did you say to Suzannah when you saw me?"

I'm happy to see him struggling to confront the reality of me confronting him.

"I said, 'Oh, shit, that's my son.' And then I yelled for you. But you ran off." He's now resigned to tell the whole story. His voice is strangely detached from the telling. "I left Suzannah in the park, telling her I had to go. I rushed to my car, hoping I could get home before you did, but you were already here when I got here." He wipes his eyes, waiting for me to say something. But I say nothing, so he continues. "I yelled at you and sent you to your room. I'm sorry."

"You told me you would beat my ass if I didn't go to my room." I let it sink in. "What happened when I was in my room, trying to help Nic not hear what was going on?"

"Your mother and I screamed at each other. I got the bottle of scotch. And I drank. I drank right from the bottle, slug after slug. Your mother left me there alone and I just drank. I got wasted."

I wait for him to continue, to admit the rest. When he doesn't speak, I ask, "What happened then?"

"I don't remember much else. I remember struggling to open the car door. I remember being blinded by headlights coming directly at me. That's it. I remember waking up in the hospital. And finding out I killed that woman." He chokes out the rest, "And her little girl." He is sobbing.

I think that fathers try not to cry in front of their sons. They don't want to seem weak and vulnerable. They think they have to set an example of strength for us. In this moment, I realize that this is the first time in my life I have seen my father cry. I have known this man for eighteen years, and although my mother told me that he cried when I was born, I have never seen his tears. It's not easy. I think about leaving it at this, telling myself that he has suffered enough, that I don't need to confront him about the rest of the story, the parts that the alcohol has erased from his memory. But I need to see this through to the end. The healing can only happen when we confront the truth.

"Dad, are you okay?"

"Yeah son, I'm good."

"You don't remember me coming out of my room that night?"

"When?"

"Right before you got in the car and drove off."

The shock in his eyes tells me that he really doesn't remember. "No Gabe. I don't remember. I'm sorry."

I think back to my conversation with Karina. Yesterday is heavy; I need to put it down, but I can't put it down if I don't confront it, expose it. So I tell him everything: "I came out of my room and you asked me what I wanted. I was hoping to fix things, so I said I was sorry. You told me that I really fucked everything up." I look at his face and this is absolutely crushing him, but I go on. "You called me a pussy."

He can't control the sob. "Oh God. I'm sorry. This was never your fault. You did the right thing. I never blamed you, never."

"You blamed me that night."

"I was drunk. I didn't mean it. I didn't even—"

I cut him off and say sharply, "Don't. Don't give me some bullshit excuse about the alcohol talking. You said it and you need to own it."

"Gabe, people say things they don't mean when they're drunk. I don't even remember half of what happened that night."

Part of me wants to stop here but I force myself to continue. He's looking at me intently as I take a breath and go on. "Well, let me tell you the rest. Let me tell you what you don't remember. Before you left, you threatened Mami. When I tried to stop you, you smacked me across the face. You told—" I don't want to sob out the words. I want them to be strong and clear, so I pause, breathe, and state plainly and clearly, "You told me that I was the biggest mistake of your life."

He gasps, "No." He repeats, "No no no no no." He's not denying that he said it; he's lamenting that he said it. He doesn't remember saying it, but he trusts me when I tell him that he said it.

He stands up and walks the short distance between our chairs. He kneels in front of me, takes my hands in his, and looks up, locking eyes with mine. "Oh my boy, I'm so sorry. I've made so many mistakes in my life but, my God, you are not one of them. I've only done a few things right in my life—marrying your mother and making you and Nicolas. That's it. I've messed everything else up, but you—you are my miracle. Please, please believe me. Forgive me, Gabe. Forgive me."

"So many times, I wished it was you who died that night instead of Mrs. Perez and her baby." I think I've landed my final, knockout blow.

But he looks me square in the eyes and says quietly, "I wished that too. Every day for at least a year. I sometimes still do."

Karina's words echo in my ears: *Forgiveness is everything, Gabe.*

It's time to put yesterday down—I can't carry its weight any longer.

I bend and hug him.

# Chapter 54

The weeks that follow are crazy busy. Up at the crack of dawn to drive dad to work, rides that have become more relaxed, where we are slowly negotiating our new relationship. We talk about the mundane and the serious, and he no longer criticizes my driving. All of us seniors are trying to make one last push, finishing projects and studying for finals, while also trying to enjoy our last days of high school—yearbook signing, senior trip, prom, senior night. I'm still trying to keep twenty hours a week at Dunkin. Billy is busy too, but we try to find time for each other every few days. Nic complains that I'm never around, but I assure him that it'll all be over soon and I'll take him to Six Flags after I graduate.

I only have two finals—Calculus and Physics. For my other classes, I have final projects. For Trevor, an essay comparing a Shakespeare play with a modern movie adaptation. I choose *The Taming of the Shrew* and *Ten Things I Hate About You.* My Social Studies research paper is about the criminal justice system and adult sentencing of juveniles.

Andres, Angel and I turn out to be a pretty cool study group in Kate's class. They're both starting to really understand concepts they were struggling with before and I'm feeling this teaching thing. One day, Angel leaves class to go to the bathroom. Andres looks up from his notes and says, "Yo Gabe, I really wanna apologize."

I just keep highlighting my notes as I respond, "Hey man, you already apologized way back in September."

He laughs, "Man, you know I didn't mean it. You didn't mean it either. Let's be real."

I laugh too. "Yeah, you got that right. I was just trying to get Zack and Karina off my ass."

"Facts," he says. "But for real, I am sorry. And not just for saying that homophobic shit, but for that ninth-grade shit about your pops. And you didn't tell no one about that. Man, I can be a real asshole."

"Not gonna lie, Andres. You can be a real asshole. But we cool now." We laugh and high five.

Angel returns and sees us laughing and says, "Okay bitches, back to work." Kate is approaching our table as he says it.

"Angel, language please!" she says.

We look at him. Andres says, "Yo amigo, seriously, you need to learn when to bring out your English curse words. There's a right and wrong time. Dang."

# Chapter 55

I've requested a final meeting with Karina. I really need to thank her because I seriously would not have gotten through high school without her. Her end of the year poster, her final inspiration for all of us seniors, is on display outside of her office. It's a crescent moon set upon a background of a black sky filled with stars. Inside of the crescent moon, the words: SHOOT FOR THE MOON. EVEN IF YOU MISS, YOU WILL LAND AMONG THE STARS.

I peek my head into her office and say, "Hey Karina, I'm a little early. Just letting you know I'm here."

"Gabe," she says with real fondness. "Come in."

How do I thank this woman? The first time she met me I was wild with anger, unable and unwilling to tell her what had infuriated me. She didn't push me, didn't press me for answers. She just let me exist in her office, brooding in a corner, until I could open up, just a little bit. And this has been her role for four years—giving space to an angry young man. Listening when he finally would speak, and then pushing him to think and analyze and cope. Today I come, not as an angry young man, but as a grateful young man.

"Almost to the finish line," she says. "How are you doing?"

"I'm doing really well."

"I'm so happy to hear that. And congratulations are in order. I hear from Kate that you aced the physics final and that your crew did really well also."

"My crew? You know about me working with Andres and Angel?"

She smiles a guilty little smile.

"Ah," I say. "I should have known. You told Kate to put me with Andres, didn't you?"

"Well…"

"Good move, Karina. Devious, but good. Fits in with your whole forgiveness is everything narrative."

She shrugs.

"Thanks for that," I tell her.

"How did everything go with your dad?"

"Good. We've worked through a lot. I think we're in a good place. There's still work to do, but I think we both understand each other a little better now."

"That's really good to hear."

"Thank you, Karina, for everything. I really…I feel like…I don't know how I could have made it without your help."

"You're welcome. You really did the hard work. I'm very proud of you." She gets up from her desk and comes around to the front. "Can I have a hug?"

I open my arms and she opens hers. We embrace and all I can say is, "Thank you."

# Chapter 56

I arrive at the Citywide High School Arts exhibit early. Before the crowds arrive, there is a reception for all of the students who have been selected and we are all walking around, eagerly looking for our own work and checking out the work of our peers. There is amazing stuff—painting, sculpture, video, and photography, and I can't believe that I'm a part of it. I turn a corner and see my two photographs. My name is in big letters, all caps—GABRIEL MEYERS—and the two black and white photos are hung side by side, each in a black frame with a white matte. On the left is "Solitaria," Mami's profile, the queen of hearts in her hand. It took a lot of convincing to get her permission to show this one. I had to tell her over and over how beautiful she looks in this photo. On the right is a new photo:

*"Reunión"*
*Black and white*
*In the reflection of a mirror*
*a man, woman, and young teen boy*
*sit at a table in a kitchen*
*gathered around a Monopoly board*
*houses and hotels on many of the properties.*
*The top hat is on St. Charles*
*the iron is on Electric Company*
*the race car is on Free Parking.*
*The young teen boy's hand*
*poised above a pile of money in the center of the board.*
*His face pure excitement.*
*The man and woman smile*
*at each other.*

Three nights after dad got out, I was out with Billy, and when I came home, they were playing Monopoly. They had just started, and they asked me if I wanted to play, told me that they could start a new game. I claimed that I was tired, that I needed to lie down for a bit, but in reality, I just wasn't ready to pretend—that things were normal, that we were just a regular family sitting around the kitchen table playing games. I went to my room and lie down. I was going to put my headphones on, but I got caught up in listening to them laughing, yelling, teasing, joking, and trash talking, and I wondered why I couldn't be more like Nic, why I can't love unconditionally like he does.

I grabbed my camera and walked back out. Nic saw me and said gleefully, "Gabe, I'm killing Mami and daddy. Look at how much money I have. And look at my hotel on Park Place!"

"That's great, Nic. Do it buddy."

Dad looked at me and smiled.

"You mind if I just take some pictures? Just pretend I'm not here."

Mami protested, "Gabriel, I look a mess. No pictures, por favor."

But dad cut her off, "Isabel, you look beautiful. Let him take his pictures."

I took pictures from all different positions and all different angles. This one broke my heart because Nic looked so crazy happy, Mami and daddy looked at each other so lovingly, and I stood on the outside, documenting it rather than being in it, a part of it. I didn't know yet how to be a smiling, laughing member of the family. I could only stare from a distance, through my lens, and try to figure out why.

The organizers announce to all of us that they are about to let people in. They wish us luck and we all cheer. As people file in, I spot Mami, Dad, and Nic. I wave at them, and they move through the growing crowd. They've gotten dressed up. Mami looks beautiful in her new blue dress, her hair up, makeup perfect. Dad is in a dark suit, his hair, which he has been growing out since he came home, is slicked back. Nic is wearing a button-down shirt and a tie with his jeans and sneakers. He has also been growing out his hair, and it's slicked back too. He looks like a mini dad.

Nic rushes over to me and hugs me. "This is amazing. I can't believe this. Wow, look at how great your photos look. Wow. Hey, it says Gabriel Meyers, not Gabe Meyers."

"Yeah, I'm trying to figure out what will be better as my professional name, so I'm trying out Gabriel."

Mami hears this and I think she may cry. She just hugs me. Dad says, "Son, I can't tell you how proud I am. This is really something."

I know that this was a big deal for him to come to this. He's kept a really low profile since he got out, but here he is in plain view. It's a small city; people know what he did, and people talk. I hug him and say, "Thanks for coming Dad. It means a lot to me."

Suddenly everyone is arriving. Lulu and Kevin arrive, and I try not to be jealous when Lulu seems happier to see Nic than she is to see me. Mami hugs them both, and Kevin introduces himself and shakes hands with dad.

I see Trevor, Karina, and Zach across the room. I say, "Hey Dad, I want you to meet some people," and we head across the room. They all smile as they see us approaching and I say, "I want you all to meet my dad. Dad, this is Zach, Karina, and Trevor. I've told you about them."

"So good to meet you all," Dad says.

Trevor reaches out his hand and says, "Very nice to meet you Mr. Meyers."

"Please, it's Josh." He shakes hands with Karina and Zach also.

Zach says, "You've got a great kid here. And we're really looking forward to having Nic with us next year."

Dad says, "Thank you. And thank you all for all you've done for Gabe. I know it wasn't easy."

After an awkward pause, Karina says, "Well, let's see these photographs."

At that moment, I spot Billy with his parents and I say, "Dad, do you mind showing them my photos? I'll be there in a minute."

"Sure thing," he says and leads them away.

Billy strides through the crowd, followed by Martin and Patricia. "Hey babe, how you doin?" he says and gives me a hug and a huge smile.

Patricia hugs me and says, "Oh honey, this is wonderful. I'm so excited for you."

I step out of her arms and say, "Thank you so much. And thank you for coming."

Martin crushes my hand as he shakes it and says, "This is quite a turnout. Congratulations Gabe. We're expecting big things from you."

Out of nowhere, we hear, "Hey Billy," and Nic is standing beside us, very excited. He and Billy shake hands as Billy says, "What's up Nicky? How you been squirt?"

"All good, all good," he replies and then turns to Patricia and Martin. "You must be Mr. and Mrs. Sachs. My name is Nic Meyers, I'm Gabe's brother. Very nice to make your acquaintance." What a dork.

Patricia and Martin smile in amusement. Patricia accepts Nic's offer of a handshake and says, "Well Nic, it's very nice to make your acquaintance also."

Martin then practically breaks all the bones in my little brother's hand. Nic must be giving him a run for his money because Martin says, "Good to meet you, young man. That's quite a firm handshake you've got there." Billy and I both chuckle.

When Nic turns to me and asks, "Hey Gabe, have Mr. and Mrs. Sachs met mom and dad yet?" I want to smack him. He knows how nervous I am about that, but he has to stick his nose into everything. I give him a quick glare and then say, hoping to hide my annoyance, "Not yet Nic. They just got here. But they will."

I thought a lot about what this night would be like if I didn't limit who I invited. At first, I thought I would just bring

Mami, Dad, and Nic. But then Lulu got all Lulu on me, lecturing me on not compartmentalizing my life, not depriving those I love of joy, and basically not being an awkward, nervous mess of a human. I worried that Mami and Dad might be uncomfortable out in public in a really visible way so soon after he got out, but when I asked them if they really wanted to go, dad looked hurt, for just a moment, and then he said, "We would love to be there for you. We absolutely want to be there. We're both so proud of you, but this is your night and you get to decide who to invite."

I remembered what Karina told me about needing to be honest, with myself and with him, so I put it out there. "I want you to be there. I want to experience this night with you, with everyone. I just didn't know if you feel comfortable being out yet, with so many people around."

"Gabe, don't worry about us. We'll be fine. And you know what? I served my time. There will be people who still judge me, but I can't live for those people. I live for me. For your mother. For you and Nic. I have to live now."

"I'm sorry," I said.

Mami said, "Don't be sorry, mi amor, it's so kind that you worry about us. But your father is right. Necesitamos vivir de nuevo." She paused and continued, "And I just bought a new dress and I'm not wearing it around the house. It's a dress to be seen in and I'm ready to be seen." We all laughed, and it was settled.

The evening has been going well. Dad has met Lulu and Kevin, Zach, Karina, and Trevor, and it's been good. If I'm being honest with myself, I'm not worried about him meeting Billy's parents because of him just getting out of jail; I'm just a kid who's nervous about his parents meeting his boyfriend's parents. There's a thousand movies where couples introduce their parents and it's a disaster. I'm just worried that I'm in a gay teen romance movie and the director has decided to turn the parent meeting scene into a total mess.

So I decide to get this messy scene over and done. I say, "Okay, if you wait right here, I'll go get my mom and dad and bring them over."

I find Mami, talking to Lulu and Kevin. Dad is walking back with Karina; she and Mami hug and launch into a Spanish conversation. I say to Dad, "Are you ready to meet Billy? And his parents?"

He laughs. "You sound like you're getting ready to face the firing squad. Yeah, I'm ready to meet them. Don't worry, I won't embarrass you," he jokes. He turns to Mami and Karina. "Karina, do you mind if I steal my beautiful wife? We need to meet the boyfriend's parents."

Billy and I introduce them and make small talk for a few minutes. They mostly talk about me and the show, which embarrasses me, but it's not too awkward and they all seem comfortable with each other. Billy then says, "I haven't seen much of the exhibit yet. Do you mind if Gabe and I walk around?" The parents all say of course not, and we escape.

"Well, that wasn't too bad," I say.

"Nah, they're fine. As my mother says, my father can talk the bark off a tree, so we're good to escape."

"Thanks for getting us out of there. I hate people talking about me, even when it's all good."

David, one of the curators of the show, approaches. "Gabriel, how's the night going?" he asks.

"It's really amazing. I was really nervous but now I'm feeling pretty good."

He turns to Billy and introduces himself. "Hi, I'm David Hernandez."

"Oh, sorry," I say. "This is my boyfriend, Billy Sachs."

They exchange handshakes and hellos, and David turns back to me. "There's a photographer who's interested in meeting you. She really likes your two pieces. Come, let me introduce you. You come too, Billy."

I nervously follow and he leads us to my photos. I'm surprised to see a number of people gathered around them, talking, talking about my photos. David stops in front of a young woman with very short black hair, piercings up and down her ears and in her nose. She's wearing combat boots and a short sleeveless black dress, her arms covered in tattoos. "Gabriel, this is Milena de Mello. Milena, this is Gabriel Meyers, the photographer. And this is his boyfriend, Billy."

She smiles at us and says, "Really good to meet you, Gabriel. And Billy. Gabriel, these are really good," she says, pointing to my photos.

"Thank you."

"I'm really impressed with your eye for angle and composition at your age. David tells me that you're starting at RISD in the fall."

"Yes," I reply. "I'm really excited."

"That's great. I'll be teaching a seminar there in the spring. But I'd really like to see more of your work soon. I'm always looking for young photographers to work in my studio. Here's my card. I'll be away on a shoot for a while, but call me in August and we can set up a time for you to bring your portfolio over."

"Wow, thank you so much Milena. I really appreciate it."

I take her card and she says, "Hey Gabriel, try to smile and enjoy the night. If you're going to be a photographer, you have a lot of these nights in your future. They can be awkward, but you can also find a way to enjoy them." She and David walk away.

"Wow, babe, that's huge. A professional photographer just gave you her card and wants to see your portfolio. Wow."

Lulu and Kevin make their way through the crowd. Lulu gives me a hug and a kiss and says, "I hope you are allowing yourself to have fun, Gabriel Meyers." She emphasizes the Gabriel.

"Yeah, yeah. I was thinking that maybe Gabriel would be better as a professional name. Trying it out."

"Well, I love it," she says.

Kevin says, "Man, Gabe, these photos are amazing. I don't know much about photography, but these are hot. They really make me feel some kinda way, like I get the emotion. And the difference between your mom in the two pictures is really incredible. Sorry, I don't really know how to talk about art and stuff, but I definitely think that your stuff is special."

"Thanks Kev. Appreciate it. And I appreciate you coming, man."

The rest of the night is a blur of new names and new faces, compliments from friends and from strangers. I begin to get a little comfortable accepting the compliments and start to believe that people are not just saying things to make me feel good. I start to believe that my work is good, that people see my photos and they make them feel, and think, and wonder.

The event winds down and people begin to say their goodbyes, with lots of hugs and kisses. I tell Billy, Lulu, and Kevin that I am going to go home with my family, and I can see that this makes them all very happy. We'll all talk later.

Mami, Dad, and Nic are waiting for me near my photos. "This is a night to remember, Gabriel," Mami says. "It felt strange seeing people look at pictures of me, but everyone loved them."

"I'm so proud of you son. What a night. Thank you." Dad looks like he might cry.

"I'm proud of you too Gabe," Nic adds. "And it was really cool to have so many people say, 'Hey, you're the kid in the picture!'"

"Thanks, goofball. Hey, I'm starving. Can we get pizza?" I ask.

"Sure thing," dad says. "Caserta?"

"Definitely!" I reply. Dad takes Mami's hand and they walk toward the door. I put my arm over Nic's shoulder, and we follow.

# SECTION 4 — JUNE

# Chapter 57

Andy and Dad laze on lounge chairs in the backyard, soaking up the late afternoon sun, drinking Coronas, listening to music on a portable speaker. They are deep in conversation, which seems to get more animated as they get deeper into their six-pack. Andy and Keith drove up from Brooklyn yesterday. I'm still replaying the image of the reunion—Andy embracing dad, a big brother hug full of comfort, protection, and unconditional love. Dad hugging him back so tightly that it looks like he may never let go. I imagine them years ago, reuniting after being torn apart by their parents. This time, with the exception of a couple of prison visits, they haven't been with each other for almost four years. I can't imagine being separated from Nic for that long.

After my graduation this morning, Andy and Keith took all of us to lunch at an Italian place owned by one of the guys that used to work at Andy's restaurant in New York. The food was amazing, and they treated us like royalty, and there was wine. Now we are back home, lazy and full. Nic is beating Keith at chess at the kitchen table, and Mami and I sit under the umbrella on the back deck.

"What do you think they're talking about?" I ask Mami as we look toward the Meyers brothers and their beer-infused interaction.

"¿Quién sabe? But it's good to see your father so happy. He's surrounded by everyone he loves."

"What about you Mami? Are you happy?"

"Oh mijo, I'm very happy. Things are not perfect with me and your father, but we're working on it. And now my baby is a high school graduate going on to college. Estoy tan orgullosa."

"Gracias Mami. I'm actually pretty proud of myself too." I squeeze her hand.

After a lengthy pause, she asks, "What will happen with you and Billy now?"

"I don't know. He's going to be really far away. He'll be living on a big campus, with lots of people. And lots of those people will be interested in him. He's pretty good looking, you know. I don't want him to feel trapped by a high school boyfriend."

She looks at me, pondering what to say. "Yes, he is very good looking. Billy's a beautiful boy. But what makes him so special is that he is even more beautiful on the inside than on the outside. And you may have first liked him because of how he looks, but you fell in love with him because of who he is and how he treats you."

"I've never said 'I love you' to him."

"But you do." Her voice doesn't go up at the end; it's not a question. She's a mother and mothers know everything. They know when you're happy, when you're sad, when you're scared. And I guess they know when you are in love. "When I first saw your father on the beach in Rincón, I thought, who is the beautiful blond boy? And then he spoke to me, asked me out, and I thought I would have a little fun with a beautiful boy before he left the island and went back home. But he was more than a pretty boy. And we fell in love. Here we are, eighteen years later, with our baby graduating from high school. And I look at him back there, on that chair, talking to his big brother, and he's still as beautiful to me as he was back then."

I fear that Mami is going to start talking about how hot she is for daddy. I'm trying to find a way to change the subject when she says, "Have you talked to Billy about what he wants to do?"

"No. I think it might be best if I break up with him. That way he can be free to just experience college."

"When I got pregnant, I thought that I should just break up with your father, just let him go back home, not hold him back. But then I thought that it wasn't up to me to make decisions about his life, so I told him. About you; you inside of me. I let him know that I would be okay on my own, that it was his decision. I gave him the opportunity to walk away but he didn't take it. He wanted to be with me. Con nosotros." She pauses but I say nothing. "Maybe you should let Billy make the decision on his own. Maybe he will want to be free in college. But maybe he has different ideas."

I know that she has a point, and I know that I am telling myself that if I break up with him it will be to set him free, but I also know deep inside what I am trying not to admit to myself—that if I break up with him it will hurt less than if he breaks up with me. But will it? This is new territory for me to navigate, and there is no map.

"Gracias Mami. I'll think on it some more."

From inside, I hear Nic. "Checkmate," he says with a little gloat in his voice. Mami and I chuckle. Down in the backyard, Andy and Dad laugh about something mysterious and clink their Corona bottles. I kiss Mami on the cheek, walk down the deck stairs to the backyard and begin to gather wood for the fire as Billy Corgan's voice blasts from the speaker and fills the backyard.

# Chapter 58

As the ferry approaches Block Island, we can barely see it through the fog. We are all standing on the deck, in sweatshirts and jackets, mist on our faces, hoping that the sun burns the fog away. Billy has been obsessively checking his weather app. "Looks like the sun will be out by 1:00," he announces optimistically.

There are eight of us: me and Billy, Kevin and Lulu, Billy's cousin Katie and her boyfriend Marc, and Katie's best friend Kelly and her girlfriend Toya. Katie's parents, Billy's aunt and uncle, own a house on Block Island. In the middle of the week in June, the house is empty, so they've agreed to let us have a graduation celebration. Katie, Marc, and Kelly just graduated also; Toya graduated a year ago and is home for the summer from Syracuse.

The ferry captain sounds the horn, and we see the rocky coast through the fog. Then the hotels appear. We go inside and collect our suitcases and bags of groceries and line up to disembark.

Katie says, "Billy, why don't you grab a cab with your crew, and we can meet at the house?" We stuff our things in the trunk and then stuff our bodies in the small cab, Billy in the front and the three of us in the back. Billy tells the driver where we are going and then proceeds to talk non-stop—the weather, our graduation, how he's been coming here every summer of his life. Kevin, Lulu, and I are looking out the windows at this beautiful island, which is part of Rhode Island, but which none of us have ever visited. As the driver climbs a long, windy road, a house appears at the top of the hill. Billy tells the driver, "It's the gray house up there on the left." The three of us in the backseat look at each other. Okay, this could be a fun few days.

What's totally cool about this house is that although it's pretty big, and it's got amazing views, it's a little run down and shabby, both inside and out. It looks comfortable and lived in. Katie explains that the house has been in the family for a long time; that her mother used to come here as a little girl.

Katie's a planner and she has everything worked out, which I love. "Kevin and Lulu, you are in my room, first room on the right at the top of the stairs. Kelly and Toya, you're in my brother's room. Don't worry, he promised me that he put away all of his porn and my mother assures me that the maid changed all of the sheets yesterday." Kelly and Toya pretend to be horrified and we all laugh. She continues. "Marc and I are taking my parents' room. It's kinda weird to sleep in their bed—I know they still have sex. Gross. But the view from their room is amazing. And Billy and Gabe, you'll be in the little guest house out back. Billy's been obsessed with that little house since he was a kid."

"Facts," Billy replies. "I always wanted to sleep out there, but my parents wouldn't let me until I was about eleven or twelve. Then we would have pajama parties out there, me and Katie, Anya and JJ."

We put all of the groceries away and agree to all do our own thing this afternoon and then have dinner together tonight. Katie's mother left lasagna in the freezer for us.

Billy and I settle into our little guest house. I make him unpack his suitcase and put everything in the closet. He groans about it but does it. He's learning. He plops down on the bed and says, "Babe, I really wanna take a nap. You up for a little siesta, amigo?"

"I really want to check out the yard and the view."

"Okay cool. You mind if I snooze a bit and then catch up with you later?"

"Nah, Billy. Get your beauty sleep. You need it." I wink at him and he sticks out his tongue at me.

He grabs a pillow and hugs it. "I'm just gonna hug this pillow and pretend it's you as I sleep. This is my Gabe pillow."

"You're corny. But sweet." I kiss him on the forehead. "See you in a bit."

I grab my camera bag and walk from the little house around the side of the main house. Dozens of sunflowers are in full bloom, turned toward the sun just emerging through the clouds in the northern sky. I round the corner and the view opens up. We are high on a bluff, and the back lawn slopes gently down, overlooking the ocean, waves crashing below. A group of white Adirondack chairs are lined up, waiting to offer occupants a beautiful view. Toya sits alone in one of them.

"Mind if I join you?" I ask.

"Why would I mind? Please." She motions to the chairs. I lower myself into the one next to hers. She offers me the joint she's been smoking.

I accept it and take a hit. Hand it back to her. She takes a hit and hands it back to me and I take another. I say, "I'm good," when she offers it the third time. I'm a lightweight and I know my limit.

"This view is amazing. Have you been here before?" I ask Toya.

"No sir. First time. I could get used to it pretty quickly though."

"No doubt," I agree.

Toya is easy to talk to. And the weed helps. She tells me about Syracuse and her first year of college. New friends, new freedom, new responsibility. And new ideas. I tell her about my photography and RISD and she checks out my Instagram page. She tells me about her and Kelly. They went to the same high school. She was a year ahead of Kelly; they got together when Toya was a senior and Kelly a junior.

"So, how did it go this year? With you all the way in Syracuse and Kelly here?" I ask.

"Kelly and I have an open relationship. I messed around with a few women at school, and a couple of guys. Nothing serious. Kelly and I talk all the time and we'll spend a lot of the summer together. But she'll be at Princeton next year, so we'll be even further away than now. Who knows?" ¿Quién sabe?

This is a mellow, contemplative weed, so I decide to take a walk on the beach. "Thanks for the hit, Toya. I'm feeling great. Gonna take a walk."

"Sure thing. Enjoy."

There's a long, steep, wooden stairway that winds its way down the cliff from the yard to the ocean. When I reach the bottom, I take off my sneakers and leave them by the stairs, and I roll up the legs of my jeans. There's something about walking alone on a deserted beach, the cold June water numbing your feet while the bright June sun warms your face, that is heavy and light at the same time. Heavy because so many thoughts rush in—thoughts of the past, the present, and the future, thoughts that threaten to overwhelm. But light because the open, vast expanse says that anything is possible; it reminds you to visit the past but to not live in it; it invites you to consider the importance of the present. And the deserted beach and the waves and the sun and the vast open sky remind you that the future is a dream and that in dreams, anything is possible.

I stop and face the water, and I watch the incoming tide wash away my footprints. I'm brought back to Horseneck Beach. I am maybe ten, Nic is maybe six or seven. We have sticks in our hands and we've made a big tic-tac-toe board in the sand. He starts with an X in the center, and I add an O. We continue until I realize that I've made a tactical error and I'm about to lose. The tide is coming in; it's lapping at the bottom of the tic-tac-toe board. It's my turn and I ponder the sand board, pretending that I can't decide which of the three remaining squares to put my O.

The tide rises and washes part of the bottom row away. Nic says, "Gabriel, hurry up. It's your turn."

"Hold your horses, Nicolas," I reply. "I'm thinking."

The next wave washes away a tiny bit more, but we can still see the O X O on the bottom row.

I stall more and Nic says, "Dad, Gabriel is cheating. It's his turn and he's letting the water wash it away. He's cheating!"

"I'm not cheating, Nicolas. I'm just figuring out my next move. Don't be such a baby."

"Gabriel, just play before the tide comes in," my father orders me.

The next wave advances and washes away half of the board.

"Oh," I say. "Too bad. Maybe next time Nicolas."

He starts screaming. "That's not fair. I was winning. You just waited so the water would wash it away. I hate you, Gabriel." He throws a handful of sand at me. Because I have bigger hands, the handful of sand that I throw back at him is bigger.

Dad yells, "Gabriel, stop it. Leave him alone, goddamnit. I swear to God…" I'm about to complain that Nicolas threw sand at me first, but I know he will still lay the blame on me, like always. I just look him in the eye and say nothing. I turn and walk into the water.

I'm supposed to stay near the shore when I'm alone. But I wade in a little deeper. Mami calls out, "Gabriel, no tan lejos. Quédate cerca," but I keep walking. A wave threatens to knock me over, but I hold strong against it and move a little deeper.

"Gabriel. You heard your mother. Not that deep. The undertow is strong. Come back."

The water is up to my waist. When Dad yells my name again, I turn and see panic on his face as he runs to the water, but I don't see the big wave that sends me crashing to the ocean floor. I'm tumbled and tossed against the sand and stones. The ocean spits me out toward the shore but then decides that it's not done with me yet and pulls me back. As kids we were always warned about the undertow, this mysterious unseeable monster in the water, this monster that we were to avoid at all costs. Now the monster has me in his tight grip as the wave tries to send me to shore.

I only know the rest of it from the "remember when Gabriel almost drowned at Horseneck?" stories. Dad managed to wrestle me from the iron grip of the undertow monster, this we know. But the story has been told and retold so many times that we don't know the actual truth of the details anymore. Was I just shaken up or was I close to death? Was I breathing or did they have to do CPR? Was it my fault for disobeying my parents? Or Dad's fault for taking Nicolas's side and yelling at me? What matters in a story? The indisputable facts? The subjective details? Here are the indisputable facts: a boy almost drowned and his father pulled him to safety. Is that enough?

Lulu is walking down the beach toward me, her red hair blowing in the gentle breeze. She smiles as she nears me. When she is standing in front of me, she looks at my eyes and says, "You're stoned."

I laugh. "What? Me, stoned? How can you tell?"

"Hah. I've only seen you stoned like twice before. You get the cutest, goofy look on your face. It's like you're trying to figure out the world and you're totally confused by it. But a really mellow confused."

"That's about right, Lulu." I hear my voice and don't recognize it. It's deeper, and blurrier. "Wait, I need a picture of you, here, right now, like this." I take my camera out of my bag, put the strap over my neck and consider the angle. I sit down on the warm sand, looking up at Lulu.

"Hold up. You're not taking a picture of me from that angle. It's gonna be all boobs and nostrils. You really are stoned."

"Trust me, Lu. Your boobs are great and the sunlight on your hair makes you look like a renaissance painting."

"You really know how to sweet talk a girl, Gabe. You sure you're gay? Okay, I will trust you on this, but I get photo approval. No posting anything on socials without my say-so."

"Deal," I say, focusing. "Turn your head a little bit toward the ocean. Not a full profile, just a little turn. That's perfect." I take a few shots from that angle. "Now, look down at me." I lie down on my back and focus in on Lulu's face, looking directly into my lens. The sun hits her red hair and, against the bright blue sky, there's almost a halo over her. Click, click, click. "Perfect," I tell her. I put my camera in the bag and stretch out on the sand.

Lulu sits beside me. She lets out a deep breath. "It is so beautiful here."

"Absolutely."

"I saw you from up in the yard. I wondered, what's he doing down there, walking all alone on the beach? You good?"

"I'm great. I've just been thinking. About how complicated everything seems, but maybe we just make it complicated when it doesn't need to be."

"What's bringing on these thoughts? Besides the pot?"

I laugh. "Probably mostly the pot." I think for a moment. "What's going on with you and Kevin when you go away to school?"

"We agreed we'd see other people. But I think it means that we're just letting this thing, whatever it is that we have, fizzle out. It's been fun and Kevin's a really great guy, but since college commitment day, I think the reality has set in that we're heading out to new adventures and we need to head there without any ties. And we've never been all that serious anyway. I'm not in love with him, and I don't think he's in love with me. We should have just broken up, but it seemed easier to just let it die on its own." She's picking up handfuls of sand and letting it slip through her fingers. "That sounds sad when I say it out loud. Not sad that it's going to end, but sad that we're just letting it die instead of being honest and properly ending it and celebrating the freedom and the future."

"My mother says I'm in love with Billy."

Lulu smiles and runs her fingers through my hair. "Oh honey, did you really need your mother to tell you that?"

"Apparently I did. I guess I just never admitted it to myself until she told me."

"Well, I knew. I knew when you came back from New York. When you told me about the trip, I knew. I remember you telling me about Billy convincing you to ride the Cyclone with your hands in the air. The way you told that story, I knew then."

"Do you think he loves me?"

"I'm not sure. I think so, but I don't know him like I know you. Maybe you need to tell him."

"Yeah, maybe. This sun is mad hot and I'm frying. Let's head back."

"Good idea."

We stand and Lulu kisses my cheek. She takes my hand, and we walk down the deserted beach back to the house on the bluff.

When we arrive back at the house, everyone is on the back deck. Marc has been manning the blender and they are on their second pitcher of frozen margaritas. Billy and Katie are dancing and singing along to "thank u, next." I take out my camera and start snapping photos. They all cheese it up for the camera. Marc hands me and Lulu margaritas and says, "Drink up. You got some catching up to do!"

And catch up, we do. We have a wild night of graduation celebration—margaritas, wine, lasagna, ice cream sundaes, pot, dancing, singing, shots of tequila. Kelly, Kevin, and Marc take turns on music, so we get every possible genre—Lizzo, Taylor Swift, Janelle Monae, Billie Eilish; Drake, Lil Wayne, J. Cole, Cardi B.; R.E.M., The Smiths, Nine Inch Nails, The Talking Heads.

Some of us take it relatively easy on the booze and pot (me, Lulu, Kelly, Kevin) while others get pretty wasted (Marc, Katie, Toya, Billy). Kelly takes Toya up to bed when she starts to fall asleep. Katie's toenails are painted bright red, and Billy keeps telling her how much he loves them. Katie finally announces, "I'm gonna paint your toenails, Billy! Be right back."

"Yes!" Billy yells. "I want red fucking toenails. I want pretty feet. Guys should get to have pretty feet too. Pretty feet shouldn't always be only for girls."

Marc drunkenly agrees, "No cap, bro. That's some sexist shit. Why do guys just get to have ugly ass feet, man? Not fair!"

Lulu, Kevin, and I laugh hysterically as we watch. Katie has to concentrate extra hard to paint the nails, like she's a four-year-old trying not to color outside the lines. She has the most serious look on her face as she works very, very slowly. Billy watches her intently—as intently as his alcohol impaired brain will allow. Marc looks over Katie's shoulder, giving her words of encouragement and advice. "Man, that big toe looks hot, Katie! Amazing. Careful Katie, don't get it on the cuticle."

When she finishes both feet, she lets out a big breath and said, "Done!"

We all clap and Billy wiggles his toes. "My feet look beautiful. I never had such pretty feet. Katie, you're the best. I love you, Katie."

"Yo bro, that's my girl," Marc said to Billy.

"Dude, she's my cousin!"

"Oh right." They both laugh and high five.

Billy gets up and stumbles toward us, catches himself on the arm of a chair and says, "Oops."

"Okay, Billy, I think it's time for us to get to bed. Let's go back to the little house."

"The little house! I love the little house. Hey, Lulu, Kev, did you see my toes?"

Kevin puts on a very straight face and says, "Your toes look great Billy. Maybe the best toes I've ever seen on a guy."

"Thanks man. Kevin, you rock man."

"You rock too Billy."

Billy drapes his arm across my shoulder as I guide him out the door and down to the little house. He plops down on the bed, and I help him take his t-shirt off. I go into the bathroom and come back with a couple of aspirin and a glass of water.

"Here, take these. And drink the whole glass of water." He obeys and lies on his back.

As I take off his pants I ask, "How you feeling there buddy? The room spinning?"

"No, no spin. I'm good. I have red toenails."

"Yes you do."

"I love you babe," he says sleepily.

"Love you too Billy."

"Really?"

"Yes, Billy. Really."

And he's asleep. He looks so sweet, so innocent. I cover him with a blanket, kiss his forehead, and say, "Sweet dreams, my love."

# Chapter 59

"Señor Gatito está muerto," Mami tells me when I walk in the door. She's not crying, but her eyes are a little red and puffy.

"Oh no. When?"

"Your brother found him dead in the closet when he came home from school."

"Where is he?"

"I put him in a box. He's out on the back deck. We'll figure out what to do when your father gets home. Can you go and check on Nicolás?"

When I enter the room, he is lying on his bed, playing on his phone. I sit on the edge of his bed. "Hey bud, how you doing?"

"I'm okay." He has the hoarse voice of someone who has been crying. "I'm gonna miss him. Especially him purring right next to my head while I'm falling asleep."

"Yeah, I'll miss him too."

We sit in silence. Then, "Gabriel, do you believe in heaven?"

"Do you mean heaven for cats, for Señor Gatito? Or heaven in general?"

"I guess I mean heaven in general. Like, I want to believe in it, but I'm not sure I do. What if when we die, we just rot in the ground and that's it? I feel like I'm supposed to believe in heaven though."

"Nicolas, you're not supposed to believe in anything. You're supposed to question things, think about them, believe what you believe."

"What do you believe?"

"About heaven?"

"Yeah."

"I'm not sure, Nicolas. I want to believe there's a heaven but if there's a heaven, does that mean there has to be a hell? Like, can one exist without the other? And hell sounds horrible, like it's made up to make us behave ourselves while we're on earth. I don't know, all this religious stuff really confuses the crap out of me, and us not being a church kinda family, we have to figure it out on our own. Which I guess is good."

"You know what?"

"What?"

"You don't know shit about this stuff either. That didn't help at all." We both laugh.

"Yeah, l'il bro. Don't look to me for the answers. I got nothing."

"I hope we don't just rot in the ground. I hope we go somewhere and get to live another life. And maybe we do it better the next time. Like, we improve on the mistakes that we made the last time. But make new mistakes for us to fix in the next next life."

"I like that plan, buddy."

"I hope that Señor Gatito gets to be in another kid's life, snuggling under his blanket, purring next to his head, licking his face to wake him up in the morning."

"Yeah, me too. He'll be a lucky kid."

I rendezvous with Billy later that evening, like so many evenings before, in Prospect Terrace, our little park on the hill. It's one of those summer nights when even after the sun sets, the heat hangs in the humid air. The statehouse below is still lit in red, white, and blue a week after the Fourth of July. A chorus of katydids provides a background soundtrack for the scene that's about to play out, occasionally drowned out by after-the-fact fireworks.

We sit for a few minutes on our special bench, holding hands and enjoying our favorite spot. Billy will be leaving with his family for a vacation in Spain in two days and then when they come back, he will head out to Northwestern. We both know this will be our last time in our park for a long time.

"Billy," I start. And then I hesitate.

"Yeah babe?"

I swallow. "I'm breaking up with you."

He turns to me, a puzzled look on his face. "That's weird," he says.

"Weird? Why is it weird?"

"Do people really say 'I'm breaking up with you' when they break up?"

"Well," I explain, "in the movies the person who's breaking up always says something vague and then the person being broken up with says, 'Are you breaking up with me?' and then it gets awkward, so I figured it was easier to just cut the awkward part out."

"Umm, okay, well that didn't really work. The cutting out the awkward, that didn't work."

"Sorry."

"What's this about? Did I do something?"

"No Billy, you didn't do anything."

"Is this the part where you say: 'It's not you, it's me'? Cuz *that* would be awkward."

"I just think...well...you're going off to Northwestern and you'll be so far away. You'll be on a big campus with all these people, meeting new friends. You'll be at parties with people throwing themselves at you."

He lets out a derisive laugh. "Are you serious right now? Are you seriously sitting here telling me that you're breaking up with me because I'll be partying and people are going to hit on me? I opened my heart to you about people focusing on my looks. And now you're saying that you're breaking up with me because people at college will find me attractive? What the hell Gabe?"

"Billy, that's not what—"

He interrupts, "Oh wait, I get it," he says, sarcasm building in his voice. "You read that quote about how if you love someone you have to set them free and see what the hell

247

happens. So you're setting me free? Is that what you're doing Gabe? Are you opening my cage and setting me free? Waiting to see if I'll come back?"

Billy doesn't normally do sarcasm, but he's doing it now and it's not pretty. It stings. It stings bad. And when the sarcasm combines with anger, it stings real bad. I think about what I've done here, and I realize that if I were in his shoes right now, I would stand up, turn, and walk away without saying another word. But Billy's not the walk-away kind. He's the open-and-honest-figure-it-all-out kind.

"I'm sorry Billy. You're right. It's not just about you, it's about both of us starting college and new lives."

He doesn't say, "Shut up," but he holds his hand up and I get the idea. "Gabe, if this was about both of us starting college and new lives, we would have talked about it. But we didn't. You just said that you were breaking up with me, so this is about you. And that's fine, but just be honest about it."

Karina's voice echoes in my head: you have to be honest Gabe.

I take a deep breath before I speak, hoping I can get this out. "You're right Billy. You're right. I should've been honest right from the get-go. So here it is." I suddenly feel like an actor, stepping to the edge of the stage to make his big speech.

"I love you Billy. I do. I guess I knew it in my heart for a while, but it took my mother and Lulu telling me that I love you for me to admit it to myself. And admitting it to myself is what makes this so hard. But I need to start new. I'm staying here in Providence while you, Lulu, and most of my good friends are leaving. College is a time to reinvent. I need to reinvent myself. You all are kind of reinventing yourselves just by going away to college. But I'm staying here where everyone knows me, and I feel like I need to start fresh.

I wait for Billy to respond but he says nothing, just stares straight ahead. Finally, I can't take the silence any longer. "So? Are you going to say anything?"

He sighs and turns to me. "Well Gabe, it seems that you've already made up your mind. I can't believe that you didn't even talk to me, tell me you were thinking this way. But hey, I guess I shouldn't be all that surprised. It's not like you've ever really been open with me unless I pry things out of you."

"That's not fair Billy. I've opened up to you more than I've opened up to almost anyone else. What would you have said if I told you that I was thinking about us breaking things off when you go away?"

"I would've said—I am saying—that we should at least give it a chance, see if we can make it work long distance. We've put a lot of work into this relationship, and it feels like you're just ready to walk away."

"I'm not walking away Billy. You're right, I should have talked to you about it, but I was afraid you'd convince me to give it a try and then you'd go away and we'd talk sometimes and we'd see each other over the holidays and then it would eventually just fizzle out."

"Well, you really have a lot of faith in us."

"Come on Billy. Imagine how you would feel if you were staying in Providence and all of your close friends were going off to new places."

"It's not like you're stuck here, like you were forced to go to RISD. You could be going to NYU. If you were going to NYU, would you still be breaking it off?"

"I don't know, Billy. How can I know that? Listen, I'm happy that I'm staying here. Sure, sometimes I wonder if I'll regret not going to New York. But I love it here. And my family is here, and we are working through all of our shit. But this new start, this reinvention—it's the beginning of me, the beginning of the adult me. Gabriel Meyers: college student, photographer, son, brother, man. I want to focus on being the best Gabriel Meyers that I can be. And I know that if we're still together, trying to make this long-distance thing work, I won't make anything work."

Again Billy says nothing for a minute. Then finally he punches me lightly on the shoulder and says, "You're making this really hard. Because you're making sense. Because I know you're right. And I don't like that. And I'm sad."

"I'm sad too, Billy." I turn and hug him, and we hold each other tight. When I release him, I pull back and we look into each other's tear-filled eyes. I smile at him as I stroke his face. "Thank you, Billy."

"For what?"

"For this year. I'm really proud of myself, for the first time in a long time. I've worked really hard. I worked hard at school and at my photography, but I really worked hard on myself, you know? On letting go of anger, on figuring out how to forgive, on being a better brother and son. You played a big part in that. Always there to listen to me, to encourage me. And to call me out when I needed to be called out. To make me let go and throw my hands in the air. You saw the good in me when I didn't see it myself." He gives me a soft, sad, gap-toothed smile and I say, "God, I'm gonna miss you."

"I'll miss you too. But hey, we can still be friends, right? You're not cutting me totally out of your life, are you?"

"No, I'm definitely not cutting you out of my life."

"Good," Billy says. We lean back on the bench. He puts his arm across my back and rests his head on my shoulder. The stars flood the dark sky, and the crescent moon floats off to the left. I stare at it, and for a moment, just a moment, I think I see the man in the moon. And he is smiling.

# Chapter 60

We don't often have a fire in August, but we've enjoyed a few days of unusually low humidity and cool nights. The a/c is off and the windows are open and Nicolas suggests a fire. "I'll get it going," he says, and heads out back.

I've said my goodbyes to the friends who are heading away to college. Kevin is already in Wisconsin, and Billy and his parents are on their way to Northwestern. Lulu left for New York last week, doing a two-week summer program before the official start. I still wonder once in a while if I made the right decision, if I should be in NYC right now instead of in Providence. But I decide to live in the present, without doubts, without what-ifs. Gabriel Meyers has a great new beginning ahead of him.

I look out the back door from the kitchen. Nicolas has a blazing fire going, better than any fire I've ever made. He is sitting all alone, staring at the flames.

Mami, Dad, and I join him.

"Wow, Nicolas! Man, this is a fantastic fire," Dad tells him. "Well done, son."

"Thanks, Daddy."

"Ay, mijo, tu fuego es perfecto!"

"Gracias Mami."

"Eh, it's alright. I could have done better," I say, as I lower myself into my chair.

Dad chuckles, Mami shakes her head and rolls her eyes, and Nicolas says, "In your dreams, Gabriel, in your dreams."

# Chapter 61

Nicolas and I decide on the rear car of the Wicked Cyclone. I promised him I would take him to Six Flags New England after graduation, and here we are. As we climb the first hill, I breathe deeply, trying not to cling too tightly to the safety bar. The climb is a little steeper than the Coney Island Cyclone, but I don't see rotting wood and protruding screws.

The front car is just about to reach the apex. Nicolas turns to me and says, "Are you really going to do it Gabriel?"

"Yes Nicolas, I'm going to do it. I'm going to show you." I'm going to let go, throw my hands in the air, take chances, embrace what scares me. I'm going to be free! I let go of the safety bar and yell, "Let's do this!"

We both raise our hands in the air and scream as the roller coaster plunges down the first steep drop.

# Chapter 62

There's an open spot right along the edge of Prospect Terrace, right where the Lyft dropped me and Lulu off the night of Billy's Christmas party. I pull my truck into the spot, park, get out, and look at Billy's house across the street. I think about that night last December, candles glowing in all the windows, white lights twinkling in all the trees. Tonight the house is dark, the blinds all down and closed, no sign of life. I look up at the third floor. For a second, I imagine Billy looking down at me from his bedroom. But his blinds are down and closed also.

In Prospect Terrace, young families and groups of friends are spread out on the grass enjoying picnics. I hear multiple languages from the tourists taking pictures of the city below. A young couple rises from a bench — the bench that Billy and I called *ours*. I claim my spot.

It's the last Sunday in August. Tomorrow I start at RISD. And next week I start as a photographer's assistant for Milena de Mello. On August 1st, I woke up to a text from Billy in Spain: *Don't forget to call Milena. She said to call her in August.* A little later, as I was driving dad to work, he said, "Hey, today is August 1st. Are you going to call that photographer lady?"

I had been trying to work up my nerve to call Milena, rehearsing what to say, worrying that she wouldn't remember who I was, and nearly convincing myself to forget the whole thing. But then I thought about all that I had said to Billy, about reinventing myself, about starting my adult life, about following my dreams.

"Yes," I said. "I'm going to call her today, Dad." He nodded and smiled.

When I identified myself on the phone, Milena responded, "Of course I remember you, Gabriel. I'm so glad you called." We arranged a meeting at her Federal Hill studio the following week.

I was nervous but confident as I walked into the studio with my portfolio under my arm. Milena showed me around the studio, which was filled with equipment I had only ever dreamed about working with. She looked through my portfolio with great interest, asking me questions about each one — Why did you shoot from this angle? Why black and white? Is this posed or candid? Each question showed me that she respected me, that she took me seriously as a photographer. At the end she said, "I'd love to take you on as an assistant, Gabriel. You need to understand that it's not going to be glamorous. It will be a lot of setting up, breaking down, organizing equipment. But I think you'll learn a lot. And you'll have access to a lot of this equipment on your own time to shoot your own work. We can work your hours around your RISD schedule. If you need time to think it over, I can give you a couple of days. But things are going to really heat up in September, so I want to hire someone soon."

"I don't need to think it over," I said immediately. "Thank you so much for this opportunity, Milena."

It's been a hot August day. The sun is going down, but the temperature isn't. The sky is pale blue and the setting sun is turning the wispy clouds amber, ruby, and coral. The lowering sun gives the state house an orange glow, and the light reflects off the windows of the Superman building, making it look like every light in the place is on. I look down at my city, at the landmarks of my life, and then move my gaze up to the wide open sky and the horizon in the distance. So many prospects. So many possibilities.

Walking back to my truck, I pass two boys on a bench holding hands, speaking in hushed tones. On the grass, a guy and two girls are tossing a frisbee; a young mother is telling a boy to be nice to his little brother, who is crying.

I open my truck door, take a last glance up at Billy's room, turn and take a final look at Prospect Terrace. I get in, close the door, and drive down the hill. Tomorrow is a new beginning.

# Acknowledgements

This book, or some version of it, has lived in my head for years. Then the pandemic arrived, we were locked down, and I no longer had the excuse of my busy life to keep me from writing it. The sudden revelation that I had nothing but time helped me find the motivation to finally put pen to paper and shape the story to share it with others. I first want to thank Gabe, Billy, Lulu, Nic and all of the characters for giving me focus and purpose during those early months of lockdown.

I told no one about the book until I finished a first draft. Then I shared it with some trusted friends and family — people who I knew would be honest and tell me if I was deluding myself into thinking this was a good book. None of them told me that, and since I trusted them, I pushed on. So a big thank you for your honest, constructive feedback and encouragement — Mark Lee, Bill McKenzie, Marc Thibodeau, Glenn Wambolt, Jeanne Washington, and Jennifer Wolfe. Thank you to Mike Howson for guiding me through the publishing process.

Finally, a thank you to all of the students in my life, both in Brooklyn and Providence. You showed me the power of young adult literature to inspire a love of reading and storytelling and words and ideas. But mostly, thank you for allowing me to play a part in your teenage years — years full of emotion, conflict, exploration, and a fierce dedication to justice. The characters and conflicts in the story are all fictional, but they are shaped and inspired by my years with all of you.

# About the author

Fred Wambolt is a former high school English teacher and administrator. After teaching English and ESL for over twenty years in Brooklyn, he relocated to Providence, where he continued to teach until his retirement. His retirement days are filled with writing, reading, volunteering, tennis, swimming, hiking, and walking the beaches of Rhode Island and Cape Cod. *The Beginning of Me* is his first novel.

www.ingramcontent.com/pod-product-compliance
Lightning Source LLC
Chambersburg PA
CBHW020105310726
48970CB00002B/487